Praise for *Shmutz*

"*Shmutz* is a dirty book with a pure heart. . . . Let [Raizl's] laptop burn forever into the night."

—*The New York Times*

"Transgressive and hilarious, Raizl's story questions everything we think we know about women, desire, and religious faith."

—*Los Angeles Times*

"In a voice evocative of Erica Jong, Felicia Berliner answers the Rothian tradition in *Shmutz*. . . . Desire and guilt, faith and ecstasy—Berliner proves that such human categories are never diametrically opposed, but rather always enmeshed together in the throes of their own combative passion."

—*The Millions*

"Seriously juicy . . . [A] compulsively readable coming-of-age story."

—*Cosmopolitan*

"[A] sharply observant novel."

—*Jewish Book Council*

"Berliner's memorable debut . . . shines in her depictions of a deeply religious life, both in its inequities and its enchantments. . . . This brave, eye-opening tale is full of surprises."

—*Publishers Weekly*

"*Shmutz* to me, as a native Yiddish speaker, is first and foremost a love note to my *mama lushun* (mother tongue). This book is a beautiful creation, both as a powerful story of a community that rarely talks about life's most basic nature: love, romance, and sex—intertwined with the richness of our language."

—Abby Chava Stein, author of *Becoming Eve*

"*Shmutz* is a precise exploration of the abject terrain between faith and yearning. Berliner finds the bridge between ecstatic and carnal and welcomes their contractions."

—Raven Leilani, *New York Times*
bestselling author of *Luster*

"Clever, subversive, juicy, and surprising, Felicia Berliner's *Shmutz* had me laughing out loud one minute and clutching my pearls the next. Raizl and her story are both so full of heart. A stunner! Raizl forever!"

—Deesha Philyaw, author of
The Secret Lives of Church Ladies

"*Shmutz* is a provocative and propulsive debut. Felicia Berliner comes to this story with a deep tenderness for her characters and a keen feel for the pain that arises when desire collides with custom. *Shmutz* probes the desperation of being caught in systems, both religious and secular, bent on telling everybody, but especially women, who they should be and what they should want."

—Sam Lipsyte, author of *Hark*

"I read this pitch-perfect debut all in one sitting, barely breathing until I'd reached the stunning, poignant conclusion. I'm in awe of Felicia Berliner's wisdom and insight into the human condition and her virtuosic ability to turn a highly specific story into a thoroughly universal one."

—Joanna Rakoff, author of *My Salinger Year*

"An engrossing, irreverent, deeply felt, and often funny story of a woman finding her place in her body, in her language, in her family, and in the wider world, *Shmutz* is perhaps the one thing I always want a book to be but seldom find: like nothing else I've ever read."

—Lynn Steger Strong, author of *Want*

"Malamud meets Melissa Broder in this deeply charming, soulful novel. Not since Eve tasted the forbidden fruit has a story about curiosity and shame felt so vital. Berliner has given us a true comedy: beautifully rendered, fully earned, and suffused with love."

—Elisa Albert, author of *Human Blues*

"*Shmutz* is like nothing else I've ever read anywhere by anyone, a thoroughly wonderful novel made on the bones of the unlikeliest of setups. It is a testament to Felicia Berliner's considerable skill that the story of Raizl, obedient daughter, Orthodox Jew, porn addict, is absolutely authentic, hilarious, and poignant. In heavier hands, this could have been a parable or a satire. Instead, it's a masterstroke."

—Jacquelyn Mitchard, author of *The Deep End of the Ocean* and *The Good Son*

"Bold, heartfelt, furious, and funny. A wonderful debut."

—Shalom Auslander, author of *Mother for Dinner*

"Berliner's debut navigates the tension of family, faith, and freedom with heart and humor."

—*Apartment Therapy*

"Insightful in moving beyond binary ideas about freedom and captivity . . . Full of funny and moving moments."

—*The Forward*

Shmutz

A NOVEL

FELICIA BERLINER

WASHINGTON
SQUARE PRESS

ATRIA

New York   London   Toronto   Sydney   New Delhi

WASHINGTON SQUARE PRESS

ATRIA

An Imprint of Simon & Schuster, Inc.
1230 Avenue of the Americas
New York, NY 10020

First Washington Square Press/Atria Paperback edition May 2023

WASHINGTON SQUARE PRESS / ATRIA PAPERBACK and colophon are trademarks of Simon & Schuster, Inc.

For information about special discounts for bulk purchases, please contact Simon & Schuster Special Sales at 1-866-506-1949 or business@simonandschuster.com.

The Simon & Schuster Speakers Bureau can bring authors to your live event. For more information or to book an event, contact the Simon & Schuster Speakers Bureau at 1-866-248-3049 or visit our website at www.simonspeakers.com.

Interior design by Kyoko Watanabe

Manufactured in the United States of America

1 3 5 7 9 10 8 6 4 2

Library of Congress Cataloging-in-Publication Data
Names: Berliner, Felicia, author.
Title: Shmutz : a novel / Felicia Berliner.
Description: First Atria Books hardcover edition. | New York : Atria Books, 2022.
Identifiers: LCCN 2021044276 | ISBN 9781982177621 (hardcover) |
ISBN 9781982177638 (paperback) | ISBN 9781982177645 (ebook)
Subjects: LCSH: Hasidim—Fiction. | Young women—Fiction. | Jewish Families—Fiction. | Brooklyn (New York, N.Y.)—Fiction. | LCGFT: Bildungsromans. | Novels.
Classification: LCC PS3602.E75795 S56 2022 | DDC 813/.6—dc23/eng/20211027
LC record available at https://lccn.loc.gov/2021044276

ISBN 978-1-9821-7762-1
ISBN 978-1-9821-7763-8 (pbk)
ISBN 978-1-9821-7764-5 (ebook)

For my mother
Thank you for teaching me and so many children to read

Blessed are You, Adonai Eloheinu, Majesty of the
Universe, by Whose word everything came to be.

—JEWISH BLESSING

It's the binary of normative/transgressive
that's unsustainable, along with the demand
that anyone live a life that's all one thing.

—MAGGIE NELSON, *THE ARGONAUTS*

תנו רבנן: כיצד מרקדין לפני הכלה? בית שמאי אומרים:
כלה כמות שהיא ובית הלל אומרים: כלה נאה וחסודה

The Rabbis taught: How does one dance before
the bride? The House of Shammai says one
praises the bride as she is, and the House of
Hillel says the bride is beautiful and graceful.

—BABYLONIAN TALMUD, *KETUBOT* 17a

Shmutz

Daughter of Israel

The doctor's nails are shiny, glittering around the pen she points at Raizl. "You don't want to get married?" Dr. Podhoretz asks.

Raizl shakes her head. "I want," she corrects. "But I can't. Mami sent me to you because I told her and the matchmaker, no meetings. No b'show." She's told her mother she's scared of sex, which is true. Scared she won't ever find a husband. Also true! Just not everything that is true.

"You can't?" The doctor's forehead wrinkles. "Why not?"

Raizl's thighs clench, her thick tights pressed so close they may as well be stitched together under her long wool skirt, guarding against the feeling that even under all this fabric, a part of her will be exposed. For the sake of finding a husband, though, she will say it.

"Too much watching," Raizl answers, but the doctor doesn't react.

"On the computer," Raizl adds, blushing. The heat of saying it rises from her temples, from the tops of her ears.

"Wait, you mean pornography?"

Raizl nods slightly, a hint of yes. Porn, that's what she watches. Shmutz.

"All right." Dr. Podhoretz is nodding her head, too, as if this isn't unusual. "Let's talk about it. What do you like to watch?"

Like to watch? Why is the doctor asking this? Raizl looks at the ceiling, where perhaps an answer swirls overhead, and mumbles to herself, "Ich veiss nisht." *I don't know.* She's not sure what happens to her during the nights of porn. Raizl thought Dr. Podhoretz would tell *her* what's going on, and how to make it stop. So far not.

Instead, the doctor's question reminds Raizl of a video she saw the night before, *College Girls Play Games*. Three girls lay on a bed on their bellies, wearing shirts but nothing below. Their bare tushes sticking up. Two of them played a silly video game, chatting and laughing, while a man shtupped the one in the middle. Weren't they too old to be playing these games? And didn't they see what was happening between them—didn't they notice the shtupping? She wasn't talking, the girl in the middle, but sometimes she reached her hand around, behind her back, and held her tush. Raizl remembers the girl's nice manicure, her bright pink nails.

Raizl squeezes her legs together even tighter, aware that the video memory has stirred sensation down there. She smiles weakly, wondering if Dr. Podhoretz can tell.

But the doctor just tilts her head to one side and asks, "Can you say a bit more? Preferably in English. I'm sorry, my Yiddish is rather limited."

The doctor doesn't sound sorry, but Raizl breathes in, getting ready. It seems an impossible task. To say what she knows.

Never mind that her knowledge is entirely virtual. The only hands that have touched her body are her own. But the videos imprinted in her memory will not be erased or sealed shut. No angel will come to wipe away her knowledge, like the angel who teaches the Talmud to every infant in utero, then pinches the baby's lips shut at birth, leaving the small hollow between nose and lip as a reminder: the child must relearn the Talmud with a new consciousness, with a free will. If only Raizl could come to the marriage bed like this—fully innocent, newborn and unknowing, as eager to learn sexual pleasure as if she had not a shred of digital experience.

It's too late, though, for this kind of purity. Raizl sinks lower in the armchair, and the wine-colored leather creaks without mercy each time she moves. Raizl fears she cannot be reconciled with the sex that awaits her: post-ritual bath, Friday-night sex. Will she take off her special bride's nightgown and be naked? Will she ever persuade her chussen, the husband of her future, to put his tongue down there? Based on the women Raizl's seen in videos, she doesn't think she can live without this, and she fears her chussen will think she's prost, a coarse girl, with ugly wishes. Sometimes she dares to hope: if she takes her chussen's cock-dick into her mouth just once, he won't be able to live without it either. Of this, porn has her convinced.

If she can just stop watching porn now, perhaps it's not too late to find a chussen. To get married.

"You can help me quit watching?" Raizl asks.

"Do you want to quit?" The doctor lowers her chin and observes Raizl over the top of her glasses, asking this question in the same even tone she uses to gather all the facts. So far, the doctor has collected the meaning of Raizl's name (Yiddish for "rose"), age (eighteen and a half), and birth order (third of five brothers and sisters).

"Only five children? Why so few?" the doctor had asked. It pained Raizl to speak of Mami's miscarriages, as if she were giving away family secrets. But according to Mami, even though the doctor is not from the community, she has worked with other Chasidish families. Presumably she has dealt with the rumored heartaches and tzuris: the schnapps-loving mother, the plate-smashing father, the bedwetting bar mitzvah boy. On occasion, a bride who does not bleed on her wedding night and has never been near a horse.

And now Raizl, daughter of Israel, porn addict.

"I *can't* quit," Raizl says. "Every night I'm looking at it." The fluttering movement of Dr. Podhoretz's pen makes Raizl forget what she's saying.

"Every night?" prompts the doctor. "You have internet at home?"

"Yes," Raizl says, and her toes curl inside her flat black shoes. Another secret, out now.

"Tati is a manager at the electronics store, and since he hurt his back they let him work from home sometimes. He got internet for his email. He doesn't know I have the password, that I open the internet on my laptop, which I'm only supposed to use to study accounting. I'm in the Cohen College honors program. I have a scholarship."

These details come out in a rush, so much easier to talk about than the videos. "Also, I work a few hours a week for a business on Forty-Seventh Street," Raizl continues. "As soon as I finish my degree, it's already arranged, I'll work full-time."

"Arranged?" asks Dr. Podhoretz. "Like a marriage?"

"I have a *laptop*," Raizl says impatiently. The doctor is missing the point. "For me it's permitted because it's for parnussa, for livelihood. I give the money to Mami, and she saves it to pay for my wedding. And in the meantime, before I get married, the money helps pay for my brothers—in a few years they'll work, like Tati, to earn a living, but for now they learn Torah all day.

"I have my computer where I want. School. Home. Bed." Raizl's cheeks flush yet again, but the doctor's face is perfectly smooth, undisturbed. "Nobody else is allowed to have a computer at home, not my brothers, my sister, my friends," Raizl says. "For them it's forbidden."

"That's very unusual, isn't it?" the doctor asks. "A young woman like you, going to college before getting married?"

Raizl nods. Tati almost forbade it.

▼

Last spring, nearly a year earlier, when Raizl showed Tati the college acceptance letter, he waved it away. Deemed it profane. "Kollej is tumeh!" he said.

Mami interceded on her behalf, arguing that it would not be improper to study accounting, and Raizl had a head for numbers. She reminded Tati of the salary for an accountant. And besides, it would cost them gurnisht. Raizl had a full scholarship!

"Gurnisht mit gurnisht," Tati said dismissively, not looking up from his Gemureh. Zero cost and zero gain.

"Please, Tati," Raizl said.

He paused his learning, pursing his lips and gazing at Raizl. He picked up his yarmulke from the top of his head, smoothed it over his nearly bald crown and the slightly thicker fringe of hair at the back, then put it down again at the top, exactly where it had been before.

He stared without blinking, a look that was a command. "Riyyyyzl," he pronounced her name the traditional way and drew it out long, a name that turned into a sentence. "Nisht kan science," he said. "No biology, no monkeys. You already know where you come from. Only accounting."

Raizl had said yes to Tati's conditions. She didn't mention things like "distribution requirements" and "electives." She didn't say that a computer was part of her scholarship. It was spring 2012 by the goyish calendar, and the great rabbis had just banned the internet. At Citi Field, with forty thousand men as witnesses, the rabbis decreed that the internet, with filters, could be used only at work. And yeshivas were not to admit any student with internet in the home. Raizl heard about it from some other students at her all-girls high school, who'd gotten the news on a livestream. The internet informed them that they were not allowed to use the internet.

Raizl was secretly grateful that her intention to use the internet could not harm her brothers' chances for admission to yeshiva. Her older brothers, Shloimi and Moishe, had been studying for years already, and her younger brother, Yossi, who'd just celebrated his bar mitzvah, had also passed the scrutiny of the rabbis and been admitted to yeshiva.

Finally, Tati gave his consent. At the end of the summer, as the first semester of college started, Raizl got her scholarship computer. It was sleek and silver, with the shape of an apple minus one bite right in the middle of the lid. Even unplugged it felt warm to her, as if it radiated from inside her book bag. Walking home from the subway, Raizl kept her arm over her bag, afraid that on the crowded sidewalk, somehow the women pushing strollers and the men hurriedly walking by with their plastic bags could discern the outline of the laptop. Could feel its heat.

She didn't know, until she got home, what she didn't know: How to turn it on. How to open, and install, and use the college's free software. How to do anything with it, besides hold it.

▼

"What did you do?" exclaims Podhoretz. "How did you learn?"

Raizl shrugs. A librarian had helped her apply to college, and now her advisor taught her how to google, how to look for life on the internet. "You can register online," her advisor had said. "Pick your classes, choose what you want."

"What I want?"

"Well, within limits. As a freshman you don't have *too* many op-tions. But a few. Here," she said, turning her monitor so Raizl could watch, and then she started typing. "W-w-w," she said. "Dot. Cohen College. Dot. E-d-u. Textbooks are online, too. You can find them used on Amazon. And the president's welcome to new students, that's on YouTube."

Everything the advisor put into the Google bar, every wish and command, was held, invisible, inside the computer. And then sur-faced on the screen.

To the doctor, Raizl says, "A few things I learned from my advisor. The software I learned from YouTube videos."

"You taught yourself. No one helped you."

"Yah." Raizl nods.

The doctor tilts her head to one side, taking this in. "Why did you come to *me*, Raizl? Why ask for help now?"

"So you can't help?"

"I didn't say that. But you could've talked to a rabbi. A rabbi's wife. It might be easier to talk about in Yiddish."

Raizl has a round face, but when she's angry, her cheeks pucker in-ward. Her freckles get redder, along with her skin. "If I go to someone inside, I won't get a shidduch. No match! Or I'll get the nebbish, some pitiful boy no one else wants!"

"You haven't told anyone—?"

"Of course not!"

"—and you're still observant?"

Raizl glances down at her turtleneck sweater covered by a cardigan and sweeps her hand through the air over her body, a see-for-yourself gesture. Maybe because it's the middle of winter and all the doctor's patients wear sweaters in January, she had to ask about Raizl's obser-vance. But there are too many clues. A bit of Raizl's thick, beige tights, like an extra skin, is visible from calf to ankle, but looks nothing like flesh. A seam runs like a faded, raised scar down the back of each leg. Plus long sleeves over long sleeves. Raizl hoping that the extra layers of clothing would be an antidote to porn, or at least provide armor against detection of her habit.

Even without a rumor like that, she is a difficult match, with many strikes against her. Although her oldest brother, Shloimi, got married two years ago and has a baby, her next brother, Moishe—her favorite—turned twenty and is still single. Raizl suspects she's not the only one who has seen him with a cigarette that turned out not to be a cigarette.

And then there is her hair, a shade of coppery paprika. Raizl keeps it in a ponytail to minimize the mass of curls, to contain the bright light. Families of young men searching for a bride might avoid a redhead unless the color already runs in the family.

Mami denied it was red. "Nisht royt!" she had protested to the matchmaker. "Cinnamon," she offered instead, pulling a strand of Raizl's hair taut, as if to change Raizl's prospects by making one ringlet straighter, smoother. Less red.

"Well," Podhoretz says. "Now you're here with me." Her chin drops in a smiling affirmative but one eyebrow lifts, the arch of a renegade question mark. A face moving in two directions. Raizl considers the doctor's perfectly straight, dark hair, combed into a neat bun, definitely her own and not a wig. Her creamy silk blouse, with long sleeves and a bow at the collar, could be modest but isn't, so tight across the front. Though she wears a wedding band and a diamond ring, she is nothing like the married women Raizl knows. She has shelves lined with books, all with English titles. On the wall is a painting of golden flowers in a vase. The office smells of false citrus, oily cleaners, dust nevertheless, a cooling coffee on the side table next to the doctor's armchair. Behind her is a desk piled with more books, and half hidden underneath are two low-heeled brown pumps, siblings of the black pair on her feet.

The doctor's prettily manicured nails, clear polish with white tips, remind Raizl again of the girl in the video she'd seen the previous night. Just before the shtupping started, when the girl's tush was in the air, Raizl saw everything down there: the oval of pink flesh, with shiny folds curling away from her dark loch, her hole a purple shadow. And the other loch, small and wrinkled, an even darker hole. With one hole right above the other like that, where does the shvantz go? Raizl watched the video to find out. She worried for the girl, felt relieved each time the shvantz went into the right hole, but also bothered, dissatisfied. Why *not* the other hole? In some videos, the man shtups tuches. How does the shvantz decide? In this video, the man's face never appeared, so it was impossible to guess anything about what he wanted, or what he would do next. Maybe that's why the girl held her tush, pink fingertips pointing at her shmundie. A signal to the shvantz: go here.

Raizl squirms in the chair. Says nothing. How can she explain this watching in any language? It would certainly not be easier to talk about in Yiddish. Words for what she's seen are not said in Yiddish by anyone she knows. She'd never heard of tuches, of shmundie! Only found them on the internet, along with the other shmutzige shtupping words.

The doctor, though, is undeterred. "Let's continue." Again she points her pen at Raizl. "How did you start watching porn?"

"I googled."

"Googled pornography?"

Raizl shakes her head no. "I googled 'Der Bashefer' to see what the internet says about the Creator, and then I googled . . ." She can't mention the holy names. It was easier to type them than it is to say them.

"I googled 'Hashem,' too." It seems silly, now, that she'd once thought the computer would explain G-d, unveil a new aspect of holiness. In those first weeks and months of having a computer, when she'd realized it could explain so much, she'd wanted it to reveal everything. But the virtual world could also disappoint. About Hashem, the internet offered the reasons for saying Hashem—The Name—instead of the actual divine name, and Raizl already knew this.

"Then I tried the English name, G-O-D, and there were so many pictures of men!" Although Raizl understood that the goyim worship a man, it was shocking to see those pictures. In one, a man with flowing hair and a beard, leaning from a cloud, stretched his finger out to the hand of a naked man.

"After I saw that, I had a different idea. I typed 'kiss.' Because the internet has pictures for everything. You give the internet a word, and it gives you back pictures. So many people kissing. And men with long hair and meshiggeneh makeup, and men kissing men, and women kissing, too."

"You liked that," Dr. Podhoretz says.

This might be a question, but Raizl doesn't stop for it. "I wanted more pictures. All the pictures of what I don't find anywhere else. I typed 'sex' and found videos. What comes up if you try to find sex, is sex. Not just words about sex."

And the videos are full of English she doesn't know, so she asks the internet to teach her Yiddish. Cock is shvantz, and pussy is shmundie. Together they shtup. The English names are so strange and ugly. Cunt? A goyishe word for a goyishe place, except that she has one, too. She googles the whole shmutzige vocabulary to find out what in Yiddish are these words. Better that pussy is shmushka, because it's always shmooshed; and loch, the hole. Where the whole story happens, the gaansa maaseh, the deed. The internet gives her pictures and videos, and, when she needs them, words for other words. An unfamiliar Yiddish that is still her mamalushen, her mother tongue, even if Mami never spoke this way.

"Okay," Dr. Podhoretz says. "I understand how you started watching pornography. But doesn't anyone in your family realize you're watching? That you're online?"

Raizl's hands feel damp, and she smooths them against her skirt, as if she can wipe off the guilt along with the cold sweat. Her sister, Gitti, does know. Because Raizl showed Gitti the internet.

▼

A month ago, during Chanuka, someone had told Gitti about a music video made by the Maccabeats. How amazing and handsome they were, this group of singing Yeshiva students.

Every night of Chanuka, Gitti begged to watch them on the phone Tati keeps for his work. Every night, Tati said no, it's not Chasidish. It's forbidden.

"It's just a Chanuka song," Raizl said at dinner on the eighth night, and Tati slammed his fist so hard against the table he knocked the fanken, an entire plate of Chanuka donuts, to the floor.

"We have the Torah! And the Chanuka prayers to sing!" He stood, shouting, while Mami got a towel and cleaned the jelly globs and powdered sugar.

"For what do we need these students to make up songs? They should spend more time studying, and less singing," he continued. "And you—" He stormed around the table to Raizl's place, shaking his finger at her. "Don't think because you're at goyishe kollej and working that you're too big to show respect!"

"Zalmen, stop!" Mami jumped up and ran toward Tati. He turned sharply from Raizl to Mami, yelling, "Shah! Don't interrupt when I'm teaching them! You're too soft, and this is the result!" Tati waved his hand in Raizl's direction.

"Does your father get angry like that very often?" Dr. Podhoretz asks. "Did he hit you?"

"Nein," Raizl says. "Never hits me." But she had felt Tati's rage against her, and against Mami. And why? Were the Maccabeats really so bad? Why would Der Bashefer, the all-powerful, worry about a few students making music videos?

Later that night, Raizl told Gitti to come sit on her bed, and clicked on YouTube. "This is the internet," she said to Gitti.

"There's no filter?" Gitti looked puzzled. Raizl shrugged. She'd also been surprised at first that Tati hadn't put a filter on, but then she had taken it as a good sign—luck or destiny—that in some strange way Der Bashefer wanted her to go to college, wanted her to have internet access.

And she gave Gitti this Chanuka gift, playing the music video at a very low volume. She didn't think those boys were any good, but Gitti went crazy over the a cappella singers in yarmulkes. Fourteen years old, what did she know? To Gitti, each singer was more handsome than the next. "Don't you like him?" she'd said, pointing at one. "How old do you think he is?" pointing at another. She begged to play the video again, and then a third time. "Raizy, please!" Again she wanted it, but Raizl said no, Mami will be wondering what's going on, and anyway she had to study.

"So you showed Gitti the video. And she liked it," Dr. Podhoretz says.

Raizl nods.

"And you like to watch videos, too," the doctor says. "Right?"

Raizl's mouth goes dry, her tongue pasty. "Not music videos," she manages to say. Like Gitti, she whispers the Shema prayer at bedtime, and turns out the light. But she doesn't go to sleep.

"No? You watch something else?"

The doctor's question conjures in Raizl an image of herself in her bedroom. Raizl sees her body, what used to be hers without having to think about it. But now Dr. Podhoretz wants Raizl to watch herself and describe what she sees. So this is therapy, a porn of the self.

▼

In her narrow bed, Raizl watches under the covers, the computer resting on her nightgown. The lid is open but angled forward so she can shut it quickly, and the volume is muted; the only sound is Gitti softly snoring on her matching twin bed across the room.

On-screen, the woman stretches over a much bigger bed, with her back arched and the crown of her head tipped into the pillows so Raizl has a view of her open mouth, the dark hollows of her flared nostrils. The man lifts her hips and pushes himself, sharp and fast, into her bald shmundie again and again. With no sound, Raizl has to imagine the woman's moan. In pleasure? In pain? The woman spits on her fingers and rubs herself in a kind of rhythm with the man. Even without sound, Raizl understands something crucial has shifted: the woman's features soften, her eyes open for a moment and then close again, as her thighs tighten around the man.

Abruptly, he stops and climbs forward over her body, points his shvantz at her lips. Smiling, she swallows him.

So this is what a woman does! Shaves her shmundie, takes a man in her mouth, eats without saying a blessing first.

▼

Podhoretz waits, her unflinching silence like an extra set of walls around the room, holding Raizl, suffocating her. Raizl can't manage to say a word.

"It must be hard to talk about," Podhoretz says. "But I can help you."

Suddenly, Raizl is scared. The doctor's promise is seductive, but what if the therapy doesn't work? Even if Raizl can find a way to put it all into words, she doesn't believe in the doctor.

"You think it's hopeless," says Podhoretz, as if she's read Raizl's mind. "You're worried about never getting married. But Raizl, you haven't even tried to go on a date. You don't know what will happen." The doctor shuts her notebook. "Our time's up for today, but I want you to consider something. Why not go on a date? You don't have to marry the first man you meet. Some young women do, I know that, but not everyone, right?"

Raizl nods, thinking of girls who had a few matches before they found their ziveg, their destined mate.

"One date. What did you call it, a show? You could just try once. Think about it, at least, and we can discuss it next time."

The doctor doesn't seem to require anything further, so Raizl stands and moves slowly, uncertainly toward the door, weighed down by all she hasn't said. In the small hallway, she puts on her coat, wraps herself in a large wool scarf, and prepares for the cold. Podhoretz wants her to agree to a b'show, but there's so much more she didn't tell Podhoretz.

▼

This is what happened last night, what happens on all the nights of porn.

While she watches bodies on the screen, her own body vanishes, but as soon as the video ends, her thighs and hips are present again, heavy, her skin tight. Tightest of all at the point where her body is joined, where the blood of one half rushes to meet the blood of the other. Raizl shifts the computer off her belly and, under the covers, pulls up her nightgown. Following the woman in the video, Raizl spits on her fingers and reaches through the coarse hair to find what's exposed online and hidden on herself. Raizl makes circles there, a strange orbit of sensation, as quiet as she can be, at the last moment biting her lips closed while her entire body shakes—a convulsion, knees drawing up nearly to her chest, aftershocks in waves. A voiceless trembling that is almost prayer.

Dream-Teller

The morning after her therapy session with Dr. Podhoretz, as Raizl rushes down the hall in a hurry to leave for school, Zeidy calls her to his room. The five siblings have always shared bedrooms—one for the three brothers and one for Raizl and Gitti—but Zeidy has his own. Tati said it was out of respect for the elderly, and Mami said it was because he snored, and Shloimi said it was because he smelled like pish, but Raizl knew that it was because he could tell your dreams back to you in the morning, and this was something Mami and Tati didn't like and certainly didn't want to encourage. No matter that Zeidy wore his tzitzis outside his shirt like the other men; no matter that he hated gossip and would bellow in anger, "Shemayisruel!" turning the prayer into an expletive if he ever heard his grandchildren make a mean comment; to Tati and Mami it was heretical that Zeidy saw the dreams unrolling inside other people's heads.

Mami admitted that this had been going on for a long time and was, in fact, the reason Babi had married him: when Babi was a girl of eighteen, Zeidy told her that she had dreamed of marrying him and scolded her jokingly, "At least wait for me to ask you!"

Was he reading her mind or merely expressing his wishes? No one would ever know, but Babi agreed, so his audacity won him a bride.

Granting Zeidy his own room doesn't stop him from dream-telling. This morning, Zeidy gestures to the chair beside his bed, and Raizl reluctantly sits. She doesn't want to be late for class, but she would never ignore a summons from Zeidy. He recounts the following dream: A horse canters up the avenue early in the morning, before the buses come to take the boys to school, the sky still black and dotted by streetlights. The horse stops in front of their apartment building, neighing and neighing, the snow melting in the steam from the great beast's nostrils. When Tati and the other men on the block try to push the horse away, it stomps and kicks until they back off. Only when Raizl emerges through the metal-and-glass doorway, wearing her old high school uniform, the horse gentles. She jumps onto the horse—her long skirt! The towering horse! None of this stops her, she's aloft!—and rides with the horse's mane flowing against her. No one tries to rescue her, because they can't, because they hear her laughing as the horse gallops away. Then Raizl is back, once more in front of the brick building, but now in daylight the street is strangely empty. The children have gone off to school, and the men to study or work; down the block, a few women head to the grocery, pushing strollers. Raizl stands alone, no horse, only the horseshit turned to straw on the snowy ground.

Raizl's dream, forgotten until Zeidy tells it, is now as vivid to her as a memory. Zeidy asks, "Raizele, when you ride off on the horse, where are you going?"

Zeidy strokes her cheek as he asks this. Following the path of his fingers, a magical heat spreads across her face. His gift of dream-telling, of pulling stories from the lost darkness of night into the day . . . how can it be? What if Zeidy made up the dream and gave it to her, as perhaps he had with Babi?

But Raizl believes him, and the warmth spreads down her neck to her back, along with the feeling that he already knows where the dream horse takes her.

The same way she always knew where he had hidden candy for her. Their game since she was a tiny girl: he tells her to guess, and she gazes intently at all of his jacket pockets until her intuition becomes solid and certain, like the shape of the candy itself, and she points, there!

Always, she picks the right pocket, and Zeidy pulls out a Paskesz candy. She doesn't wait until after dinner as Mami insists—she unwraps the candy and pops it into her mouth faster than she says the blessing, the sweet-tart fizz on her tongue before the words are finished. Zeidy smiles and does not scold. He loves her anyway.

Signs

Finally on the subway, Raizl fishes her sidder out of her purse. She holds the pocket-size prayerbook with its ornate silver cover like an amulet or shield in front of her face, open to the pages of psalms though she knows the words by heart.

Psalms don't stop the infiltration of porn.

The woman standing in front of Raizl, is she about to dance? Her grip on the metal pole is suggestive. In a minute she will twist a knee around the slim silver rod. Perhaps she will unbutton the businesslike blouse visible at her neck where she has unzipped her down jacket, the heat in the train an invitation to further heat, to a physical encounter with a seeming stranger. Raizl lives now in a system of signs, which, weirdly, seems familiar to her. Religious life is also a system of signs. Every item—an apple, a new skirt, a good grade—had been presented to Raizl as evidence of the hand of G-d. As an opportunity for prayer or blessing. If she tripped and fell, that, too, was a warning from Der Bashefer. Pornography operates in a different, but parallel, fashion. Every object is a sexual prop, every gesture an invitation to the senses. Now an apple is something to eat sexily, in case a man is watching; a red mouth, a red pout; a skirt is there to unzip.

Had sex always been behind everything, and she just hadn't seen it? The way people who aren't religious don't see the G-d in everything. The way for some people an apple is just an apple, a subway pole just a thing to grab when the brakes screech.

O'Donovan Here

Math and accounting come easily to Raizl, and she takes as many of these classes as the college permits. But she can't avoid the required English class.

In comes the professor, a man without a beard. "O'Donovan here," he says on the first day of the spring semester. Jeans and a necktie. He hangs his jacket on the back of his chair but doesn't sit. He paces, giving ample exposure to both profiles. Raizl is fascinated by his jawline. By his skin, pale as any yeshiva boy's but speckled with tiny, dark pores. Finally he sits, locating the most professorial corner on the table at the front of the room. He hinges forward alarmingly in the direction of the front row of students. "I want to hear your voices, not just mine," he says.

This is the first sign of trouble. On the syllabus is the fine print, requirements for class participation, the rules after the rules; the demand not only to learn, but also to fit in. Raizl despairs of making an A. She has studied English throughout her schooling, but it's not her first language. Only after the mama-tongue of Yiddish and then the sacred-tongue of Hebrew for prayer did Raizl begin to learn English. First grade. To supplement the approved school textbooks and permitted Chasidish novels, she has consumed unholy English in secret—romance novels found on the street, magazines discovered at a doctor's office. During high school, Raizl made up stories about going to see friends, and went to the library instead.

So many words Raizl has read but never said!

At home, she guards against giving away that she knows more than she is supposed to. In college, she worries that she'll slip and reveal the gaps, all the ways that she knows less than the students around her, wearing their T-shirts and jeans, constantly cradling their phones. She keeps her kosher flip phone—free of internet, with blocked camera and no messaging—hidden in her bag while she's on campus. In class discussions, Raizl's over-enunciated consonants, the slight music of her Yiddish, are audible to the others, who sometimes stare at her curiously. No matter how well O'Donovan-here teaches her to write, she will never look or sound like the other students.

He loosens his tie, and then it hangs slightly sideways. His casual gestures all seem false. Raizl much prefers the teachers she had all through her religious schooling, rebbes and the wives of rebbes, the rebbetzins who insist on respect and teach with no pretense of friendliness.

"This is your first college English class," he says. "The foundation for your future as students. I don't care what you major in, what else you study, you need to be able to think critically, read analytically, and write compellingly." He points to his head, then his eyes. He swirls his hand in the air, as if his finger is a pen. As if anyone writes papers with a pen.

Then he jumps off the table and stands, suddenly solemn. "The work you do in this class will prepare you not just for the university, but for life."

Raizl realizes, too late, that she has chosen the wrong seat, that what's directly in front of her is the zipper of O'Donovan's jeans. She keeps her eyes down, studying the syllabus, trying not to admit anything higher than his knees into her field of vision, and wonders if what he predicts, or promises, will be true—if she will ever be able to use what she reads and writes outside of school.

"I'm very easy to reach," the professor continues. "If you have any questions, you can always message me on Facebook."

Now Raizl is alarmed. She doesn't have this internet book. Going to college is one thing, hiding a computer in her backpack and secretly taking English . . . but Facebook would be even more dangerous. She could be found on Facebook and reported to the modesty committee.

Professor O'Donovan has the students introduce themselves. As they say their names, he asks everyone with an accent, "And where are you from?" With his most generous, welcoming smile.

Raizl doesn't usually think twice about speaking English, but now she wonders if any Yiddish will seep through. "I'm Raizl from Brooklyn," she says, as quickly as she can, so the professor won't have to ask.

For an agonizing moment, she feels the eyes of the professor and her classmates taking her in. The long pleats of her skirt, down to her shins, her blouse buttoned all the way to the collar, the sleeves that swallow her wrists. Then they move on to the next student.

What she wants to say to the professor: *From where are you?* She wants to take away his English, leave him stranded without language, without place. She wants to take classes with only numbers, and no words.

Just Try Once

"Raizele, take your head out of your books! You have to get ready!" Mami comes rushing into the room.

Raizl hastily shuts her computer and covers it with some papers. "Ready farvus?"

"The matchmaker called, she found someone. The chussen is coming to meet you tomorrow evening."

"Tch tch," Tati, standing in the doorway, reproaches Mami. "Don't say 'chussen,' not yet."

"You were *my* first," Mami says. "The first could be the one." Mami goes into the closet and returns with three of Raizl's dresses. There is no time to shop for new clothes before the b'show, so the finest Shabbes dress will have to do.

"Zalmen, shut the door so she can try these on. I want to see how beautiful she'll be for the chussen!"

"Beli ayin hora," Tati says as he leaves, warding off the evil eye.

Mami waltzes with one of the dresses, a white one. "A blessing, this Podhoretz. A miracle worker," she says.

Raizl stares at the dress Mami holds, then at the others laid out on the bed. A false choice, between so many dresses that are, in the end, all the same. Why isn't she excited, like Mami? After Podhoretz said, "Just try once," Raizl had agreed to a meeting, but she doesn't want it to happen this fast. Not tomorrow.

"It happened so fast!" Mami laughs.

This gives Raizl a chill. How can Mami know what she's thinking? Will she start to tell Raizl's dreams, too, an inherited gift from Zeidy?

"Not that I'm surprised," Mami adds, and comes over to Raizl at the desk. "Wear this one, it's white, to bring you mazel," she says, looking dreamily at Raizl, imagining her good fortune. "Ah sheine maidele. Ah yiddishe kop. Pretty and smart!" She puts the dress down on the desk and gently strokes Raizl's head, this time letting the curls be curly.

Suddenly she grips Raizl's hand with a terrible pressure, as if to pull her somewhere. "I don't want you to be alone," Mami says.

She stares fiercely at Raizl. "I want you to be happy, Raizele. The studying, it's what you want, fine, you should study. A gift from Der Bashefer, your seichel! For now it's enough, being smart. But it won't always be. I want you to have more."

Another squeeze, so tight Raizl's knuckles ache.

Raizl twists her hand free and leans in to hug her mother. Her head sinks into the cushion of Mami's chest, which frees her from the awful gaze, that look of love and expectation that Raizl is certain she cannot live up to. The pain of being one of her mother's five born children, raised all these years, and no more able to fulfill Mami's dreams than the miscarriages who never took a breath. "Mami, I'm not alone."

"Not now, Raizele. But after Tati and I are gone—"

"Oy, Mami," Raizl says instinctively, not wanting her mother to conjure her death, to bring that future nearer by speaking of it. "I won't be alone then either!"

Raizl doesn't say how she comes by this not-aloneness. Her secret world online. Instead she says, "I *have* a family."

"You love your sister, your brothers. Of course! And they love you! But you don't want to be an old maid. They'll have their own families, and you'd be the alte moyd in their homes!"

Raizl hugs her mother tighter, trying to erase the distance that separates them even when they are so close.

"Oooof, Raizele. Stop. Put on your dress, and I will give you a necklace to wear. And put that thing away." Mami points nervously at the computer, which is only half hidden by the papers.

Back in September, when Mami had first seen the computer open on Raizl's desk, a look of raw fear came over her face. "Tumeh," she said, pointing at the forbidden machine that tainted their home.

Raizl put her finger on her mother's lips. "Shhhh, Mami. I need it for school. All the homework is here, see?" And she'd turned the screen toward Mami, nothing to hide back then, the computer showing a bright, green-bordered Excel spreadsheet, numbers all neatly in their columns. But the blood drained out of Mami's face. She shielded her eyes with the palm of her right hand, as if she were saying the Shema for protection.

Raizl took Mami's hand away from her face. "I need it also for work. So I can help with the expenses while Shloimi and Moishe learn Torah. So I can pay for my wedding dress."

Eventually, Mami agreed she could keep it. "But when you use it, shut the curtains," Mami warned her.

Now Raizl quickly puts the computer away in her bag, which is where it will stay during the b'show, too. Not that the young man will be allowed anywhere near the bedroom she shares with Gitti, or anywhere at all without parental supervision. But it would be bad luck to have it out while this man, maybe her chussen, is in the house.

The Dress in the Tub

"Nice dress," Moishe says, holding it up so that his long, black coat disappears behind the white dress. "But it would look so much better on you."

It's nearly time for the b'show, but Raizl and Moishe are in the bathroom, where Raizl has taken refuge for the last two hours. Though she agreed to the meeting, agreed on the dress selected by Mami the night before, now she cannot go through with it. She refused to open the door for Mami. But when Moishe knocked, Raizl relented, and here he is, her favorite brother, joking around and smoothing the dress against his chest. He pins it to his collarbone with his chin so that his hands are free to flounce the white woolen skirt from side to side. The bathroom is narrow, and the hem of the dress ends up in the tub.

"Stop," Raizl says, her voice muffled. She sits on the lid of the toilet with her legs drawn up and her head sunk against her knees. She's wearing her everyday clothes, a long dark sweater and a long dark skirt. Moishe's sly humor is not what she wants right now.

"Help me get out of here," she says.

With one arm still holding the waist of the dress, he digs with the other hand into the pocket of his long jacket.

"Smoke this," he says, putting a lighter and the stub of a skinny homemade cigarette on the shelf above the sink.

"Mami is right there!" Raizl shifts her knees so they point at the door.

He shrugs. "What's a little pot smoke in the bathroom compared to the scandal of a girl who won't dress for her b'show? Just take it, relax. In the end you'll be doing a mitzvah by saving Mami from the embarrassment of turning a chussen away at the door."

Moishe is a year and a half older than Raizl. They were inseparable as small children, and even after he went to yeshiva, he could always make her laugh.

But she doesn't touch the cigarette-not-a-cigarette.

"Don't be scared, Raizy."

"I'm not scared," she says, still talking into her knees. "I *want* to get married. But I can't. Ich ken nisht."

Moishe picks up the stub. "Light it for me," he says, and for the first time Raizl lifts her head, doing as he asks, flicking the lighter as he purses his lips around the sliver of paper. He inhales, squints at Raizl through the exhale. She coughs and fans the smoke away.

When the red glow gets close to his lips, he lets the rest fall into the sink, rinsing the ashes down the drain. "If you're not scared, then why not get married?"

Raizl almost tells her brother. She wants to tell him. To tell Moishe what's in her heart, this is her chance.

But what can she say?

The image of a long, U-shaped couch comes into her head, from a video. A half-dozen naked women sit on the couch, and each one has a man before her, a shvantz inside her, in the moal or the shmundie. The women reach for each other, too—they stroke each other's hair or, if their mouths are free, lean sideways to kiss. The scene is chaotic, the U of the women and the U of the men crossing over each other, bodies bending in rhythms Raizl can't predict. This is what she would have to tell Moishe, if she says why she can't get married. She would have to explain the choices, the shifting configurations of shmutz. The messiness and possibilities. The chance to discover what she doesn't know. Won't a husband mean giving up all this—the pleasures she has already found, digesting the images and exploring her body, plus the gnawing certainty that there is still more she hasn't seen?

Moishe interprets her silence as modesty. "You don't have to worry about the bedroom," he says. "The chussen should please the bride. Not just make babies. It's not like the old days."

This advice, sweet and bitter, makes Raizl weep again. How many Chasidish men think like her brother? It *is* the old days.

Moishe gives an uncharacteristic sigh. "You know that Mami will blame me if you don't make a match."

This is true. Moishe's wedding was called off, which cast some doubt on Raizl's own prospects. "I don't want to have Mami's double disappointment on my head, so please, Raizy. Get dressed. Give this chussen a chance."

The B'show

With fresh makeup hiding the afternoon's tears, Raizl sits at the dining room table, waiting for Itzik, her maybe-groom, to arrive. When the buzzer sounds, she doesn't go to greet him at the door the way she would for a friend, the way she would if he were already her husband. She isn't allowed to greet him this way; it isn't done.

It's a strange time, this b'show limbo, when there are even more rules than usual about what she can or can't do. So she sits, not walking past the long rows of holy books, shelves upon shelves of sfurim, the library of Tati's learning that extends from the living room all through the house, down the hall to the front door, and in the other direction to Tati and Mami's bedroom. Books wait everywhere. Books chaperone everyone. Books say there is no such thing as boredom, or even free time. Every second is purposeful, Raizl right now listening for the footsteps, watching in her imagination the progress of this maybe-groom's body, alien, a man who is just a man but is also her future. She doesn't have to marry the first match she meets. But if she says yes? They will be engaged tonight! Raizl knows by the creaking of the hallway floor exactly where this trio is, Mami leading the guests. Raizl follows the man in her mind's eye if not her heart, welcoming him but also doubting him even before he steps into the room. And it seems to Raizl that this maybe-chussen is surely taking a long time to walk down the hallway, his shoes are possibly made of lead, or more likely he doesn't really want to meet her, or if he does want to meet her while he's still in the hallway, he won't want to meet her, not at all, once he finds her.

"Raizele," says Mami. "Mrs. Kahan is *here*. Itzik is *here*." As if she has not merely escorted them, but created them out of thin air.

Raizl stands but keeps her eyes lowered, taking in their shapes without their faces. Mrs. Kahan wears a dark skirt paired with a surprisingly bright silky blouse, white with black polka dots. Itzik will make a tall chussen—his mother's head is only a bit higher than the buttons on his rekel—and this long coat is stiff, as if it's never been worn before, perhaps purchased for this occasion. The newness flutters in Raizl's stomach. She bows her head slightly in the direction of Mrs. Kahan. "Shkoyech," she says accidentally, and then blushes, not sure why she is saying thank you. Thank you for possibly providing a husband? For agreeing to the meeting? She doesn't know what to say to this woman she will call shvigger, the way Shloimi's wife calls Mami shvigger, the way Moishe's almost-wife, a near miss, would have, too, if Moishe hadn't canceled the wedding. Putting Raizl into this wrong-order matchmaking of herself before her big brother.

Mami's head turns back and forth between Raizl and the guests. Smiling, eager, Mami looks faintly concerned that already the introduction hasn't gone well. Considering that Itzik is standing there and hasn't said anything. From Raizl, also nothing more. Things could go wrong so easily. It's much easier for things to go wrong than go well. Even with all the rules about what they can discuss (not much) and what they can do (even less), there is still too much left to chance, to the idiosyncrasies of a boy who has not talked to girls since kindergarten, and of a girl who has dreams. A girl who has secrets.

Mami, flustered, clasps her hands together and welcomes them again. "Burech ha-bo," she says.

The game Raizl agreed to now seems as if it's being played without her, even though she's the main character. She certainly doesn't feel at all like a wife, or like a bride, or even like an about-to-be-engaged girl. The only thing she knows with certainty is that she's supposed to say something.

"Yah, burech ha-bo," she murmurs, wondering if Mami will feed her more lines. Wanting Mami to stay just a little longer and wanting Mami, and Mrs. Kahan, to go, go, go.

Mami ushers Mrs. Kahan to the living room, leaving the double doors open, and immediately they are chatting side by side on the couch, turned toward each other with broad smiles and happy tones, never looking toward the dining room. They could almost be sisters, Raizl thinks, except that Mrs. Kahan's small hat is perched farther back on her sheitel while Mami pins hers right on top.

"Shulem aleichem!" Tati bellows, joining them.

"Aleichem shulem," Itzik says, extending his hand.

Tati proceeds to the living room and sits in an armchair off to the side, the only one without a match at this meeting.

It's quite warm in the apartment, and Raizl wishes the b'show would start in earnest. She and Itzik are wasting precious time, standing around in silence while their mothers get to know each other. She assesses him in her peripheral vision. He is a long tall string bean, so gaunt it's startling. Will he ever come sit? Will he ever speak? He has to speak first! Suddenly their eyes meet, and Raizl gasps slightly, not meaning to, and tries to mask it as a sneeze. The gasp of looking directly at a man who could become her husband. She loves him and hates him for this. He is handsome, with large dark eyes and his hat at a fractionally jaunty angle. He is a little ugly, too. His hands dangle out of his cuffs like a straggling plant, too many years without sunlight but growing nonetheless. His skin is whiter than his shirt. One thing that's immediately strange about him is that he's not wearing glasses. Every man she knows wears glasses. Can he even see without glasses? But he's already spotted the box of tissues on the sideboard and placed them on the dining table for her.

"Asisa," Itzik says, his first word to her, as he takes his seat across from her. Not a greeting, but a response to her mock sneeze. Is he wishing her health and giving her tissues because her brown eyes are still red from the crying, and he thinks her sneeze was real? Or because he knows it was fake, and he's calling her bluff? Or reassuring her that he won't call her bluff?

She sinks back into her chair, finally, and thanks him for the tissues. "Shkoyech," she says.

Though they aren't really by themselves, and won't ever be until they're married, this moment of space, with its shimmer and hint of aloneness, is intoxicating. Itzik's tall torso leans forward over the table, as if there is a Gemureh lying before him, but there is no Gemureh— she is the sefer, he is leaning forward to read *her*.

Being this close to a man is terrifying, thrilling. Suddenly she imagines Itzik naked beside her, the string bean without a shirt or pants, the outline of ribs above the long belly, a shvantz aimed at her. Her shmutzig mind! Stripping him before they've had a conversation!

They are not actually close, of course; no matter how much he leans forward, there is still a table between them. That and the box of tissues, sitting in the middle like the augur of their future child, or some other emblem of all that ties them together but also keeps them apart. Still, Raizl is acutely aware of his body, the points of his broad shoulders elegant in the dark coat.

"Are you feeling sick?" he asks.

"No, not sick. Not at all."

"Burech Hashem," he says, thanking G-d for her health. "I'm happy for us. For our meeting."

Us? The word sends a little electric shock through her. It seems a terrible impropriety, and she likes it very much. It's almost mathematical: Raizl + Itzik = Us. She is simultaneously inside and outside the equation, accepting him, accepting the inevitable elements of matchmaking that would transform their seats at her parents' dining table into seats at their own table, in their own apartment. Turn the electric shock of a word into the sustained current of touch. She tries to guess whether she likes him. He hasn't said anything offensive. He was thoughtful about the tissues. Yes, she guesses, she could marry him. She wonders what else her mother heard about him that might make him a good match.

"Burech Hashem," she agrees.

Immediately she blushes. Repeating Mami, now repeating Itzik.

Hasn't she at least one original thing to say? Her mind fills with algorithms. With shortcut formulas, as if her imagination is a giant spreadsheet waiting for cells to be filled with numbers. As if there is a formula for a shidduch conversation, if only she can decipher the words needed to make the match.

Meanwhile, the radiator behind Itzik clangs, pouring steam heat into the room and covering their awkward silence with a noisy dialogue, as the pipes ask questions and the hissing valve answers. Tall, pale Itzik begins to redden. He melts faster than a candle, the sweat at his temples rolling into his nicely groomed beard.

He looks around, as if he wants to change seats, but he has to stay on his side of the table. The seating arrangements cannot be altered. Taking two tissues from the box, he lifts the brim of his hat and wipes his brow and cheeks. Evidently this isn't sufficient relief; he removes his hat and sets it on the table, mopping his forehead and patting his hair.

Raizl is startled to see his entire head. The hat-flattened brown hair on top, cut close to the skull. The tender sides, above his ears where his twisting payes begin. Not things a girl would normally see on a man before she marries him.

But Itzik doesn't put his hat back on over his yarmulke, returning to propriety. Instead, he unfastens the top button of his shirt. This doesn't loosen the collar, as far as Raizl can tell. Still, she glances nervously toward the living room. Fortunately, all the parents are occupied: Mrs. Kahan and Mami engrossed in conversation, and Tati reading a sefer.

Then Itzik scoops up the damp tissues, and his hand disappears below the table.

Did he put them in his pocket? Drop them on the floor? Raizl suppresses a laugh, imagining that he has disposed of them like a boy who makes the unwanted peas disappear from his dinner plate by throwing them to the ground.

She can't hide her grin entirely, though, and Itzik returns a smile. Encouraged, he asks, "What are you studying?"

Raizl is relieved that he knows she's in college. It's impossible to guess what else has been said about herself, what embroidered truths might have been designed to make her the most appealing bride.

"Accounting," she says. "Other things, too," she adds daringly.

She recalls what she was told about Itzik: that he is tall, which is true, and handsome, which isn't untrue. But was there something halting about his gait? Though she hadn't looked at him directly, kept her eyes modestly cast to the floor as he crossed the room, something didn't seem right. A limp? A sway? One foot smaller than the other, one leg longer than the other? Omissions are not lies, in the field of matchmaking. Omissions are facts waiting to be discovered.

"What other things?" Itzik asks.

Just then, thundering footsteps announce Tati. In the doorway, he draws himself up, his belly inflating with anger. "He gets undressed in front of maan tochter? Like a little cheder boy, in his yarmulke!" Tati bellows. And, pounding on the dining table, he yells, "Why is he bare like that in front of my daughter?"

Bolting into the dining room, Mami takes it all in—the hat on the table, where it doesn't belong, a button undone, Tati's and Itzik's faces equally red. "Let me open the windows," she says, trying to salvage the situation.

"Zaa mir moichel," Itzik apologizes, grabbing his hat and putting it quickly on his head. He stands and bows slightly to Tati. "I didn't mean to offend you or your daughter."

But Tati grants no forgiveness. "What kind of vilde chaye takes off his hat like that?"

▼

After Itzik has gone, after Mami has rewound him and Mrs. Kahan through the hallway and out the door, wishing them well, kol tiv, and the door has shut on Raizl's not-future, she continues to sit in the dining room. She has an impulse to get up, and she can visualize going to her bedroom. She would have the relief of solitude there—Gitti has been sent out to visit Cousin Ruchy, because of the b'show—but Raizl can't move. Paralyzed, held in place like a semiprecious stone set in a ring, as if golden points reach up from the chair and hold her securely, a golden bar around her right thigh and another around her left, a golden bar over her right shoulder and another over the left. She's not a diamond, not brilliant and hard. More of a pearl, round and soft, the luster wearing off the longer she sits. In the company of the memory of Itzik. The man-ness is still in the room, the smell of him, a phantom sitting across the table.

She considers what she might have talked about with Itzik, in those few minutes they'd had to themselves before Tati ended the b'show. What she might have asked him: Why he said yes to meeting her. Whether this was his first b'show, or if there'd been any others before her. Whether he had faith in Der Bashefer always, or sometimes doubted. Whether he remembered his father, who, the matchmaker had said, had died when Itzik was six.

At least Itzik wouldn't have Tati as his new father.

▼

"Farvus?" Mami whisper-yells at Tati. "Why did you drive him away?"

"Our tochter I'm protecting! If you don't say no to a thing like that, taking off his hat, such disrespect, he will bring shame on us!"

"Shame? Shame is driving away a good young man. Your protection is going to make her an old maid! Bad enough Moishe isn't married, and now you want to make it two? People will understand if Raizl goes before Moishe. It's not so terrible. But if Raizl doesn't go, we will have also Gitti home without a match."

"Calm down, Mami. Come have a tea with me." Tati heads for the kitchen.

"Nein!" Mami says in an angry whisper. And goes to Raizl, still frozen at the dining table.

Raizl is more certain than ever: she will never get married. She's already decided. No more b'shows. No more meetings. She's not going to discuss this disaster with Podhoretz, or her mother.

But Mami regards her with squint-eyed determination. With her usual uncanny precision, she knows Raizl's despair, and dismisses it.

"Today was not your time. Next time, the chussen doesn't come here. It's not customary to have a meeting outside, but it's impossible to make a match at home, with Tati. Next time, you go out."

"Really?" Raizl can't believe Tati will agree to this. Can't believe she'll find a chussen this way. "I can go out?"

"And how!" Mami exclaims with a definitive nod. Convinced and convincing.

Cold Turkey

"Have you ever tried to quit?" Dr. Podhoretz asks at the appointed hour the following week.

"Of course," Raizl says.

Once every seven days, Raizl must quit her obsessive watching. The longest day of the week, the porn-free Shabbes.

On Friday before sundown, while Gitti bathes and Mami is in the kitchen, Raizl takes a few private moments for her blue-green sunset in the rays of the laptop. The lid is low, the volume off, so that if anyone walks through the door, not a peep or a moan would be heard. But Raizl listens closely to every bit of it. Even with her head tilted at a crazy angle, in that sliver of vision Raizl knows what she sees, and learns what she feels. She has no shvantz in flesh or plastic, like the women in the videos, but fingers she has, and the ones not shielding the computer are inside herself, finding an internal anatomy to match what has been mapped out for her on the screen. Her longest finger she sends in deep, again deep, fast and quiet, into her vilde loch, the dripping wild hole. *Hurry, Raizl, it's almost Shabbes!*

Gitti returns from the bath, and Raizl stows the computer under the bed. The Shabbes queen cannot be kept waiting any longer. Raizl showered earlier but washes her hands again, splashes water on her face. She watches in a haze as Mami lights the candles, and the flames dance. *Yes, Shabbes, yes.* Her whole body still subtly humming.

When the murmur of Mami's blessing ends, Shabbes has arrived, and Raizl goes with her mother and sister into the kitchen to prepare dinner. Too quickly, the humming ends. Raizl begins putting food on serving dishes, ladling the chicken soup into bowls, sprinkling fresh parsley over the broth fragrant with onion and carrot, over the thin noodles and chunks of chicken. Her fingers look odd to Raizl as they do the normal tasks, as if their other purpose must somehow be visible, too. As if her body's pleasure might be discovered. The afterglow of porn fades, and the drama of the arriving Shabbes queen is lost to the twenty-five long hours of obeying her commands. No electric switches. No synaptic pop. No zeros and ones, no turning on what's off, nor turning off what's on.

▼

"So how does it feel to quit like that?" Dr. Podhoretz wants to know.
"Cold turkey."
"Cold what?"
"It's an expression. Quitting all of a sudden, completely, instead of tapering off gradually."
Raizl weighs these alternatives. They both seem foolish—and impossible.
"Sometimes I say I'm sick on Shabbes so I can stay home while everyone else goes to shul in the morning." She imagines then, home alone in the Shabbes stillness, what it would be like to hear the suck and slap of the porn videos, the moans. To turn on the blue light, though she'd turn on no others.
But she can never bring herself to do it. Even when she's alone in the apartment, Shabbes still surrounds her. "I don't turn on the computer. I keep Shabbes. That's when I *am* sick."
Quitting porn means Raizl puts on her nice Shabbes dress and walks a few blocks to shul with her mother, silent and glum as a lovesick girl. The computer eats away at her. With each step toward the synagogue Raizl lays down invisible wire, her brain networked to the laptop in its bag, in the dark under her bed.
"Is it any better once you're at the synagogue?"
"Not better. It's just different. . . . I pretend I'm like everyone else."
She prays and kisses the sidder, then whispers with Gitti and Cousin

Ruchy at the back of the women's section, as if she is still the school-girl version of herself. After the leisurely Shabbes lunch, Raizl loves to sing zmires too loudly, and clap the table too forcefully during the grace after meals. Her mother glares at her, Gitti tells her to shush, but Raizl doesn't stop.

"When they tell me shush, I bang the table harder. Gitti says I'm as loud as a man."

"So you don't fit in, even when you're not watching porn," Dr. Pod-horetz says.

Startled, Raizl searches the doctor's face for a sneer or angry eyebrow, for the cruelty that must come with such a comment, and doesn't find any—but the words pinch, and all the air that was in Raizl while she told her story rushes right out and she sinks, tired, into the chair. She has always been different. She has always stuck out from the other girls. Her red hair, and the brains underneath. Her good grades. In elementary school she won the contest to memorize the names of all the weekly Torah portions in order, and the contest to name the correct blessings on all the foods. She wasn't the only girl in her class to finish high school, just the only one to start college. Still, until now, she didn't have to hide her difference. Until she started watching shmutz.

It seems that the doctor is waiting for her to say something, but what? Isn't the session over yet? Soon, surely, please; Raizl shuts her eyes to stop staring at the clock. The empty, waiting feeling is one she knows from Shabbes afternoon. After the long lunch, her parents take their Shabbes nap. Zeidy, who used to be Raizl's Shabbes afternoon reading partner, is too sick now, too tired to open a book. Exhausted but unable to sleep, Raizl tosses on her bed, back to belly and belly to back. The Shabbes nap eludes her.

In the absolute peace of the seventh day, Raizl does not dare open the laptop. The only computer is in her mind, which goes to Replay—a mental History of Recently Visited Sites. Though her mind registers the porn, her body stays still. On her bed a few feet away, Gitti barely rests, reading and humming Shabbes songs to herself. The dim after-noon light coming through the drawn shades is still too bright for Raizl to touch herself.

And so the Shabbes goes, a minute-by-minute, second-by-second cycle of self-awareness and denial, of certainty that she can quit porn *anytime* because she is quitting *now*, and despair because she knows she can never quit. She is less alive, less human, without her computer. The initial post-pornographic sunset glow at the start of Shabbes gives way to the itching, anxious, bargaining, clock-baiting wait for Shabbes to end.

"Time's up for today," Podhoretz says.

A Blessing for Traif

As Raizl walks up Lexington Avenue toward campus the next day, the doctor's words play in her mind: she doesn't fit in—not in Manhattan, not in Brooklyn. Not in college, not in her community. Porn, though, has taken her in. Porn welcomes her; porn wants her. Women with bodies of many shapes and sizes, living in their bare skin. Smiling at Raizl, happy to have her there.

She hunts in her memory for a time when she did fit in, wishing she could prove Podhoretz wrong—*you're wrong!* But Podhoretz has gleaned that porn is not all that makes Raizl an outsider.

In its usual spot in front of the main campus doors, a food cart fills the sidewalk with a smell that taunts her. Every day she slows her pace just a bit to breathe it in: a distant cousin of pastrami but warmer and richer, spicier, the dream of a deli roll just out of the oven, a scent so dense it fills Raizl's nose and throat.

Today she gets in line behind the other students in their jeans and Cohen College sweatshirts, and when her turn comes, she points inside the cart's little window toward the sizzling strips of meat.

"Baconegg?" the man asks.

"Baiknan*degg*," she echoes. Hoping it doesn't sound Yiddish.

Raizl doesn't wait to get to campus, opens the paper bag, and falls instantly in love with the little puff of meaty steam when she peels back the foil. She takes a bite and licks her lips for the salt, and Der Bashefer doesn't strike her down, and she swallows to make room in her mouth for more. The egg soft, almost custardy, around the crisp chazzer. She's not supposed to know what this is, but Google showed her: a pinkish animal with a pushed-in nose and big ears. Yidden have died not to eat pig, but she is alive! The sandwich is peppery and buttery and the flavor is not just in her mouth but her nose and ears, too, seeping from her throat and belly into every part of her body, consuming her as she eats.

Too quickly, it's gone. An empty feeling overtakes the fullness, with the nonkosher food finished and no customary way to give thanks at the end of the meal. Of course, she didn't make a blessing before she ate either. If only there were a blessing for traif: *Blessed are You, Hashem, Who creates the fruit of the swine. Who brings forth bacon from the pig.*

At the glass doors to school, pulling out her ID, she searches in desperation for an extra napkin, convinced that grease on her chin will give her away. She rummages in her bag, fingering first some extra sanitary pads and then her sidder, the miniature prayerbook, which she quickly drops back to the bottom of her purse.

▼

Later, after class, Raizl goes to the food court, where students eat burgers and fries and vending machine lunches. Raizl always brings her own kosher lunch from home, and she scans the tables for an empty spot where she can sit with her thermos and open a book, too. She's putting her backpack down in a perfect place, in the far corner of the room, when she realizes a girl all in black, from her hair to her sweater to her shoes with enormous black soles, is staring at her. Her skirt is long and black—even longer than Raizl's.

Raizl takes a deep breath and nods at her. "I can sit here?" she asks.

"It's a free country," says another girl. Or is he a boy? Everyone is wearing black mascara.

Raizl balances on the edge of the empty chair, too uncomfortable to take out her lunch and too self-conscious to leave.

"Why are you wearing everything black?" Raizl asks, suddenly feeling bold.

"How sweet," the girl says to the others, rolling her eyes. "She doesn't know goth." Then she turns back to Raizl. "Amiright?"

Raizl nods, though she's not sure what she's agreeing to. Is this some new word for "goyta"? Does a goyta know she's a goyta? But why would a girl who's not Jewish call herself this?

"Black clothes—that's one part of it. How we find each other," the girl says. "Just like you find your people." She points at Raizl's long, dark skirt.

"I'm not goyta, I'm Chasidish," Raizl says, and they all laugh and Raizl's cheeks redden.

"We know about you," the goyta-goth says. "Your people rule in Brooklyn. Plus Oprah had Hasidim on her show. Oprah loves your people."

Raizl keeps quiet. She's not going to ask what is Oprah and her show.

"I'm Sam," the goyta-goth says. "That's Spark and Kurt." She points across the table.

They both grunt. Introductions are always a worry because Raizl doesn't shake hands with boys. But instead of a handshake they both make a signal with their fingers, and Raizl doesn't have to touch them at all; it's not even a choice.

Kurt and Spark have a phone on the table between them. One white wire goes to Spark's ear, one goes to Kurt's. Their bodies pulse and their shoulders lean together, as if they are holding each other up.

Sam hoists a large, worn satchel onto the table. The bag is covered in metal chains and has a large silver cross at the latch, and Raizl instinctively recoils. Sam doesn't notice this, digging intently through the bag but not finding what she needs. "Damn, I'm hungry," Sam says.

Raizl unpacks her lunch and offers Sam her spoon.

"What is this anyway?" Sam points at the thermos.

"Chulent," Raizl says.

Turns out goyta-goths love chulent.

"Jew-chili," Spark says.

"Look at those potatoes. It's Irish Jew-stew," says Kurt.

Sam keeps going with Raizl's stainless steel spoon from home. The others find plastic and fork in.

"What kind of sausage is this?" asks Kurt.

Raizl doesn't know about sausage. Only Mami's kishke: flour and fat, pepper and paprika.

They eat bite after bite of the tender, falling-apart flanken meat, the beans and barley plump and shining after cooking so long with the marrow bones, the golden potatoes dense with the flavors of onion and garlic and more paprika.

"Aren't you going to have some?" Sam asks.

Raizl nods but isn't sure. Is she allowed to eat with them? Can she make the bruche with them? Is this the same as praying on the subway on the way to campus, an anonymous davener surrounded by goyim? They will all see her lips move, maybe think she's crazy, if she blesses before she eats.

So Raizl just watches, taking them in as they take in her lunch. Sam wears a heavy chain with keys on it. Black liner circles her eyes but they are still a soft brown, the hunger showing in them as she eats Raizl's food. Her hair, dyed a fierce blue-black, falls straight on one side, is shaved short on the other. The freckles rising through the white powder on her cheeks make her look more innocent than ghostly.

There is a stud through Sam's left nostril and a loop through the center cartilage. More metal loops through her eyebrow, like a form of hair stitched there as reinforcements after a severe plucking. When Sam opens her mouth for another bite of chulent, Raizl can see that her tongue, too, is pierced.

In Raizl's world, the only piercing is through the middle of the earlobe, for a diamond or a pearl.

"It hurts?" Raizl points at the stud in Sam's cheek.

"Nah," Sam says. "Even if it does, it's not a problem. Life hurts." For Sam, pain is not an issue. Maybe it's the goal. "God was pierced," she says, looking thoughtfully at Raizl.

"You believe in—?" Raizl can't say Yoyzl, because Sam won't understand that, but she can't bring herself to say the other name, forbidden.

"Jesus? Sure," Sam says. "I don't have a problem with Jesus." And then, "Want me to pierce you?"

"You do that for me?"

"Yeah, babe. Unless you want a clit piercing," she adds. "Then you need a total pro."

Raizl has seen those piercings—online.

Growing up, Raizl never had a word for the place at the center of her body other than *there*. Dortn. Or *that place*. Yene platz. A whole region sending out smells and liquids, with no name. Online, there are names upon names, places upon places. The cunt has also the clit. And the fleshy bead of the clit has, sometimes, a metal bead.

"How much will it hurt?" Raizl asks, trying not to let her voice waver.

"Just a pinch," Sam says, nonchalantly. "Feels gooooood after. Totally worth it."

"Oy." It pops out of Raizl's mouth, and Sam laughs.

"You still haven't said your name, oy-girl."

"Raizl," she says.

Sam gives Raizl another, more intense scan. "Wow. That's a very goth name."

"It is?" Raizl says, bewildered.

"Hell yeah. Razor? You're a walking bloodbath."

Raizl doesn't bother correcting her.

Raizl accepts her new name, and Sam accepts her—her long skirts and long sleeves, her absolute difference from all the other students.

After that, Raizl often joins Sam and her friends in the food court, where they don't eat anything, or at least don't buy anything, because they don't have the money or occasionally because someone brought Ritalin for lunch, and Raizl because she has her kosher food from home.

"Hey, Razor, you got any leftover brisket today?"

Her new friends accept her food as kindness, and they don't ask questions when, sometimes, Raizl falls asleep with her head on the cafeteria table. They put on black eye makeup in the bathroom when they get to school, and take it off before they go home. They understand the exhaustion of not fitting in.

The Rebbetzin

Raizl's boss at the office on Forty-Seventh Street is a woman in a pitch-black sheitel who seems old enough to have great-grandchildren, but as far as Raizl knows, never had children. The Rebbetzin keeps no family photos, other than one of her departed husband, on an imposing desk in the back office. There is a second, smaller desk along one wall of the office, presumably where she worked while her husband was still alive, where now her assistant, a young woman, sits. Raizl heard a bit of gossip, lushen hora, that the Rebbetzin's husband was not in fact a rabbi, but he's been dead so long no one in the office can confirm or dispute this. So the Rebbetzin stays a Rebbetzin.

Raizl's desk is in a back hallway, not far from the ladies' room. Occasionally the Rebbetzin passes by, nodding but never speaking to her. Today, however, she's been told to deliver her weekly invoice report directly to the Rebbetzin.

On her way to the office, Raizl crosses the long corridor of men and women absorbed in setting and repairing jewels. The vendors' stalls occupy a full floor of the building. Behind a row of glass-topped cases, where the finished pieces are on display, they sit at simple worktables. Light pours out of gooseneck lamps onto the fingers of women who string pearls and men who fit diamonds—men whose wardrobes consist only of white shirts and black suits but who carry briefcases of gems in every color, rubies and emeralds and sapphires and opals. The semiprecious men never deal diamonds, and of course the diamond-dealers never touch pearls, as separate as milk and meat.

Most of the diamond business has moved to India, and of all the Rebbetzin's real estate, this is the last property still filled with Jews and jewelry.

Once a week, an armed guard arrives to walk her to the bank. She stoops under her shoulder bag, right shoulder higher than the left, pinning the bag tightly between her body and her elbow on the opposite side from the guard, as if she doesn't trust even him.

In Raizl's bag, the sole jewel is her laptop, with its comforting, anxious weight. She doesn't dare leave it behind at her desk, not while she's in the ladies' room nor on this errand to the Rebbetzin. She walks quickly past the vendors, always polite but telling them nothing.

"Vus machsti, Raizl?"

"Burech Hashem." Praise G-d.

"How's your mother?"

"Burech Hashem."

"And your father?"

"Burech Hashem."

"And your brothers?"

"Burech Hashem."

"And your sister?"

"Burech Hashem."

Perhaps it's true that the Rebbetzin's husband was not a rabbi. Perhaps he was not even pious. His ambition is the only certain fact of his legacy. When they started in business decades ago, Raizl has heard, the Rebbetzin herself was a pearl-stringer, but then her husband leased the stall beside hers and found a subtenant, and same for the stall on the other side, and so on down the line until they had the floor, and eventually bought the building. Why worry about international trade, revolution in South Africa, mining in countries they would not care to visit, currency fluctuations, the dangers of keeping gems on the body? Why all that, when they can collect rents? The bricks and mortar of Manhattan are diamonds to the Rebbetzin.

The office door is open, but Raizl knocks anyway and waits to be called inside before offering the report. The Rebbetzin takes it without a word, squinting briefly before she tosses it onto her desk.

She is exceedingly proper and well-dressed. She wears a triple-strand pearl necklace with the fattest pearls Raizl has ever seen. Gorgeous as they are, they do not serve the Rebbetzin well, their luster making her front teeth more noticeably yellow.

Her squint is perpetual. Even looking straight at Raizl, she still squints. Raizl feels as if she's under a loupe, as raw and unfinished as any pearl the Rebbetzin ever strung.

"Turn around," the Rebbetzin says.

"Vus?"

The Rebbetzin is a strict boss. Everyone knows this. What mistake did Raizl make, what calculation did she miss to be scrutinized like this?

"Turn, sheine maidele," she says again, a bit more gently.

Slowly, looking at her toes as they clock their way around on the carpeting, Raizl turns.

"Good," the Rebbetzin says when Raizl faces her again. "All the invoices are paid?" she asks.

"Yah, Rebbetzin."

"Have they shown you the accounts receivable? The full ledgers? Have you read the bank statement?"

Is this a trick? Is she in trouble, or going to get in trouble? "Nein," Raizl says.

The Rebbetzin shakes her head, disgusted. "Zicher nisht!" she says. "Of course not!" she repeats in English. "Why would anyone teach you something useful like that?"

She holds a statement toward Raizl, as if the paper is an extension of her hand, beckoning. She holds it between her index finger and her thumb, which sparkles with a diamond band. Raizl's never seen a ring on a thumb.

"I will teach you. It won't be hard for a girl like you. Bring the chair here." She nods in the direction of a small wooden desk off in the corner and the plastic stacking chair beside it. Her assistant is not at work today.

The flimsy seat is easy to lift, and when Raizl places it to the side of the large desk, the Rebbetzin pulls it right up against her own chair, thin plastic against dark wood. Raizl sits where she is told, tucking her bag under the chair. The Rebbetzin smells of rose water, like the old women in shul, and something else, astringent and minty. The flesh is loose at her neck but her chin is still strong. What is that other smell?

Raizl has never sat so close to anyone who isn't family; only Mami sat this close, reading to her years ago from the Yiddish book of Torah stories for girls. And Gitti, when Raizl had read her that same book, which Raizl had memorized but she still made sure to point at each word, just as Mami had.

The Rebbetzin points, too, takes her through the columns of credits and debits. Teaches her how the monthly inflow of rents becomes an outflow into other investments, accounts receivable transformed into capital, the down payment on a mortgage for the next new building. Teaches her the Torah of money. Gives the principles of her accounting classes new meaning. The Rebbetzin is surprisingly patient and doesn't get mad when Raizl asks, "If you're always in debt, how do you make any money?"

"Why not look at it the other way around?" she replies, leaning back in her chair for a moment. It's clear from her full smile of unpearly teeth that she likes this question. "I'm always making money, so what's a little loan going to hurt if it lets me make even more?"

She smooths Raizl's hair, tucking a particularly wayward curl around Raizl's ear. It gives Raizl a chill, the scrape of the Rebbetzin's fingernails against her earlobe. But the Rebbetzin's hand goes away, and the moment passes so quickly, it's as if it never happened.

They continue reviewing the statement, and soon Raizl understands that she is to start doing more than recording invoices and paying bills. Receivables will be hers now, too.

"Very good," the Rebbetzin says as she finishes the lesson. "I need a sharp girl like you. A girl with seichel," she adds approvingly.

Raizl takes this as a cue that she can move her chair away, and begins to stand.

"Stay." The Rebbetzin holds Raizl's thigh with surprising strength, so she cannot rise. "There is more."

Raizl has the impulse to push the hand off her thigh and move her chair back to the other desk, where it belongs. But she stays. Surely such odd behavior won't last long. And Raizl does want to know more, wants to be successful like the Rebbetzin. Her accounting classes tell only half the story. The money she studies in college is ephemeral, vanishing the minute the textbook closes or the spreadsheet screen turns off. The Rebbetzin's money is real and never stops. It flows even when the ledgers shut and the office light goes dark.

Each time Mami read to Raizl from the Yiddish Torah stories, when they arrived at the end of a chapter, Mami hugged her tight. That's how Raizl knew it was finished, and Mami, done reading, would put the book aside. For a moment, Raizl worries that the Rebbetzin will embrace her. But all she does is keep her hand on Raizl's thigh, a continuing pressure, as if the money and accounts they are discussing flow through the Rebbetzin's body, and now this information will be pushed into Raizl.

The Smell of There

"Raizele, you go study," Mami says after dinner that night. "Gitti and Yossi will help me."

So Raizl goes to her room, relishing the privacy to get into bed with the computer instead of sitting at the desk, keeping the volume all the way down so she can hear what's going on in the rest of the apartment: Tati complaining that Yossi spends too much time in the kitchen, that he's too old to be helping Mami. He berates Yossi for daydreaming in school. "It's time to grow up, take your studies seriously! Why can't you be more like your sister? Always studying. Always making A's. What kind of parnussa will you earn? What kalleh will we find for you to marry?"

Raizl wonders whether there will be a bride for Yossi, and not because of his grades. Raizl suspects what he is, even if he doesn't. There is a club at college where boys walk out of the office holding hands. She has seen boys kiss there, and online. Things that were beyond her imagining, and surely beyond what Yossi has imagined for himself. Tati calls him weak. There is no room for Yossi's differences. Not in their family, their community. Her father's yelling distracts Raizl from the video, and all she feels as she watches the naked people is sadness knowing that Yossi can't be free, as they are, that his identity will be masked in inverse proportion to their exposure. He will have to fight his insides, his kishkes, to be who his father wants him to be. Or he will hide himself, as Raizl is hiding.

A cupboard slams; the fleishig china jangles. Plastic dishes, for dairy meals, make a totally different sound when the other cupboard slams. The after-dinner fights are always fleishig. And the fight is always the same fight: Tati pounding and insulting; Mami smoothing it over, telling Tati that Yossi will do better, telling Yossi and Gitti that Tati didn't really mean it. Those things he said, Mami tells them, you should forget.

Then, suddenly, it's not the same fight as always. Gitti yells, "Leave Yossi alone!" A high-pitched shriek that Raizl has never heard. And Tati comes around the table, the walls shaking as he bellows, "Chutzpadik maidele!"

Gitti's footsteps come so fast down the hall that the bedroom door swings open on Raizl, and *Sexy Supermodel* is on the screen. Gitti doesn't notice, though; she throws herself on Raizl's bed and sobs into the blanket. Raizl left hand X's out of the porn and clicks into Excel.

"Gitti, please, don't cry!" Raizl wishes she could slide her thighs closed under the blanket, but that won't be possible. Gitti's piteously shaking body is right between her legs.

"Tati is so mean," Gitti sobs. "I hate him." She pounds the mattress with her fist. The shaking bed is just what Raizl needs. Slowly, unobtrusively, she pulls her right hand out from under the blanket.

Gitti stops crying and sits up, giving Raizl a strange look. Her nose crinkles, and then she asks if Raizl's sick. Puts her hand to Raizl's cheek.

"Heiss!" she exclaims, shaking her fingers as if Raizl has a fever hot enough to burn them. "I'm getting Mami."

"Nein!" Raizl says, grabbing Gitti's arm so she can't leave.

Gitti sniffs, uncertain. Sniffs again. It's the smell of there. Like the smell of herring, plus a hint of yeast from the little packet that Mami mixes with water and sugar for the challah. The smell of a whole kitchen on her fingers! That smell gives Raizl away.

Again Gitti sniffs, disbelieving. Raizl and Gitti have always been close. They are the only girls, after the two boys and before the last boy. For years they've worn matching dresses, and Gitti is tall for her age, too, so they could almost be mistaken for twins except that—lucky for Gitti—her hair is a light brown, barely tinged with red.

Raizl puts her hand to her own head, bringing the smell of there right to her face.

"You're right, Gitti, I have a little fever. I'll take some aspirin, I'll be fine."

Gitti's chin goes up. Boldly she points at the computer. "That's making you sick," she says.

"Nein," Raizl says. "Working doesn't make you sick." But she shuts the computer right away as if it's the lid on a can, as if she could lock the smell of herself inside, between the keyboard and the screen.

"Yah," Gitti says, "you work too much." She reaches for the computer. "You should let me help you."

Now Raizl's temperature really does rise with the heat of this possibility: Gitti, watching porn.

For a half second she imagines it. What if she could tell Gitti about the porn? What if it were as simple as showing her the Maccabeats, a stupid song, something she could see once and then never again?

"You're getting the aspirin?" Raizl prompts Gitti. Even in weakness, Raizl is still the big sister; even when Gitti is taking care of Raizl, it is Raizl who gives the order. "Shkoyech," she calls from the bed, thankful and relieved, as Gitti heads to the bathroom.

Broken Time

When Tati got injured at work, it felt like more than just his back was broken. It felt like a piece of their life was broken, like time itself was broken, completely out of order. It made sense for Zeidy, who was old, to be sick. Not Tati.

Three years ago, when Raizl was in tenth grade, it happened. Mami called her on the phone, on a day Raizl was at her job as a mother's helper for a family with six children under eight. Mami had given her the kosher phone to call her for forgotten groceries and other emergencies. That night, Mami asked Raizl to get a prescription for Zeidy's kidney troubles.

When Raizl came home, the kitchen was empty, no dinner was ready, nothing but the kettle whistling away on the stove. From down the hall a moaning joined the whistle, a deep note much lower than the whistle, pressing in on it. Raizl quickly prepared a tea to bring to Zeidy, along with the medicine. But she found Zeidy alone in his room, snoring away until the noise of the tray on his dresser woke him.

"You brought a tea! Shkoyech, Raizele," he thanked her. "Such kindness." Zeidy closed his eyes again but continued speaking. "It's the zchis of your mami, her great merit, that earns her such a daughter. You even guess when I'm thirsty!"

"Where is Mami? Wasn't she making tea for you?"

"Ach, no," Zeidy said.

The moaning began again, coming from her parents' bedroom. Raizl sprang toward the door, but Zeidy called after her. "The tea!"

Raizl backtracked, retrieving an extra cushion and hurriedly plumping the pillows so Zeidy could sit upright. She put the tray on a chair beside his bed, jostling it in her rush so that a bit of tea spilled over the edge of the glass.

"Nisht geferlech," Zeidy said. "It doesn't matter. Go ahead now." He waved her off.

The moaning got worse. The anguished rumble of Tati's voice, different from his usual tone, scared Raizl. Tati had always been strict, but he mixed the strictness with sweetness. If he warned her often in his stern, low voice that something was not permitted, he also brought toys for her and Gitti. He'd burst into their room with his hands behind his back, challenging them to guess what delights he held for them. He'd stop at Toys2U on his way home from work and surprise them with a pack of bedtime mitzvah dolls, a family of figurines with their hands over their eyes for the nightly Shema, or a Shabbes Mami doll with toy candles and tiny plastic challahs.

Now there was no hint of sweetness. The low growl of pain reminded Raizl of Tati's determined voice when he rumbled through the grace after meals. Even at Shabbes lunch, when he was in a hurry to get to his nap, he said every word. This night's rumble still had the hurry in it, the sound of trying to get through one thing in order to get to something else, but also a despair. Raizl sensed that he didn't know how to find the ending of whatever pained him.

Mami, sitting beside the bed with a worried look, didn't seem to know either.

"You didn't bring the tea?" Tati scolded.

"I brought it to Zeidy."

"Zeidy? Why? Don't I need a tea, too?"

A scowl of disappointment creased Tati's forehead. His mouth turned down as if he'd just taken a bite of something he thought he'd like but instead found it rotten and wanted to spit it out.

"Yes, Tati." Raizl turned so she didn't have to look at that bitter face she didn't recognize. "I'm making you a tea. Right away," she said as she left the room.

Mercifully the light was off when she came back with the tea. She put it on the dresser but didn't stay to help with it; she let Mami spoon it into Tati's mouth.

For days Mami went back and forth between Tati and Zeidy, making teas and compresses and bringing the medications with milk or with water, with food or without food as required, pausing only when Raizl came home from school and her job; then, Raizl filled in and helped Zeidy at least. If she went in to see Tati, he yelled, "Go get Mami!"

Tati's voice echoed in her head, even after she scooted out.

Raizl emerged from Tati's sickroom of pain and anger to find Mami resting on the sofa in the living room. Shockingly, Mami's feet were up on the armrest.

"I'm going to quit my job," Raizl said. "This is too much for you."

Mami rejected this idea. "Nein, nein. You'll continue. It's fine. I'm just a little tired tonight."

"I can start working again next year. That family will still need me."

But Raizl stayed at that job. It was Tati who took a leave from his work, and Raizl added a few more hours, to earn her own bus fare and buy a few things for the family, too. When Tati eventually went back to work, he never lifted a big box of merchandise again—no more fifty-inch televisions! ("Why did he lift the television? Twenty-five years at that company! He's a manager! And still carrying boxes like a Shabbes goy!" Mami exclaimed to Raizl, shaking her head. Of course she never said this to Tati. He would be angry, and for what?) Tati got some painkillers that didn't make him throw up and didn't make him constipated, at least not so badly that prunes wouldn't work, and so, slowly, he began coming out of his room, walking, going to shul. Taking a special van to the store in Manhattan on days when the pain wasn't too sharp. But his gruff way of talking didn't go away, and his patience steadily diminished. No one wanted to make Tati mad. When he yelled, there was less and less air in the room, until it seemed as if the room would have to crack open for Tati's yelling to escape and the oxygen to come back in. While he shouted, the creases deepened across his forehead, and little beads of sweat shone on his face. They got used to his pounding on the table. And they waited quietly for him to finish. No one spoke, not just because they hoped for the anger to pass, but because if they didn't spark any more rage, then maybe the old Tati would return.

V-neck

In the bathroom at Cohen College, Raizl pulls off her cardigan and unbuttons her blouse, shoving them into her backpack. For a moment she stands in white skin and enormous beige bra, Chasidish even when undressing, the modesty somehow glued to her so that she can never truly get naked no matter how many layers she peels off. This bra, certainly, is designed for concealment rather than revelation.

Raizl pulls a black V-neck sweater out of her backpack. She had to lie to Mami to take the money out of her paycheck—said she'd lost her MetroCard—to buy it at a store near campus. She shimmies her way into the shirt and, emerging from the stall to examine herself in the bathroom mirror, sees that the fabric is even more sheer than she'd expected, her pallor visible through the top. The line between her breasts is visible, too, right at the center of the V. A shiver runs through her. People who had never really seen her before might now notice her. Certainly she is seeing more of herself.

The dread rises in Raizl as she heads for class. Her face generates heat but her fingers, clutching the straps of her backpack, are cold and numb. Her top half, in the tight sweater, feels like a different body from her bottom half, still wearing the usual long skirt. She might be sliced in two; those might not be her legs, or perhaps it's her front—what the internet calls tits—belonging to someone else.

She gets to class early and sits farther back. More students enter, including a particularly tall student making his way along the row of chairs with one-armed desks attached. He's wearing a shirt emblazoned with a large number ten, and Raizl knows this means he plays a sport. As he passes, Raizl feels his eyes on her, looking down her top. Or did she imagine it? The minute he's behind her, she doubts it. She's never had this experience before. It's scary to feel exposed but also exciting to be seen and possibly desired by a man whose wide hands are so large, they make his computer seem like a child's toy. His long white fingers could send the laptop soaring into the air and then catch it gracefully on the way down. His shirt is tight across his shoulders and chest, just as tight as her sweater. What would it be like, if he took off his shirt? If he took off hers?

She keeps her eyes down on her desk and busies herself with her notebook, taking out the reading assignment: "Superman and Me" by Sherman Alexie. Alexie writes about how he learned to read when he was three years old, how he imagined what the bubbles in the *Superman* comics said, based on the action in the pictures. Raizl wonders anxiously if there might be bubbles above her own head, if the other students can sense that she is starting to strip them in her mind—imagining them, for a moment, without books and backpacks and jackets. Which ones might be willing to hold each other, or her? Whose jeans might be shed? Porn fosters in Raizl a disorienting sense that any clothed human might be waiting for only a wink or a single caress to undress.

But feeling top-half naked herself is so distracting, she can't bear it. It's impossible to focus on anything when she wears this black-but-somehow-transparent V-neck. She slides her arms into the sleeves of her jacket and zips it shut as though the snow outside has piled up inside the classroom. She doesn't care how hot she gets, with the sweat trickling down her spine in a damp line of shame that melts into the tight sweater.

Professor O'Donovan has students read the essay aloud and then puts questions on the board for class discussion. Question 1: When did you learn to read? Question 2: What was the first book you read? O'Donovan wants to know. He wants to know everything! But mercifully, this time he doesn't call on Raizl.

After class, Raizl goes to the library to ask the internet what Sherman Alexie looks like. He calls himself an Indian, and Raizl isn't sure what this might mean. The internet shows photos of him, and that's all she needs to imagine her three-year-old self sitting next to Sherman Alexie's three-year-old self, both of them learning to read. What's in her hand is not *Superman*, though; it's not even a book. It's a three-by-five index card, the only text in the house that's dog-eared and flour-speckled and not holy, part of a collection of cards kept in a box on the kitchen counter, recipes told by Babi to Mami. Next to the box are the eggs and flour and margarine, sugar and yeast and chocolate. Raizl knows the order of the ingredients, so she points to the words in the recipe and reads the index card. Crack the eggs. Add the flour. Mami makes her Shabbes cakes, and Raizl reads. As soon as she learns the recipes, Raizl learns the prayerbook, and then the little booklets containing Shabbes songs and the grace after meals. To follow the sounds of songs and prayers back into words on a printed page is not hard.

In the library, alone in the small study carrel, Raizl finally takes off her heavy jacket—it doesn't matter if she strips down to the V-neck here, where no one watches—and rereads the essay. She has to ask the internet what is Spokane Indian Reservation, and what is Catholic school, but she already understands what it means to be a child who wants to learn when adults around you expect you not to learn certain things. Don't want you to learn too much. And what it means to keep learning anyway.

Bruches Bee

One night, after Gitti turns out the light, Raizl pulls her blanket over her head and makes a private tent for the internet. Barely has she begun to peek into the World Wide Web when the tent sags as Gitti jumps on her bed.

"What are you doing, Raizy? Staying up all night studying, ready to receive the Torah?"

In an instant the tent is collapsed, and Raizl slams the lid of the computer shut.

"Gitti, don't be such a tzadeikes, so righteous and annoying. Go back to sleep."

"I'm not tired!" Gitti announces.

"Fine, stay up if you want, but go back to bed. Leave me alone." Trying to sound disinterested rather than angry.

Gitti stomps off to her bed, harrumphing so Raizl knows she's not sleeping.

Raizl waits for her sister to give in, to fall asleep. There's no question that her own desire—what new video scenes will she find tonight?— will keep her up for hours. Listening for Gitti's breath to even out and deepen into a slight snore, Raizl remembers how studying used to keep her up at night.

▼

Raizl studied day and night, flash cards by flashlight under the covers. "Don't tell Mami," she warned Gitti.

The bruches bee was a big contest held in her elementary school, like a spelling bee except that instead of spelling words, the students had to name the correct blessings to say before and after eating different foods. This contest was not customary in the Chasidish girls' schools, but their principal, Rebbetzin Fried, decided it would be proper for her students to be even more rigorous in saying these blessings. Raizl studied long lists of foods, all the categories of blessings, and the many exceptions. Under the blanket each night, she whispered the names of the foods and their bruches, aiming her words into a huge funnel of listening, Der Bashefer, who hears everything.

For a week there were preliminary trials in each classroom. Then the winners from different grades competed in an assembly before the whole school. Each time it was Raizl's turn to answer, her heart beat so loudly in her head, she could barely hear Rebbetzin Fried name the food—her cue to call out the blessing. She didn't say the entire blessing, just the shorthand, the one word at the heart of the blessing: hu'eitz, the blessing for all the fruit she visualized growing from one great tree in her imagination, and hu'adomo, the blessing for food growing in rich, dark dirt like the shore of the lake in the Catskills. Mezoinois, the blessing like a sprinkling of flour over everything that needs to be baked except bread, which gets the special blessing of Hamoitzi, bringing bread forth from the land. Shehakoil, the everything else blessing like a giant shopping cart that holds all the foods that don't fit into the other categories. And then the blessings to make after eating. Raizl fit all of it into her mind. Her secret, there on the stage, was to imagine the taste of each food, even the things she'd never tried, and swallow before she named the blessing.

Raizl was determined to answer correctly. She would not make the mistake she'd made when she practiced with Cousin Ruchy— saying hu'eitz, the tree blessing, for peanuts when she should have said hu'adomo, the earth blessing. "Wrong!" her cousin had sung, gleeful over Raizl's error. She would not lose because of peanuts! She would win first place and take home the prize: a beautiful pocket-size prayerbook. It had a silver cover with two lions standing on their hind legs, the tablets with the Ten Commandments braced between their paws, and a crown above them. The school will send a letter home to notify her parents. Her mother will open the letter, and her father will be proud. Zeidy will give her a wink that says, *I knew you'd do it.*

That was what she prayed for, standing on the stage that raised her a little closer to himel, and strengthened her sense that Der Bashefer was not only listening to her from heaven but would speak to her, would put the right blessing on her lips. The Creator would help her triumph over the other students, including her rival Dvorah, who said she'd been studying every day. She came from a family of esteemed rebbes, and everyone expected her to win.

Rebbetzin Fried called out the names of the foods and then pursed her lips and stared at each girl in turn. And as she said the foods, Raizl questioned herself:

Pretzel buns—more pretzel or more bun?

Potato knishes—more potato or more knish?

Banana splits—more banana or more split?

The foods got trickier as the contest went along, winnowing out the girls who knew only the most obvious blessings. But the students who had memorized all the lists remembered that the banana and the ice cream had equal weight, and so two blessings were required.

On the stage, Raizl felt woozy, the lights hot on the top of her head. She looked out to the sea of faces, the girls from all grades sitting in rows, bored, fidgeting, whispering to each other. The teachers couldn't keep them all quiet. Over on Rebbetzin Fried's table, the light glimmered off the lovely silver siddur, as if the prize were not a book but a star.

The contest narrowed down. Rivky had to leave the stage after mistakenly saying the bruche on caramel popcorn was hu'adomo instead of shehakoil. Then Leah somehow forgot the bruche for mushroom barley soup. Now only Dvorah was left, until she forgot that the important part of cheese blintzes was not the cheese.

"Mazel tov!" Rebbetzin Fried congratulated Raizl, inscribing the siddur with her name. "May you continue to bring naches to your family and honor to your school!"

And Raizl's last bruche: *Blessed are You, Hashem, Who makes me remember the blessing.*

Too Much

Now that Raizl has found the students wearing all black, their paths cross regularly.

Sam is a senior. She and Raizl don't have any of the same classes. But they have classes on the same days, in the same buildings. When Sam is ahead of her in the hall, Raizl recognizes the blue-black hair from behind.

Raizl runs a few paces, slides in beside Sam.

"Hey, Razor," Sam says. Raizl's heart skips a beat, to be acknowledged, even by the wrong name. "You're looking good today. Nice skirt."

A plain wool but it's black, so Sam likes it. Raizl makes a mental note to wear it again soon.

Raizl realizes that when she walks next to Sam, she becomes almost invisible—as close to normal as she has ever been at college. Usually people stare at Raizl, questioning her strange clothes and her slight accent. But Raizl's long skirt and tights are nothing special compared to Sam's gothic maxi dress, yards of black lace over black boots that have thick rubber soles and steel at the toes. Sam clinks as she walks, the chains around her neck beating time against a studded belt with her every step.

"I'm heading out. See you at lunch," Sam says as she shoves open the emergency exit. An alarm goes off, and Raizl has to decide whether to follow Sam and have people think she's the one who set it off or walk along with the rest of the students as if she had nothing to do with Sam. Raizl keeps walking. Why did Sam do that? Raizl has a moment of anger, but it's immediately swallowed up in sadness, a feeling that she is not a good friend, that she has betrayed Sam by not sticking with her.

▼

At lunch, Sam says nothing about what happened. Sam and Spark and Kurt share Raizl's brisket leftovers. Afterward, as they walk through the food court, Sam motions Raizl to go outside.

Raizl wants to hang out with Sam. It's a delicious thrill to be asked, especially since Kurt and Spark both have class, so it will be just the two of them—the first time they've ever gone off campus together. But it's freezing outside. Though the sun is shining, it's cold enough for snow. And if Raizl goes to the library as planned, well, there's the warmth waiting in her laptop.

"It's too cold," Raizl says.

"Too cold is good," Sam insists. "Just like too hot, too sexy, too loud. 'Too much' means you know you're alive. C'mon. We're going to let our fingers freeze so we can pinch them and it won't hurt. And then, when we come inside, the blood will pour back into the frozen cells and prickle, and it will be amayyyzing." She shudders, delighting herself.

Raizl stops walking. This doesn't sound so good, really.

"You're not going to die," Sam cajoles. "This isn't the arctic circle. If it's really too cold, we'll come right back."

They walk and walk. "Where are we going?" Raizl asks.

"Somewhere we won't get hassled." Sam knows a spot that's hidden, a pocket park where no one will bother them. Where she can light up the tiny stub of a tiny not-cigarette. They sit on a bench and Raizl sees what a treasure it is for Sam, to hold something burning hot between her freezing, numb fingers, to take the heat of it inside herself. By the time the spicy-sweet smoke blows across Raizl the heat is gone; it's just another draft inside the bigger draft of the day. As cold as she is, though, Raizl doesn't leave. She likes the way Sam's eyes drift lazily, the way her thick beige tights are set against Sam's tall black-leather boots, the way Sam casually knocks one knee against Raizl's knee, warding off the cold, a sign of easy friendship.

"You've really never been stoned?"

Stoned? It makes Raizl think of the punishment in the Torah, stoning, which could happen if you were chutzpadik to your parents, or broke the Shabbes, or, chas v'shulem, had relations with not your husband. Or is the punishment for that one burning?

"No one stoned me yet," Raizl says, and Sam laughs.

"But seriously, did you ever get high?"

"My brother does that," Raizl says quietly, as if someone might overhear.

"Oh?" Sam's interested. "Your brother's in college?"

"In yeshiva."

"If he's funny like you *and* he gets high, he'd be a good guy to hang out with."

This is a new perspective: Moishe's smoking as an asset, as something to recommend him.

"Hey, you see that guy over there?"

Raizl sees a man with a beard. Not a Chasidish beard.

"Go ask him if he'll front us some weed. Tell him we'll bring the money tomorrow."

"Tomorrow?"

"Just ask him for some weed. I'm all out." Sam opens her hand to show a streak of ash on her palm, nothing more.

Raizl shakes her head.

"Damn!" Sam huffs. A line of rage crosses her face. "I'll ask him myself."

Sam disappears around the far side of a shed, and Raizl worries that she won't come back. Sitting there alone, Raizl's mad at Sam for asking and at herself for saying no. What if she had gone over to the man, would that have been so bad?

Sam does come back. And after she's puffed on the odd little cigarette, wrinkled and pinched like a finger too long in the bath, Sam isn't angry anymore.

Raizl recognizes the smell from Moishe's clothes, sweeter and without the choking dust of a regular-cigarette tobacco. Now she smells it deeply, Sam alternating between big, quick gulps and the long, head-tossed-back exhalations that shower smoke over Raizl.

"I don't blame you for saying no. I mean, why would I ask you to do that? What's in it for you? You don't even want any, right?" Sam waves her arm in a great arc toward Raizl.

Raizl shakes her head. No way.

Sam takes another gulp, pulling as if the cigarette is a straw, sucking the fire into herself. She doesn't catch fire, though; she sweetens, her head tilted to the side. "You're lucky, Razor," she says through her streaming exhale. "You don't need this shit to get through. I wouldn't last a single day without weed. Not a night. Not five minutes."

Sam gently rubs the glowing end of the cigarette on the bench beside her until the fire goes out. "Got anything left in the lunch box?"

"You're hungry?" Raizl asks. This is something Raizl can do for Sam. Quickly she opens her bag, takes out a foil-wrapped slice of chocolate babka, and hands it to her.

In Sam's hands, the delicate coils of cake pull apart like a braid unweaving, the doughy flesh falling away from the veins of gooey chocolate. Sam tosses piece after piece into her mouth. "Ohmygod, Razor, this is soooooo good. You're amazing. You know just what I need!"

Joy fills Raizl as she watches Sam devour the babka. Yes, she does know what Sam needs.

When the cake is gone, Sam puts her hand out toward Raizl.

"Sorry, that's all I have. I'll bring more tomorrow," she promises.

Sam doesn't take her hand away. The open palm, the reaching fingers are still there, a little bit of chocolate stuck under a fingernail. She's reaching for Raizl, not cake.

It's not forbidden, to touch a goyta. Anyway, she's already touched Sam, passing the babka, and if she had more, she'd touch her again. This is just like touching to give her food, only without the food. Raizl grasps Sam's hand, a quick squeeze.

"You're all right, Razor," Sam says.

The Girls Inside Her

The ornate candelabra stands tall: a wide base of swirling polished silver, like a single magic shoe, and a solid silver body rising to hold seven glowing white candles. The separate flames burn, every Shabbes, with the same light.

"We light not just for ourselves," Mami had said when Raizl was a little girl. "We light for the six million. We light for every Jewish mother and daughter killed by the Nazis. Your light is their light. Your strength is their strength. Your life is their life."

After Mami lights the candles, she pulls Raizl tight against her silky Shabbes dress and holds her for a long time. The whole week flies away—the week that was, Mami cooking and cleaning all the time. In the breath at the start of Shabbes, the world slows down. Mami's belly rises against Raizl's cheek; Mami's fleshy hands squeeze her shoulders. Raizl wishes she could feel like this all the time: certain. Mami's hands squeeze Raizl into herself, make her solid in her own body, remind her that Mami's energy travels through Raizl's shoulders into her spine and then down her legs to her feet. She remembers that she loves herself, too. Mami's love makes her feel lovable, and the unease of the week vanishes.

"Do you understand?"

"Yah, Mami."

"Yah? You're crying, farvus?"

Raizl feels those bodies, the elbows and knees of the girl bodies inside her own. Hugging Mami, she feels the other Mami bodies inside her. They make Mami full and thick and busy, too crowded. She wants them to get out of Mami, and the girls to get out of her. It's terribly selfish that she doesn't want to give up a little bit of space inside herself for them. But she doesn't. She imagines them escaping through her skin. How they dance out of the room, how much lighter she feels as they leave. She squeezes Mami more tightly, urging those Yidden to go, and she loves to have Mami squeeze her back.

Mint Schnapps

Raizl packs her things; she's moving to the small desk in the Rebbetzin's office. The other assistant announced she's getting married and quit.

From her corner, Raizl tracks the Rebbetzin's income (always more) and expenses (always less). Columns of black numbers, uninterrupted by columns of flesh. Raizl would never dare to watch porn at work. The Rebbetzin has eyes in the back of her head, eyes even where her body is not. From her throne of heavy wood and worn leather behind the large desk, the Rebbetzin knows what's going on out in the far corners of the business: who has customers, who doesn't, which jeweler is crying from heartache and can't see pearls for tears, which jeweler is substituting a cheaper diamond into an engagement ring. Surely, if she knows all this, she would glean any tiny flash of porn on Raizl's screen.

When the Rebbetzin calls, Raizl goes reluctantly to her desk. It's a Friday, a short winter day, when everyone in the office goes home by two o'clock in the afternoon to make Shabbes. But the Rebbetzin, rumored to have a helper make all the Shabbes meals for her, stays longer than the others and keeps Raizl working a bit longer, too.

"Kim du." She gestures to Raizl to bring her chair around the desk, the familiar side-by-side arrangement for reviewing weekly reports.

"The rent report's not finished," Raizl says, but the Rebbetzin beckons impatiently.

When Raizl is seated, the Rebbetzin looks at her sternly, and she wonders what she forgot to do, what the Rebbetzin has found missing.

The Rebbetzin leans toward Raizl, delivering a cloud of terrible breath, both astringent and too sweet. "Hub nisht chasseneh," the Rebbetzin says. And clicks her tongue, *tch tch*, for emphasis.

Raizl recoils from what she hears. Did she even hear right? Usually she is subjected to teasing encouragement when news arrives of other couples getting engaged. Mirtzeshem bei dir! *If Hashem pleases, a wedding for you, too!* But the Rebbetzin has a different message. Hissing just inches from Raizl's ear the most unromantic words—a prophecy? a curse?—ever uttered in Yiddish: don't get married.

"A girl with a head on her shoulders shouldn't waste it," the Rebbetzin admonishes. "Let the other girls make babies." The Rebbetzin waves her hand to show how useless these girls are.

Then, perhaps taking into account the pain this might cause Raizl's parents, the Rebbetzin inquires, "Daan shvester, Gitti, is she going to college, too?"

"Nein," Raizl replies.

"Good. Let *her* give your mother babies." The Rebbetzin sips from a tea glass, quarter-filled with a clear liquid. From there the harsh, medicinal smell of mint schnapps. "A son's babies belong to the mechatunim"—the in-laws—"but a daughter's babies are yours."

As if you would know, thinks Raizl.

The Rebbetzin puts her arm clumsily around Raizl's shoulder and squeezes hard. She squints at Raizl, appraising her, as if she's double-checking a receipt. "You're very smart, ah yiddishe kop." The Rebbetzin nods, agreeing with herself. "You are better than three bookkeepers!" Then her hand falls from Raizl's shoulder and she tilts, off balance. The Rebbetzin's lips smear Raizl's cheek, the edge of her mouth leaving a little trail of spit.

Instinctively Raizl pops up from her chair. She says nothing but goes quickly to her desk, wipes her cheek with a tissue, grabs her pocketbook and shoulder bag to pack and go home. Raizl doesn't care that her work isn't done.

But then the Rebbetzin is standing beside her. The Rebbetzin steadies herself by putting her hand on top of the computer, which is closed on Raizl's desk.

"Where are you taking this? My records are here. It does not leave without my permission."

Raizl panics. She can't leave without the computer. "I will finish some extra work at home. And my schoolwork," she stammers.

"Such a sad face." The Rebbetzin lifts her hand from the computer to caress Raizl's cheek.

Raizl doesn't dare move; her face is glued to the Rebbetzin's dry palm.

"Don't worry. Good news for you today, Raizele. I'm increasing your salary. Would you like that?" The Rebbetzin's eyebrows go up, which, oddly, makes her sheitel move a bit, too.

There is something dizzying about the wig's slight rise and the cloud of schnapps. An urgent wave rolls through Raizl's stomach: nausea and the desire to leave. But her legs feel heavy and tingling, a pins-and-needles sensation, a warning that they might not be able to move when she needs them to.

"You have no answer? Don't make me reconsider, sheyfele. Don't make me wonder if you'd like that."

"Shkoyech, Rebbetzin," Raizl says, barely a whisper. "Thank you."

"Git." The eyebrows go down, the sheitel settles on her forehead. Finally the Rebbetzin takes her hand off Raizl's face, ending the caress. "Good. It's decided, then. But it's just between us, Raizele. The extra. Not for your parents. I know they take your salary, and why should a hardworking daughter have nothing for herself?"

"Yah," Raizl says, trying to speak without breathing, to affirm without inhaling any more of the Rebbetzin's smell than is absolutely necessary. Raizl senses, in that moment, a future in which she will need cash. "Between us," she agrees.

"Git Shabbes." The Rebbetzin turns her back on Raizl.

Fast, fast, before the Rebbetzin can set conditions, or call her back, or stop the sun from getting lower in the sky, Raizl clutches the computer and forces her legs to run out of the office, past the empty stalls, past the glass display cases with their empty fields of velvet and the small oval mirrors reflecting no bejeweled ears or necks, until she makes it out the door.

Dead from Forgetting

Raizl sits straight up in bed. Morning rushes over her like a cold wave, knocking her back to the pillow. She forgot to say Shema last night! And is she truly awake now? Or dreaming she is awake, when really she is dead from forgetting G-d?

Since she was four years old, she's said this prayer every night. Even in a delirium of fever she's said it, even when she had bronchitis and each word made her cough. Believing, since she was four, that if she doesn't say Shema at night, she won't wake up.

She throws off the covers, hops out of bed, frantic. Making sure. Standing in the dark, she shivers. Too cold to be dead, but not relieved to be alive. She faces east out of habit, praying in the direction of Jerusalem, and also of Gitti's bed. Raizl listens to Gitti's deep, even breathing. The radiator is silent. How could she forget to say Shema? Last night, she watched video after video, touching herself until . . . she drifted off to sleep. The skin there is still tender, a slight hum in the folds. An image returns to her of one beautiful girl kissing another. They are sitting outside by a swimming pool, their two lounge chairs pushed together, and one girl takes off her friend's top and then holds her friend's golden tittes. Raizl doesn't like the shmutz words she's heard, when she is alone and can turn the video volume on low—tit tits titty—and she doesn't know a better word in her mamalushen so she makes up her own—titte—not a Yiddish word and not an English either. A new word in Raizlish. Titte for one and tittes for two. She watches the whole video of touching and kissing tittes that look so different from her own, a sickly white. The video girl's tittes, out in the sunlight. The color of honey.

This! This is how she forgot to say Shema!

"Forgive me," she whispers, closing her eyes to pray. Raizl curls her right hand into a fist and brings it to her chest, knocking on the door of her breastbone. *Ushamni, bugadni, guzalni.* She makes the deep confession of Yom Kippur but then stops, ashamed. What right does she have to say this communal confession—*We betrayed! We stole!*—when last night's sin is hers alone. *I watched*—she hits her chest. *I saw the girls*—she hits her chest. *I watched, I touched, I found, I watched more.* Hit, hit, hit, hit. *I forgot to say Shema*—she hits again. *I forgot You.* Shivering, her nightgown just a thin nothing against the cold.

How can she make sure this falling asleep too soon never happens again? Should she switch from saying Shema after the porn to saying it before? This is a dilemma. If she says it before the porn, it's as if she's tucking Der Bashefer into bed to sleep so no one (not even Der Bashefer!) will see what she's up to after her prayerful "good night." If she says Shema first, then her night is already protected by Der Bashefer, no matter her misdeeds . . . But what if watching porn invalidates the Shema? What if, by flipping from the Shema to the screen, she is putting all that she prayed for—the safety of her parents and Yossi and Gitti and Moishe and even Shloimi, the assurance that all will wake up the next day—in jeopardy? No, she'd best continue to say Shema after the porn. And when she does, the smell of deep inside her will mix with the powerful words, as if the prayer, too, has a scent, her eyes closed but her nostrils open to the smell of herself and her lips open with prayer.

She hits her chest again, sealing her commitment to staying awake for Shema.

"What's wrong, Raizy?"

Raizl's eyes open. It's still too dark to see Gitti's face clearly, but there is the outline of her sister's body, sitting up in bed. An edge of worry in her wakeful voice.

"Why are you klopping, hitting yourself like that? Are you having a nightmare?"

"Nein," Raizl hushes her. "I'm davening. Go back to sleep."

What did Gitti hear? As cold as it is, Raizl feels a hot shame rush up her neck and cheeks. It's not enough to stay awake for the Shema. She has to stop watching.

Raizl turns her back on Gitti and continues praying. She faces her own bed now and moves her lips without sound.

I'm not going to watch again.

I'm done. No more.

She didn't die this night; Der Bashefer has given her another chance. If she repents, she can earn back her life. Her fist stays stuck to her chest, but she doesn't knock—doesn't want to alarm Gitti further—just presses hard, knuckles against flesh, as if she could drive her hand through breast and bone to her heart below. As if pressing these words into her body can make them so.

Her fist drops to her side. She knows her prayer isn't true, and Der Bashefer knows it, too. A hole opens in her stomach, the diarrhea sensation of her insides shifting. She grabs her robe and runs down the hall to the bathroom.

Borsalino

There are so many Jewish students at Cohen College. Girls wearing jean skirts and boys wearing knit yarmulkes, sitting together on the couches in the Hillel office lounge. They cluster in classes, too, and trade assignments for efficiency. Some of them nod at Raizl, but they don't speak to her. They are modern Orthodox, not Chasidish, and she is relieved that they don't see her as part of their clan. She agrees with their judgment: she's not like them. They live on their smartphones and the internet is just another feature of life, like air and bagels. She's even seen some of these couples holding hands. Going to college, getting a degree, working—these are all expected, for them. They don't take classes on Shabbes, but they pick their own majors and make their own matches for love.

There is, on campus, one hat-wearing young man, more religious than the other Yidden. He's in her calculus class, and right away she admires his bold headgear. Not a black knit yarmulke, blending in with his hair, nor a velvet yarmulke. He wears a black Borsalino, guaranteed to block the view of the whiteboard for any students sitting behind him, so he always takes a seat at the back.

Though his hat is not the kind worn by men in her family, she feels a kinship. Could he be her ziveg, her soul mate, her kollej shidduch? She's not allowed to make her own match, yet a magnetic force seems to pull them together. They are always in the hallway at the same time. Or does everyone in the hall have the sense of being with him constantly, since he is so remarkable?

Today, thrillingly, Raizl gets on the elevator just after him and sees that he presses the same floor she is going to. The library. Normally she would not speak to him, but this week is Purim, and she has two small holiday gift packages, extras from the pile she and Gitti made for their family and friends. Raizl brought them to school for Sam and the other hungry goths, but now she has a reason to speak to Borsalino.

As soon as he sits at a study carrel, she introduces herself. "Ich heiss Raizl."

He barely glances at her. "Calculus," he says in recognition. "Azoy." Then he turns to his business—opens his backpack, takes out a stack of books, and, finally, takes off the Borsalino and sets it down carefully on the desk.

Some girls might be put off by his meager response, his "is that so?" But this is all the encouragement she needs to continue. She doesn't mind his not looking at her, his curtness. These are all typical yeshiva behaviors, signs that he is just what he should be.

"Shalach munes," she says and puts the little package, two humentashen and a mini wine bottle, on the desk. This gets his attention.

"Very nice," he says, with much more enthusiasm. "Is that so!" He unties the ribbon and opens the thick plastic wrap. The wine he puts in his backpack; the two triangular cookies filled with prune jam he leaves on the desk. Returns his focus to his textbook. Only when Raizl begins to move away, figuring she'll get nothing more from him, does he say, "Shkoyech."

She acknowledges his thanks with a slight nod. "Ah freilechen Purim," she replies, hoping that he will return the greeting and make her holiday happy, too. Feeling bold, she asks if he's seeking a match. "You're listening to shiddichem?"

This time he looks up from his book. "Yah. The shadchen is finding me a girl who is at home. No school, no work. Only at home."

Raizl's cheeks go red. His words sting worse than any slap.

Did he notice her wincing? He goes on, his tone softer, but not too soft. "For what should my kalleh work? That's why I'm here, studying."

A sharp regret stabs her, that she gave him the shalach munes. Raizl wants more than anything to grab the gift back, but it's too late, he's mumbled his blessing and popped the humentash into his mouth, a few crumbs of Mami's sweet dough trapped in his beard. He is indeed exactly what he should be. Only she is not who she should be, and this is her trap, wanting this man to be what he is, but also wishing he could be just a little different.

Piggy Bank

Sam has no patience for most students at Cohen College, who are there, Sam says, to "turn a buck."

"You don't want to make money?" Raizl says.

"To move out of my father's house and get my own place, yeah, sure. But the money's never gonna run me. You can see, on people like that, they're just human-size piggy banks, they want to be stuffed full of cash and that's it."

"Piggy banks?"

Sam looks at her. "Seriously? Please tell me you had a piggy bank when you were a kid."

Raizl shakes her head. "Pigs aren't kosher," she explains.

"You don't *eat* a piggy bank. It's how you teach kids to save money. It's a pig shape but empty inside, with a slot on the top, like the slot for quarters on the vending machine. Got it?"

Raizl nods.

"You put your coins in there, and when it's full you take it to the bank, and they give you dollar bills. Well, if the pig's big enough, they might give you tens or twenties. Mine were never that big. Anyway, I stopped putting anything in the piggy because my mom would raid it to buy loosies. It was like a bank that ate my money. Smoked it."

"Loosies?" Raizl asks.

"Jesus, Ray-Ray. You need a translator for everything."

Raizl blushes. It's true. She learns more in one lunch with Sam than in all her classes. If only Sam doesn't give up on her. If only Sam doesn't decide translating is too annoying.

"Loosies are cigarettes you buy individually. Not in a pack. You ever smoked?"

Raizl murmurs a yes, hoping Sam doesn't ask for details. Because she didn't really smoke a whole cigarette. Once Shloimi had left the burning paper tube on an ashtray next to his open Gemureh on the dining table, before Mami said no smoking in the house, and Raizl, seeing it there unattended, so close to the book, decided to move the cigarette and ashtray farther back. But the minute the slender thing was between her fingers, she felt older and more sophisticated, and even though girls aren't allowed to smoke, she put it up to her lips and drew in air through it. The burning in her throat made her gag: it was bitter and awful. She rebalanced it on the edge of the ashtray.

Does one puff count as having smoked? For Raizl, yes.

"Okay, then, so you know. If you've got the bucks, you buy a pack. If you're broke, you buy a loosie. Fifty cents from the piggy."

Raizl imagines a bank in the shape of a pig. An actual bank on the street, a building, all pink with a flattened nose on the front and ears stuck on the sides like wings.

"I don't get it," Sam says. "You're studying accounting, you're great with numbers. You never had a place to save your money when you were a kid? Something to put your money in?" Sam pinches her thumb and index finger together and mimes dropping a coin into a slot in the air.

The gesture reminds Raizl of putting coins in the tzedakah box, but instead of going to charity, the money goes from the pig to the bank. Or the pig to the loosie.

Why would people put money inside a pig, even a toy pig? It seems strange. But maybe it's no stranger than hiding money inside bras in a drawer, or rolled up in socks, or tucked in the spine of a book.

Taking Out the Not

The next day, Raizl stands in the cold dark for the morning prayers.

Blessed are You, Hashem, Who clothes the naked, opens the eyes of the blind, sets the captives free.

Without these blessings the winter day cannot begin. The habit is deep. Not only Hashem's requirement, but hers. No matter what she did the night before, and no matter how much of the coming day will be stuffed with porn and then with hiding porn, she still believes Hashem hears her prayers.

Even if the things she prays for haven't happened yet, Raizl fervently wishes for them. Believes she can add her urging to Hashem's own will and bring them closer.

But blessing Hashem for making her the way He wants her—according to His Will—today, she can't say this.

Hashem cannot want her to be addicted to pornography.

She'd never heard this word, "addict," before Dr. Podhoretz said it. But she googled it and, as usual, the internet gave her the information she wanted, but also too much more. Information about people who want something so badly they will make themselves sick for it, or hurt others for it, even kill for it. People are addicted to money, to gambling, to clothing, to shoes. To houses and cars and handbags. To drugs and drinking and food and smoking. To things that are good for them sometimes, and things that are bad for them always. People are addicted to actual sex, not just videos about it, the way she is. People are addicted, according to the internet, to everything. There are cures, or at least treatments, but between the people who don't want help and the people for whom treatments don't work, the addicted vastly outnumber the cured.

How *does* Hashem want her to be?

To be as she is, addicted, seems a cruel thing for Hashem to want. To be as she was, before she saw the porn, seems impossible, too great a miracle even for Hashem.

A sin to think this! Sin over sin! Watching porn and then thinking Hashem can't destroy porn! When she's the one who didn't follow the rules, didn't safeguard against her own weakness. She should have listened to the rabbis who banned the internet.

Raizl looks down at the prayerbook, reading the words she'd memorized long ago.

It's so much easier to know what Hashem wants for a man: not to be a woman. Unlike the blessing women say, in small print, the men's blessing appears in the regular, large typeface of the prayerbook. *Blessed are You, Hashem*, men say every day, *Who did not make me a woman*. This is what her brothers say, her Tati and Zeidy.

It's true that if she were a man, she could sit in the front of the shul. She could hold the Torah, and lead prayers for the community. She could become a rebbe, she could study Gemureh all day. And at night, Raizl-man could ride the subway!

But Raizl doesn't want to be not-a-woman. Men's lives are more public but not more free. The men she knows seem hemmed in. Borsalino goes to college, and has the power to reject her, but he still has to choose a girl sent by the matchmaker. Raizl's brothers are allowed to discuss which yeshiva to attend, but Tati still picks for them in the end. When the men lead prayers, is it because they want to, or they have to? Meanwhile, a woman doesn't need a group of ten to pray! Raizl likes the option of privacy, of being on a private call with Hashem. Plus a woman can, on occasion, go to the city unnoticed, as Raizl does. To work, or on an errand. Raizl sees her small corner of freedom and isn't about to give it up.

Please, Hashem. Tell me how to be.

And the answer, from Hashem or from inside her: the man's blessing, tailored specially for her, by taking out the not. *Blessed are You, Hashem, Who did make me a woman.*

Purim Shtick

"He needs a dress," Moishe announces, dragging Yossi into Raizl's room. She doesn't answer, doesn't breathe, until Moishe disappears inside her closet. Quickly, silently, she shuts the laptop, hides it under the papers she keeps on her desk for this purpose. It's Purim night, everyone will be leaving for shul soon to hear the story of Esther, and Raizl hopes, in all the bustle, that she will manage to stay behind, home alone. She's never missed the Megillah reading before.

"Raizy, a little help here?" Moishe calls from the closet, his voice half-muffled.

Raizl peers into the closet, where a sweetish smell fills the small space—wine for the holiday, already?—and a few of her dresses are scattered, off their hangers. Unexpected irritation rises in her. Why is Moishe playing like this, making a mess like a three-year-old? But then he brings out the lilac satin gown she'd worn to Shloimi's wedding and helps Yossi pull it on over his pants and his tzitzis. Yossi looks glorious. After Moishe zips the back, the bosom sags away from Yossi's thin chest, but it hardly matters. His smile is radiant, his pale skin incandescent with pleasure.

"Ah sheine maidele," Moishe says, his arms out in an extravagant gesture toward Yossi.

Raizl's annoyance with Moishe fades. In its place is a gulf of sadness, a tug in her throat—for the delicate way Yossi holds the satin skirts in both his hands, his fingers gently lifting the fabric to keep it off the ground—but she doesn't cry. She laughs, and claps her hands, and understands the magic of Purim, when everything is upside down and backward, and all the children wear costumes, and so, in the holiday spirit of pretending to be what he is not, Yossi has become, for a moment, what he most truly is.

From her dresser she takes out some balled-up tights, to fill in the sagging at Yossi's chest.

"Maidele," she says, "here, put these inside." She sees a flicker of uncertainty light across both boys' faces, and a small splinter of fear twists in her gut. Is she taking this Purim joke a step too far? Then Moishe—ah, Moishe, for whom joy trumps the law, joy is the law!—takes one nylon foot and holds it overhead, unspools the ball, and begins dancing with it. While Raizl grasps the other foot, Moishe spins himself underneath the stretch of fabric. Raizl follows suit, turning under the tights, and they dance together without ever touching, the split legs aloft between them. Yossi sits on Gitti's bed, arranging the folds of satin skirt around himself, and stamps his feet with glee while Raizl and Moishe continue their twirling duet. "Keitzad merakdin lifnei hakaleh," Moishe sings. *How one dances before the bride!* Yossi claps, and Raizl joins in the song, in this wedding party of three: she and Moishe are the proud parents of a finally happy bride-boy. And Raizl, too, a kind of bride, married to her family this way.

Then the door opens, and Gitti rushes in. "Why are you dancing? We're going to be late for Megillah reading!"

Then she sees Yossi. "Oy!" she says, and demands, "Take it off!" Turning to Moishe, she insists, "Make him take it off!"

"Gitti, it's Purim! He's a Purim maidele!" Moishe lets go of the tights and continues twirling around the room, his long, black coat-tails rising and flying behind him. He puts a finger to his skull and spins against it like a top, coming to rest at the windowsill.

"You're shiker!" Gitti says, voice trembling with the accusation.

With Moishe too drunk to restore order, Gitti appeals to Raizl. "Mami will come in—you have to make him take it off!"

Raizl will do no such thing. "Step into my office," Raizl says to Yossi, and they both go back into the closet. From a hanging shelf she grabs a few pairs of socks, the thick ones she wears with boots when it snows. "Put these in the front." Yossi giggles and tugs on the left sleeve of the gown.

Raizl leaves him to dress and takes up her position as sentry outside the closet door, while Gitti paces back and forth.

"Nisht git," Gitti says, shaking her head. "This is no good!"

Raizl has an inspiration. "You should do his makeup," she says.

Gitti stops her worried march. She loves cosmetics, so this proposal is delicious—but also, certainly, forbidden. Gitti's face twists in confusion.

"Use my new makeup case." Raizl sets it on her desk and lets Gitti open it. Two tiers of powders and glosses in a gold and shimmering pink palette, with rows of special brushes in different sizes for different tasks, and a mirror on the inside lid. A gift from Mami before Raizl's b'show. Along with a box of tissues, cotton balls, and a small bottle of remover.

Gitti's eyes grow large as the doubt is extinguished. She sits at the desk and in quick, greedy strokes begins to apply shadow to her own eyelids.

"It's for Yossi, remember?"

"Don't worry, when he comes out of the closet, I'll do for him."

While Gitti busies herself with the makeup and Moishe stargazes—he opens the window, sticks his head out to get a better view up the air shaft—Raizl moves her schoolwork, along with the laptop, out of the way, tucking them into a narrow slot on the floor between the desk and the wall.

Out comes Yossi from the closet, triumphant in the newly fitted gown. "It's good, Raizy?" he asks.

Moishe turns around, coughing.

"What's that?" Gitti sniffs.

Raizl knows that aroma, the secret behind Moishe's extra holiday happiness. She rushes to the window and uses a sweater to fan the smoke out into the night.

"Stop that," Raizl scolds in a whisper and pulls Moishe away from the window.

Then she beckons her little brother. "Yossi, my Purim bride, have a seat." Raizl pats the edge of the bed nearest the desk, where Gitti is waiting. "Your makeup will be done by the lovely Gitti."

The color drains out of Yossi's face, from regular pale to Shabbes candle white. He sinks onto the bed and props himself up with his hands, as if he is suddenly old and has not the strength to sit upright.

He looks at Moishe. "It's permitted?"

Moishe holds open his right hand, making his palm wide enough to stroke an enormous flowing beard, though his is sparse and scraggly and not terribly long. He smooths what beard he has and closes his eyes to recall a citation. "Permitted, yes! As Reb Moishe Isserles, the holy R'mo, brings down: since the masquerade's only purpose is merrymaking, we should not view it as a transgression of the laws of men's clothing and women's clothing."

Moishe opens his dreamy, red-rimmed eyes and tilts his head to Yossi. "You are beautiful," he says, "and beauty is permitted to beauty."

Gitti and Yossi both look doubtful. If this is a quote from the rabbis, they've never heard it before.

"What he means is you're making the mitzvah even more beautiful," Raizl reassures them. "But hurry now," she reminds Gitti, "there isn't much time until the Megillah reading."

Gitti goes to work. Gives her brother lashes as long and thick as a girl's, eyelids shaded as delicately pink as two sunrises. Cheekbones rising from rosy skin.

"Ah ziesse kind," Raizl says to Yossi. "Sweet, sweet child." She wants to hug him, but hugs Gitti instead.

"Careful," Gitti admonishes, "your sleeve is getting in the powder."

Raizl again smells smoke from the vicinity of Moishe, who coughs near the window.

Crossing the room to him, Raizl hisses, "No smoking in here!"

"Vus far a smoking?" Moishe smiles impishly.

For the second time tonight annoyance rises in her, now a gathering force of anger. He's going to smoke in her room and let her get blamed! A little wine on Purim is one thing, but smoking is another. Suddenly she senses the danger in letting Yossi dress up like a girl and giving him makeup. Where will all this end?

" 'Vus far a smoking,' " she imitates him sharply. "What you choked on just now!"

"You're being such a hothead, just like Tati."

"And you're shiker, just like Gitti said! Nothing good can come out of this. Yossi will be happy tonight and sad tomorrow. This is fake, the dress and the makeup! He will think it's real, but it's not!"

Moishe gives her the eye. "You're a meshiggeneh! Worse than Tati!"

"Yes, a meshiggeneh," she says in an angry whisper. A minute ago she saw the fun in it, too. "But it's cruel. Giving Yossi this little celebration, teaching him to hope that he can wear a dress and be beautiful. You think this will stay in some box in his mind, a box special for Purim? You think he'll take off the gown and put it back in the plastic and leave it there, not want to wear it again?"

"This is just one night, Raizl! He can't dress up like it's Purim every day!"

"He can't," Raizl agrees. "But what if he wants to?" Raizl doesn't dare say what she thinks about their younger brother, not even to Moishe. Doesn't Moishe see it, too? They both watch Yossi close his eyes as Gitti applies the third color of eye shadow. His bliss is palpable, his lips smiling in anticipation, his head thrown back. "He will be tortured until he has this again," Raizl says. "And he can't ever have it again."

Moishe shrugs. "He's happy now, let him be. It's not so terrible."

For the first time Raizl feels contempt, and even pity, for Moishe; those feelings are usually reserved for her other older brother, Shloimi.

"You smell like smoke and wine," she says. "Take some Shabbes mouthwash."

▼

"Siz git?" Yossi asks. "It's good?" He puts on his glasses and squints into the mirror that Gitti holds up. Gently he holds his payes away from his face and turns slightly right, slightly left, taking in the vision of his bride. He smiles in satisfaction. "Git," he confirms.

"Yes, so good," Raizl says. "Let me take these." She lifts his glasses off his nose and sets them on the desk. While everyone stares intently at Yossi, Raizl puts makeup remover on a tissue. Quickly whips it across Yossi's face.

"What some permit," she says, "others forbid." With a few ruthless strokes she wipes the rest of the makeup off his face. Yossi's tears speed the cleaning. "Take off the gown," she tells him, pointing to the closet.

The Purim shtick is over. In silence Gitti removes her eyeshadow, and Moishe waits for Yossi to change.

"Better," Raizl says when Yossi reemerges, returned to his pants. "Now let's go. It's time to listen to the Megillah."

Fire

The computer is in Raizl's hands. She's in a secluded corner of the library, which is especially empty because it's morning and most students are in class. She has a class now, too. English class, a paper due, unwritten. Her fingers tremble, and she grips the laptop more tightly to keep them still. She opens the lid. Closes it. Opens it.

The Creator is not stopping her from watching porn. Will not stop her.

Raizl understands at a new level what is meant by evil inclination, the yeitzer hora, and why the rebbes and rebbetzins have always been so afraid of it. Hashem doesn't fight against this inner evil, or anyway doesn't care to win.

Why doesn't Hashem stand up, pound a fist on the table, and shout, *Enough!* The way Tati yells when he's out of patience—year-round, not just on Pesach—*Dayeini!* Hashem could break her computer, or break the internet, so that it's not even possible for her to watch. Hashem could make her blind, just for a little while. Hashem could have prevented shmutz from ever existing! Hashem has so many ways to stop her from watching porn, but chooses not to.

Either it's not that bad, to singe her eyeballs daily with these bodies. Not bad enough for Hashem to take the time to intervene.

Or it *is* that bad, but Hashem doesn't care about *her*. Maybe, to Hashem, her troubles and upset are like a distant buzzing fly.

But Raizl knows in her heart that Hashem does care. Hashem is just waiting for her to call out. What's lacking, Raizl decides, is her own will, her good inclination. Letting go of the computer, clasping the edge of the table for strength, Raizl prays. *Hashem, shut my eyes to this, remove it from my thoughts. Turn my heart to You.*

This day, she makes it without watching. She puts the laptop in her bag and goes to class. She promises Professor O'Donovan she will turn in the paper tomorrow. Returning to the library after class, she sits just inside the entrance, the most public spot. She lets the eyes of the other students wash over her, examining her, accepts their scrutiny as the sacrifice she must make to avoid entering the secret internet. She takes out the old-fashioned tools, the pens and loose-leaf notebook paper. When it's time to type, she disables the Wi-Fi. Home for dinner, she feels victorious. Hashem is with her! Her heart is wrapped around her body, protecting her on the outside, while Hashem fills her inside.

"Go lie down," she tells Mami after dinner. Mami starts to say no, but Raizl pushes her out of the kitchen and proceeds to scrub the meat sink and the milk sink, clean the oven, wipe down the fridge. Humming to herself as she works, *V'taheir libeini l'ovdechu b'emes. Purify our hearts to serve You in truth.*

When the kitchen is spotless, Raizl begins to study—not at her desk or on her bed, but at the dining table. She leaves the laptop in her bag and continues her work longhand. She finds a calculator and graph paper for math problems. Past midnight, when all of her assignments are done, she pulls a Chimesh off the shelf. In stories of the great rabbis plagued by their evil inclinations, they didn't fight such fires with math; they fought evil with the word of Hashem. For this, Moishe Rabbeini, our great teacher Moses, brought the Torah from Sinai—not only for the daytime learning, yeshiva learning, partner learning, for contests to see who could recite by heart the titles of all the Torah portions. The first letter of each weekly portion like a number, a very long number that Raizl had memorized in elementary school. She was immersed, as a girl, in that daytime Torah. But the Torah is also for night-learning, a long amulet-book to ward off what tempts her. She opens to the chapter of the burning bush, a strange plant in the wilderness that catches fire but is not devoured. A voice calling Moishe that calls Raizl, too.

Raizl! Raizl!

Here I am.

She reads the passage again, and finds that O'Donovan Here is reading along, goading her on with professor prompts. *So why does Moses take off his shoes before he approaches the bush?* asks O'Donovan in her mind. *What does that tell us about the culture of the time? What can we learn from the experience of Moses, growing up with a speech impairment, about the supports needed for people with disabilities?*

College questions can't help her. She reads for a deeper knowledge, searches the verses to find relief for her aching spirit. Questions that reveal not context but human drive and purpose, that could help her understand her own way forward. Where is the moment when Moishe Rabbeini stops fleeing from his people and from Hashem? When does he decide he can't be a refugee shepherd anymore and instead becomes Moishe Rabbeini?

Raizl reads the chapter again, and then deeper into Exodus, until she folds her arms on the table in exhaustion and lays her head down. "Shema Yisruel," she whispers as sleep rolls over her. Periodically she wakes with a start, her neck sore and her arms without blood flow, but it doesn't matter, she feels strong. At 5:00 a.m. she hears Mami visit the bathroom. The night is over. And the bush burns with fire and is not devoured.

Kokosh Cake

Over and over since the disastrous b'show, Raizl has said no to her mother. She will not have another b'show. Not even one.

On the day after she conquers porn, she tells Mami yes. But she begs Mami to let her have a shidduch-date—a meeting in a public place, with plenty of people all around, so she and her possible-husband will never be alone. She'll even go out with a chaperone! Just no b'show. Please don't bring anyone to meet her at home.

So now Mami takes a different tack, trying to convince Tati to let Raizl go out on a marriage-date.

"Purim is over," Mami says as she tidies up the kitchen after dinner. "In a month will be Pesach, and Raizl will be nineteen. It's time for her to go out on a shidduch-date!"

But Tati will not allow it. "It's not done," he shouts. "The parents make the match, and the b'show is in the home. It's for her own good!"

From her bedroom, Raizl listens to the argument. Gitti surely hears it, too, though she avoids looking at Raizl, bends her head into the Tanach she is studying. But Raizl can't focus on her homework. She sets aside her accounting and creeps down the hallway so she can hear every word. Raizl hardly dares to breathe, wondering how Mami can possibly win this debate.

But Mami doesn't give up so easily. "What are you talking? 'The b'show is in the home.' 'Her own good.' Open your eyes! She's already scared, and then you come in and scare off the chussen!"

While Mami dries the dishes, Tati sits at the dining table, stirring his tea. Mami serves him a slice of kokosh cake so he won't have a dry tea. To sweeten his mood. "Don't hold back the next generation," she gently scolds.

Absorbed in the dessert, Tati pulls the plate closer. He pushes his fork into the dense swirl of dough and chocolate, takes a bite, then uses the bottom tine of the fork to scrape up the chocolate that has oozed onto the plate. "It's not done," he repeats absently.

"Zalmen, would you disobey the Rebbe?" Mami plays her best hand. "The Rebbe says, above all else, the maidele must get married!"

Tati sighs and puts down the fork. He lifts his yarmulke, replaces it: his slightest gesture of relenting.

"I can't say no, and I can't say yes."

That's all Mami needs. She goes back to the kitchen, a smile on her face, to put away the silverware in the fleishig drawers.

Marriage-Date

Mami gets Raizl ready. Straightens Raizl's hair, then re-curls it. As if the straight hair is naturally hers, and the curls are added.

Raizl is keeping her word: yes to a shidduch-date, to trying again, only this time not in the house.

She enjoys herself in the mirror. In her new marriage-date clothes. There is no skin showing, no collarbone and no wrists, just her face and her hands. What kind of porn would that be, a video of a fully dressed woman, a long-sleeved blouse with a cotton sweater over it, not even a tight sweater, and a skirt down to her boots, not even high-heeled? The modesty-porn video. She is walking, her skirt moves, her shoulders understand where her body ends and the space around her begins. All the porn is in her face.

▼

Duvid isn't bad-looking.

Give the matchmaker and Mami some credit. He's tall, but not too tall. His beard is combed. At first his eyebrows seem a bit bushy over his glasses, but then he has such a nice smile when he greets her, she doesn't mind the eyebrows at all.

Their shidduch-date is indoors, in public: they stroll through the elegant lobbies and halls of the Waldorf Astoria. His eyes are not a common brown, but she doesn't want to seem rude so she can't stare to analyze the color. More green? More gray? He reminds Raizl of her brother Moishe, who likes to play pranks on his friends. At the end of a long corridor with marble floors, they peer in the window of the gift shop, now closed for the evening, and he points at a miniature golden replica of the hotel.

"Look at that," Duvid says, grinning, standing perhaps a bit close to her. "Don't bring too much luggage," he jokes, and then, when she laughs, his arm falls to his side, and his sleeve brushes her hand.

It happens so fast. She flinches, and he moves away immediately.

"Oh, I'm sorry, excuse me," he says. "I didn't mean . . ."

Porn has taught her this much: a man doesn't touch what he doesn't want. She takes her own step away from him but looks unabashedly at Duvid's face now, to determine what, exactly, he might want.

"I'm sorry," Duvid says again. The smile is off his face, and he dips his head as if he is bowing to her. "Do you want to leave?"

"Leave?" she says. "Why?"

His head is still down.

"Why should we go? We just got here."

They sit at a table near the bar, and he orders two seltzer waters. He tells her about his family of seven sisters. The five older ones continued their studies and became teachers. He says his sisters are very smart.

"Yah," Raizl says. She keeps her voice even and watches him closely. Why is he telling her this?

"I heard you were different," he says then.

Raizl gulps the seltzer too fast and fizz goes up her nose. A crazy fear races through her, as she coughs and sputters into the napkin, that somehow he knows about the porn.

"I heard," he tries again, "that you were not going to be like the other girls?"

"Really? What are the other girls like?"

He shrugs. "I haven't been on many dates."

"How many is that?" Raizl asks. This is one of the forbidden questions of shidduch-dates, but they are not following the rules, are they?

"Only three or four. Maybe five."

"So what are the other girls like?"

He shrugs again. "Nervous, I guess. Laughing too much, because they are afraid."

Raizl had laughed earlier, at his joke. It wasn't a fake laugh, because she was told she should smile and be friendly. It was real.

"Are they afraid of you?"

"Chas v'shulem!" He is adamant, his eyebrows rising. *Heaven forbid!* "Of course they're not afraid of me!"

"Well," she says, stirring with the straw as if she's got a cup of coffee, not bubbly water. "Maybe they should be."

A slash of hurt crosses his face, and Raizl regrets what she said, wants to take it back.

"I'm not afraid," she says.

Duvid brightens. "Good," he says. "They told me you go to college. Some guys wouldn't like that, but I think it's good." He sits taller, proud of his modern views. "A wife who's not afraid to work, who can help with parnussa."

When their seltzers are finished, he pays the check, and they cross the lobby. But Raizl isn't ready to go.

"Let's walk around more," she says.

"After you," he replies.

They head toward the ballroom, swept up in the flow of guests arriving for a black-tie function. The long chiffon skirts and fancy hairdos, the men in tuxedos, make Raizl feel giddy, as if the banquet is in honor of her and Duvid.

At the ballroom entrance, where the invited guests retrieve their table assignments, Raizl and Duvid turn back, retracing their steps toward the gift shop. There are just a few people in the hallway now. Soon Raizl and Duvid will have to leave in order to avoid being the last ones there. They cannot be alone. But Raizl lingers at the gift shop window, studying postcards with painted illustrations of the grand ballroom whose interior they'd just glimpsed.

Raizl wants to touch him back.

But how? How to touch him without looking at him, touch without anyone seeing her do it, touch without touching? She turns suddenly away from the shopwindow so that the tips of her hair swing past his coat, and her skirt brushes his pants. The wind of her, a kind of energy, the fleshless touch. She leans her back against the glass, her shoulder blades drawn together. If she were in a porn video, naked, her bare breasts would be thrust toward Duvid's face.

Even with her clothing on, this is too much for him. Duvid steps to the side, his shoulders hunching to his ears. The matchmaker calls the next day to say there will be no second meeting.

Shvantz-Fresser

Raizl yawns the minute she settles into her usual armchair.

"You're tired." Dr. P states the obvious. "Staying up late?"

Raizl confirms the diagnosis with a nod. After the date disaster, an all-night date with her computer—no fighting with her inclination. Since then, she stays up two or three nights a week at least, watching porn. She drags herself out of the house, gets to campus, naps in the library. Head on the closed top of the laptop, in a quiet study carrel where it's easy to follow the no-talking, no-cell-phone rules because she falls asleep as soon as she opens a book.

"I had a date with Duvid."

"And?" Dr. P wants to know.

"No second date with Duvid."

"All right," says Dr. P, waving her hand as if to brush him aside. "There are more fish in the sea."

Raizl ignores this. What does she care about fish? "All night I stayed up. After Duvid."

"Watching porn?"

"I didn't know the time until I heard Tati in the hall, going to his early minyan. The dawn prayer service. It was still dark outside. That's when I closed the computer and changed my clothes."

"And you went to class? How did that go?"

"How did that go?" Raizl repeats. "Having the professors call on me when my tongue is numb and my brain frozen?" Raizl's face had felt so tight, as though the skin across her cheeks and nose could peel off. It feels worse now, even tighter.

"That sounds bad." A pause, and then: "What about the night of the date? Let's go back to that. What made you stay up until dawn?"

Raizl says nothing. Let Podhoretz jiggle her pen, or doodle in her pad.

In the silence, Raizl remembers a video of a woman sucking a man's shvantz, licking it and swallowing it up. Eating and eating, fressing the shvantz as if it were the most delicious thing she'd ever tasted. Then another woman enters the room, and the first woman doesn't notice; her back bent toward the man, holding on to his hips, she's so busy fressing there is nothing else she *can* see. This new woman comes up behind the first one and hugs her, rubs her tittes from behind, and a flicker of distraction rolls across the face of the shvantz-fresser. That's when Raizl feels the tingling in her own tittes, and the wet starts down there, and Raizl's body gets connected to the people in the video, riding the same wave of sensation. The shvantz-fresser's pleasure goes to the man, who moans and pushes her head down harder on his shvantz. The second woman lets go of the tittes and squats between the thighs of the shvantz-fresser. Mostly Raizl can't see what this second woman is doing down there because her long hair covers her face, but every so often she shakes her hair to the side and Raizl sees her tongue licking the purple folds. And when the second woman leans away for a breath, Raizl sees the whole story. And the wet pours out of Raizl. The computer is flat and the world before her is virtual, but her wet is real and drippingly dimensional and she sends her fingers down there to find her own story, and the juice is all over her thighs, too, so she wonders did she pish and not realize it? But this is more filmy and sticky than pish. She is as wet as if she were in the video, too, and of the four of them she is not acting, she is the one feeling every bit of pleasure for no money and for no one watching.

This is how it happened, video after video until daybreak.

And what can she offer Dr. P?

"I wanted to watch," Raizl says, finally.

"Our time's up for today," says Dr. P.

Raizl stands, zipping her raincoat in a stupor of memory turning quickly to frustration. Why does this process that should help her stop watching, instead make her relive it? She turns idiotically to the door where she is supposed to exit in a state of repair, a fixed person, or at least mended, mending, but she is still broken, more broken than when she'd arrived. Dr. P stands up, too, which she never does, and comes to the door, which she never does, and puts a hand on Raizl's shoulder.

"Don't give up," Dr. P says. "Go on another date."

Plum Pie

Raizl dreams that Mami is making a plum pie. The pale dough is laid in the dish, crimped along the edges and flat along the bottom, ready for the fruit. Mami has cleaned and pitted the plums, and now she slices them and sets them across the dough.

Suddenly Zeidy appears in the kitchen, his voice rough, warning her of danger. "Stop! Stop!"

Instinctively, Mami runs toward the hall to get the suitcase from the top shelf of the closet, but Zeidy shakes his head and asks, "For what the suitcase?"

Mami lets go of the handle and looks at him in confusion. "You came to warn me! Don't we have to pack everything and leave?"

"Tch." Zeidy points at the kitchen counter. "Don't leave, come here," he directs Mami. "Right here, look at this!"

Mami bends over the counter, her face hovering mere inches over the pie like it's a mirror and she wants to look at herself.

But when she stands upright again, she is even more puzzled. "What is it? What's wrong with it?"

"The plums are flat! You've laid them flat instead of standing them up!" He strikes his head with incredulity.

Mami's face blanches. "Zaa mir moichel," she says. "I'm sorry."

As soon as Zeidy sees Mami pulling the dark purple plums by their skins and setting them upright in the dough as if they are all standing at attention, his face brightens. Mami's fingers move quickly to create dense spirals of plums, circling the one plum in the center, the plum that stands alone.

▼

When her eyes fly open, Raizl is frightened. The plums lying flat in their pie-grave! Quickly she gets dressed, praying as she pulls on her clothes, and races down the hall. At Zeidy's door, she hesitates. It's still dark, not yet morning. Raizl doesn't want to wake Zeidy if he's asleep. But she has to check on him. Slowly, gently, she turns the knob, opens the door a few inches, and listens.

At first the darkened room holds only the hiss of the radiator. But then, as her eyes adjust, she sees Zeidy sitting up in bed. "Git morgen," Zeidy says.

Raizl is so relieved her knees feel weak and she clutches the doorknob. "Git morgen, git yoor," she says, fervently wishing this will be true for Zeidy, a good morning and a good year.

"I was waiting for you, come sit with me."

Raizl sits beside him and reads the Yiddish paper. His eyes shut and she pauses, and he immediately tells her, go on. He doesn't mention her dream.

Paid-for Jeans

"What do you mean you can't?"

"I can't."

"What's going to happen if you do?" Sam tugs at a belt loop on Raizl's forbidden jeans. Jeans so tight that Sam's tug creates a shock of pleasure where the inseam rides between Raizl's thighs.

But the sensation quickly ebbs into shame, and Raizl steps away, scanning Sam's face in the mirror. They've locked the door on the third-floor women's bathroom so that Raizl can try on the pants without anyone seeing.

"Anyway," Sam adds, "why do they care so much about what you wear?" Sam is quite serious about this question, which is ironic, since Sam cares as much about how she looks as any religious girl. Possibly more. Sam has four different shades of black nail polish and even more black eye shadows. Raizl's never heard a Chasidish girl complain that a black top and black skirt don't match, but for Sam, clashing blacks are a big sin.

"If Tati sees me like this"—she gestures at the pants that show the outline of everything—"he'll throw me out."

"So?" Sam's face hardens. Sam's brother left home when he was fifteen. Sam herself has lived in and out of her family's—her father's—house since she was thirteen.

There are days when Raizl feels ready. That she could do it, too: be free as Sam. Take three pairs of underwear—that's the minimum, Sam says, so you can wash a pair, wear a pair, and have a backup for unexpected periods; three is also the maximum because you need space in your backpack for T-shirts and a hoodie; one bra is all—and go.

She could live at work until she finds another place. She'd wait in the bathroom until everyone leaves for the day, and then let herself back into the office after the Rebbetzin, too, is gone. She could be free. She could plug into the outlet at her desk and let the images wash over her all night long. Watch what she wants, with the volume up.

She's not sure, though. Freedom isn't chocolate kokosh cake or cinnamon. Freedom isn't her sister's fingers threading into hers. Freedom isn't the smell of burnt jam and three corners of dough. Freedom isn't any*thing*—it isn't. Freedom isn't hers to give up or to have. A freed girl walks into a sea of grief and possibility, and never finds land. There would be no dry land.

Still, maybe she could do it. She could leave. A few others have left, so they all know how it's done. A suitcase goes missing. A mother weeps once, and never again. A name unspoken. A name extinguished like the candle in grape juice on Saturday night—one brief *hssssst*, and she's finished.

Her family would never speak to her again.

"It's not as hard as you think," Sam says, shrugging. "Besides, you *paid* for the jeans."

But Raizl's already yanking them down, fast, shaking them off her ankles. Her legs itch as the denim peels away and the air makes her skin prickle. She wanted those jeans! But she can't do it, she can't wear those tight blue legs. She has to put something else on. The long wool skirt hangs over the bathroom stall door, the shapeless form of her old self, and her thick stockings, peachy in the fluorescent light. The tight new skin of jeans now sits in a stiff pile on the floor. Why is it easier to eat bacon than to wear jeans? The pants are on the outside of her, while the bacon is inside. Still, it's the jeans that make her want to vomit.

Sam is watching, waiting to see. Sam says a lot to Raizl without saying anything. Now, for example, Raizl knows by the magic of Sam's voice inside her head—*Aren't you going to wear them?*—that she will wear the jeans. Even if she can't do it today. Raizl feels naked, though it's only her legs uncovered. She's embarrassed for Sam to see her fleshy thighs and plain underwear. And ashamed to be disappointing Sam. Raizl zips herself into her skirt and pulls her stockings on underneath. Folds the jeans neatly and slides them into her backpack alongside the laptop.

And then the bathroom door's swinging open, and three girls are huffing about how rude it is to lock them out. Before Raizl can say anything, Sam's gone.

By Whose Word Everything Came to Be

Professor Starr announces the class will be working in small groups, and Raizl's heart sinks. Grading will be weighted heavily not only on class participation, but also on a group project. How is this math? What does this have to do with accounting? Why can't she just keep working with numbers, those friends in her head? It seems that the work she does by herself is only a small piece of the great puzzle that is college.

Raizl is in a group with Brian Johnson and Jason Lee. With clusters of students already spread across the classroom, Professor Starr tells them to go meet in the hallway. Raizl follows the others outside and becomes part of a strange triangle, Asian-Black-Chasidish. There are many Asian students at the college, and far fewer Black students. Almost no Chasidish. Besides Borsalino, Raizl has counted two men with hats and beards and tzitzis and dark suits—Raizl assumes they are Lubavitcher—plus her.

Raizl has no idea what to say in this small group. Jason is looking at the assignment instructions on his laptop; meanwhile Brian stares at her. The backs of her knees itch under her tights, but she doesn't want to adjust them, to call attention to her covered legs. She stares at the ground, at her own black flats across from their sets of white sneakers, Brian's up over his ankles, and waits for the spell of silence to be broken.

Jason says hi and sticks out his hand to shake. Raizl edges away—she's not supposed to touch his man-hand—but then she stops, uncertain what to do. She doesn't want to offend him.

Jason quickly covers for her. He swerves toward Brian, who slaps the outstretched hand with his own sideways palm. On campus Raizl's seen all kinds of palm-slapping, high and low, and other signatures in the air that she's not sure how to read.

Brian laughs while Jason exaggeratedly shakes his fingers as if they are sore. Raizl smiles at their joking around, but keeps her hands carefully at her sides.

Brian reaches into his backpack, rummaging around and then swooping his arm toward them, holding a candy bar. "Want some?" he asks.

Raizl stiffens as he waves it at her and Jason. Chocolate in a brown wrapper with silver letters glinting in the hallway's fluorescent lights. She watches Brian's face to decide what to do. He gives her a welcoming smile, also a knowing smile, almost laughing. Laughing at her? He might be. She feels laughable, with a tight, frightened face, ready to hop away from a piece of chocolate.

It's a kosher brand—she knows the taste of this candy. Jason doesn't want any, and of course she's going to say no, too. A polite no. And modest: "No, thank you," and look away. No, thank you, and no touch.

But she doesn't look away. She doesn't want to offend him either. With one normal breath, her shoulders drop an inch. Her face relaxes.

What if she says yes?

When she holds out her hand, Brian passes the chocolate. Somehow, miraculously, she doesn't touch Brian in this process, only the candy. Opens the wrapper and breaks off a piece. She whispers a tiny blessing: Shehakoil nihiye bidvuro. *By whose word everything came to be.* And that everything now includes candy from Brian.

A familiar, too-sweet flavor. She should say thank you, but the gluey texture makes her tongue stick at the top of her mouth.

"Cool," Brian says. "I didn't think you were going to have any."

Raizl nods, still freeing her tongue from the pasty fuzz of chocolate.

"I figured you'd say no," Brian says. "You wouldn't even talk to me if we weren't assigned to this group. Jews are racist," he adds.

Raizl swallows. "Ray-cist?" she stammers. She knows this word. It's in the student handbook, and a professor has talked about it. She can be kicked out of Cohen College for it.

"Yeah, racist," he repeats. "Definitely anti-Black."

Raizl considers this. It's never bothered her that she doesn't know anyone Black—never even occurred to her to wonder why, she just accepted it. But now she remembers a Pesach outing to the Bronx Zoo many years ago, when Mami grabbed her purse from the handle of Yossi and Gitti's double stroller and tucked it in the basket underneath, below the baby blanket and the formula bottles, as a Black family passed them. And all the times Mami stands for the entire train ride to midtown, never saying why, when the only seat available is in a row with a Black man.

The candy churns heavily in her stomach. It might come back up, like these things she remembers.

"Yah," Raizl admits. She wishes she could say it's not true, but it seems that Brian might be right, at least about her family. The realization sets fire to her cheeks, flaming red up to her forehead and through her scalp. It's as embarrassing as admitting that she loves him, to say this thing that is the opposite of love.

"Truth," he says, his chin going forward. Raizl looks down at the partially eaten candy bar in her hand, as if the answer to this shame lies just inside the wrapper that hasn't been peeled away yet. Jews are anti-Black and she is a Jew, so is she anti-Black? But not anti-Brian? Could Brian be anti-Jew and not anti-Raizl?

"Here, thankh-you very much," Raizl says, slightly more enunciated and Yiddish-y than she wants to sound, and hands the candy bar back to him. This time their fingers connect, giving Raizl a shock. Brian's fingertips somehow reach into her gut and push the air out of her lungs. His easy posture, the stretch of his sweater across his shoulders as he takes the chocolate—all this is inside her now instead of air.

The touch doesn't seem to register for Brian at all. As soon as the candy is back in his hands, he pulls down the wrapper and eats the rest.

Raizl watches him closely. His cheeks and lips are still laugh-smiling as he chews, his beard moving with his jaw. It's not like the wild beards of her brothers, the long beard of Zeidy, the neat beard of Tati, or the many unshepherded beards of rebbes that she is accustomed to. Brian's beard is trimmed very close, shaped along the edge of his jaw. Designed. A beard chosen as carefully as fancy clothes.

Jason begins tapping on his open laptop with a pen, signaling that it's time to get to work. Brian rummages again in his backpack and pulls out a laptop. Raizl, too, digs around in her bag, pretending she's looking for her computer when it's already at her fingertips.

She's certain she closed out of all the porn windows, but what if she didn't? She doesn't want Jason to see her porn. And she most definitely doesn't want Brian to see. The idea of it makes her blush all over again. So she moves aside, stands with one foot propped up behind her on the wall, and balances the laptop on her thigh, her long skirt still hanging well below her knee. When she opens the lid, no porn appears. She's safe. She holds the laptop steady, and mostly she steadies herself.

A Golem Between Every Man's Legs

That night, Raizl holds off on the internet long enough to finish her portion of the group project. She doesn't dare leave it undone and risk disappointing Brian. But her English paper, her stats exam? Nein. No time for those. As soon as she sends the assignment for Professor Starr, she's back on the internet.

Even after several months of watching, she still breathes thirty seconds of fizzy strangeness inside when she sees a naked man. Sees his shvantz: giant, extreme, a shock like the time she plugged in Zeidy's old lamp, until she goes quiet and has her body back again. Raizl reminds herself that this is just what lives inside the pants, and returns to the pants. But it still takes getting used to, seeing the way it inflates, the way it moves on its own, a golem between every man's legs. And the internet says the biggest is Black. For no other man does the color of his skin announce the size of his shvantz. Raizl searches for a reason or at least a way to understand why, on the intershmutz, the Black man is the mannest. Why the dark bodies are chocolate, coffee, mocha but the white ones are never milk or butter. Why the labels repeat—big and giant and even monster. Why monster? The man in this video does what so many men do. He is gruff; a white woman lies on her back at the edge of a bed and he unpeels her without ceremony and pushes into her loch. The woman lifts her hips to meet him, wraps her legs around his waist, her body absorbing each jolt. She isn't trying to get away. No, she holds him tight with her legs, her eyes taking him in as much as her body.

Raizl has an intense craving to touch this man. To feel the muscles as they move under his skin, to rub his shoulders and thighs where the perpetual light of the internet shines, the shmutzlecht. In her imagination she borrows his gruffness, thrusts the white woman out of the way, substitutes herself in the space between his arms. Let him unpeel, let him push in. This man tells her nothing about Brian or how she could ever be his friend. But watching the man tells her about herself.

The man flips the woman from her back to her belly, continues his rough shtupping, and Raizl cannot mimic that, just holds her palm flat against herself, pressing hard, sending the force of the man's body through her own hand, her hips tipping to meet him.

Eighteen and One

Having a birthday on erev Pesach is almost like not being born. There is no birthday cake worth eating; on the eve of Passover, the regular cookies and cakes are banished for the holiday along with every leavened food, but it's too soon for the special nut cake and sponge cake that Mami is saving for the seder. The day is a hiccup in time, not yet yontif but not a normal day either. *Remember the Pesach when Raizl was born*, her older brothers remind each other at the seder every year, after their four cups, when Eliyuhi the Prophet has come and gone and the women are washing the dishes Eliyuhi forgot to take with him, and then it's inevitable, between drunk and dawn, to be a little mean. *That Pesach, when we had to go to Meema Freidy?*

Meema Freidy, whose food tastes like cardboard and glue, who makes mortar of every dish, not just the charoses. The cousins always ask to have seder by Mami and Tati, but on the year Raizl is born, finally, Freidy must reciprocate because Mami is barely back from the hospital before the seder, has to plead with the doctor to let her go home in time for the holiday. Shloimi and Moishe blame Raizl for robbing them of Pesach, not only that night different from all others but that year different from all others. Her fault. And baby Raizl the only one who got a good meal, her brothers tease.

"Mazel tov!" Gitti shouts early on the morning of Raizl's nineteenth birthday. Raizl is still asleep when Gitti congratulates her with a squeeze. The laptop under the covers is sandwiched awkwardly between them. "Me zol hern gite b'seeres!" she says. *We should hear good news!*

"You're trying to marry me off?" Raizl says, giving Gitti a playful zetz on the tush for waking her up, for her presumption.

Still, she's grateful for Gitti's hugs, for her high-volume exuberance that drowns out the sound of Mami in the kitchen, the sound of heavy, brimful pots being shifted from the front burner to the back. They both know Mami has been up all night, not giving birth but cooking and cleaning and cooking. For Mami, the night Raizl was born was not so different from all other nights-before-Pesach: awake, whether giving birth to a daughter or a yontif, always a night to labor.

Soon Raizl will have to be in the kitchen, too, will be there all day, no matter the birthday, stopping only for a moment to watch Tati set a match to the last crumbs, in the alley behind their building. So Raizl shoves the laptop out of the way and clutches Gitti to her, and Gitti holds her just as tight, putting off the unavoidable for a minute or two.

Usually, Mami stops cooking long enough to give Raizl a hug and a slightly abashed promise of chremzlech, her favorite Pesach treat of fried potato pancakes sprinkled with sugar. This modest birthday celebration will take place later in the holiday. But today, nothing. Just a brisk kiss on the cheek.

But Gitti chants and skips around the kitchen. "Mazel tov! Mazel tov! Nineteen!"

"If you're going to dance, at least bring the potatoes over here!" Mami's long ladle, deep enough to reach the bottom of the giant soup pot, clangs on the foil-covered counter. She doesn't have patience for Gitti's exuberance right now, not with the clock ticking down the hours until the seder starts.

"Achtzen mit eins," Mami says. *Eighteen and one.* Calling on the good luck of the number eighteen, whose letters in Hebrew are the word for "life." "May your mazel bring you to the chuppah."

Then, relenting, Mami pulls Raizl close, and Raizl breathes in the scent of the kitchen on her skin, the air itself a steamy broth of chicken and onion and petrishka root.

When Mami lets her go, Raizl feels a terrible heaviness. She recalls her eighteenth birthday, which seems so much longer ago than a single year. Somehow porn has added extra time. Hours that might have been dedicated to her studies, to accounting or Torah, or to sleep, instead spent in silent watching, making her older even than Mami knows.

If she could go back to that long-ago, year-ago, birthday, she'd whisper into her own ear and warn herself: *Don't start. Don't turn it on.*

A tear rolls down Raizl's cheek. Quickly she wipes her face, not to let anyone see her grief. She knows a warning would never have stopped her from watching porn.

▼

When all the cooking is finally done, the seder table laid with the special, twice-a-year china, the silver Kiddush cups that have been dunked in boiling water, the enormous goblet for Eliyuhi, and the round handmade matzos that look like circles of burnt parchment paper, Mami tells Gitti to go put on one of her new dresses for the holiday. Raizl, though, she holds back. "Get another little candle, quickly, it's almost yontif," she says to Raizl.

The silver tray is loaded with the seven-branch silver candelabra, lights for Tati and Mami and for each of their children, plus a small bonfire of votives for Mami's particular practice of lighting extra candles on yontif not just for her mother and Tati's parents, who all passed away years ago, but also six more, one for each of her miscarriages.

Clustered around the base of the candelabra, the little lights generate a fierce heat that bothers Raizl: it's not right that these miscarried ones—who were never even alive—should also get a candle, should have the same claim on Mami's heart and spirit as Raizl, who is alive and needs Mami as only a living child can.

"Put out one more," Mami repeats.

"I put the six—"

"One more," she insists.

"Why do you need more?"

Mami gets annoyed and puts the candle on the tray herself. "There was another one," she says.

"Another miscarriage?"

"No."

Raizl's brow wrinkles. "You had another child?"

"No."

"Vus?" *What?* Sometimes Mami could be infuriating. Tati was furious; Mami, infuriating.

"Abortion."

The shocking word stops Raizl's breath. She wants to run from the room, or maybe run to Mami for comfort. But she's frozen in Mami's stern gaze.

"After Gitti. I was pregnant again. It wasn't a miscarriage. But the doctor said the baby was sick, was dying inside me. That it would kill me, too." Mami sighs, and the corners of her mouth pull down.

"It was permitted?" Raizl asks. She doesn't dare repeat the word.

"Of course!" Mami clicks her tongue. "Permitted, to save my life. I was bleeding and bleeding, it wouldn't stop, even with them putting blood into me, more was going out. I would be dead. It wasn't a question. The Rebbe told them, hurry to do it!" Mami strikes a match and gets busy lighting the candles. Soon the flames are dancing under her efficient hands.

"For this, I am here now. The doctor told me not to get pregnant again, but when we asked the Rebbe, on this shaayleh, it was not such a clear answer. Tati was disappointed, only four children. So, burech Hashem, one more came, Yossi, and he didn't make for me any troubles inside. I was already zeks in draasig, thirty-six, but this baby Yossi, he waited for me."

Mami shakes the match and the flame goes out as she tosses the burnt stub onto the tray. All the candles are lit.

Raizl is still cemented to the spot, her feet numb. More shocking than the abortion is Mami telling her about it, discussing what has been unspoken for so many years. She pictures herself, a small child when it happened, and Gitti still the baby of the family. Now Raizl has a strange feeling about her long period of unawareness, her not knowing it happened coexisting alongside the fact that it did. Sensation returns uncomfortably to her feet, pins and needles, and Raizl shifts her weight side to side.

"Don't *you* wait, Raizele. Start when you're young, in case it's not so easy for you. In case the babies make tzuris for you. If you start young, and you lose a few, you'll have time to make more, to make the ones who will stay. Start early so you'll have time for the family you want."

Raizl peers into the extra candle, the flame of blue light at the wick, the yellow that grows around the blue. She looks away and spots of orange ignite her vision no matter where her eyes land: Mami's silky green dress, the window just beyond her that opens on a brick wall and the window into their neighbor's apartment. Raizl stares again at the strange, extra candle, the abortion come to life in a flame. The family she wants is what family? She tries to picture it, five or six girls, matching pinafores, all of them with some version of her own freckled cheeks, and the crazy red hair. Five or six boys with red payes framing their pale faces. She's not sure if she wants this family. But what if Mami is right—what if she risks having no family at all?

"Farshteist?"

"Yah, Mami."

"Now, quickly, blow out the candle before your brothers and sister see it. And you, don't mention."

Raizl blows out the extra candle, hefts it into the trash, and returns to watch Mami say the blessing on the rest of the candles.

Birthday Creampie

That night, after the seder is finished and trays of food covered in tinfoil are stacked in the fridge whose shelves are also covered with tinfoil, when every surface is sealed and every body, overstuffed with the required amounts of wine and matzo, lies sleeping, Raizl defies yontif. She lies under the covers with her laptop on, sound off. The red wine purrs inside her. It's not too late for a birthday party online. Raizl doesn't want to sleep, doesn't want to let go of the dream that there is a gift for her on the other side of the screen as she searches birthday videos.

But *Birthday Creampie* is not what she expects. No whipped cream and no meringue, no icebox cake made with non-dairy creamer. Only videos of men shpritzing into girls' faces, sometimes in a girl's mouth and sometimes up her nose or in her eye. Why would a girl in a video want this face-shpritzing for her birthday? Until Raizl realizes, it must be the man's birthday.

Raizl doesn't give up. And the internet obliges her. There's always another video to try, and another. Raizl finds *Girlfriend Boyfriend Birthday Party Sex*, which starts with girlfriend sitting alone on the edge of the bed, smiling—*at her boyfriend? where is he?*—and a helium balloon, HAPPY BIRTHDAY in red letters, floating behind her. The party is in the bed! On the nightstand there's a bottle and a half-eaten slice of chocolate cake, a stub of white candle, a flame blown out. Silvery glints from the balloon move across the wall. In the shadowy light, the girl's large eyes are made up lavishly in heavy black pencil and her lips are noticeably red against her pale skin, which makes her face not perfect at all, just eager and a bit nervous. She rocks slightly forward and back, as if she's on a chair not a mattress, waiting. Raizl waits with her.

Suddenly boyfriend comes diving onto the bed, knocking girlfriend over. He's naked already, his long white back rounding forward as he tugs her jeans off her hips, down her legs. Then she sits up again, holds her arms straight overhead so he can pull her shirt off, and her skin emerges in a bottom-to-top order: belly, tittes, neck. For a second, her body is there without her face, but then she frees herself from the inside-out shirt and kisses him.

Boyfriend draws her down on the bed beside him and yanks a quilt over them both so only their heads and shoulders are visible. She reaches her arm around his neck and they kiss deeply, for a long time, as if they want to be together, as if they might actually be boyfriend and girlfriend. Their movements are so subtle and slow, Raizl checks whether the video stopped. But no, it's just an odd kind of video with a covered-up couple, this modesty like a picture of her future. What she will have, if she can find a chussen!

But she hates that she can't see everything. *What's happening under the quilt? What's boyfriend doing with his hands, and girlfriend with her other hand?* Again Raizl can't tell whose pleasure is it, whose birthday is it?

Raizl watches closely, peering into the screen, wishing she could move near enough to look right through their quilt. Under her own blanket, Raizl crosses her ankles and squeezes her thighs together. Each time girlfriend's hand pulls boyfriend's head down for a deeper kiss, Raizl feels a tug inside herself, a tightening of her loch.

Then the top of boyfriend's arm moves, his collarbone moves, and Raizl draws in her mind the invisible line from his shoulder to where his hand must be on girlfriend's body, if only she could see it.

Finally the triangle of his knee rises under the quilt and boyfriend kicks the cover away. There, yes, his hand is dipping into the shadow below girlfriend's hipbone, his fingers making a gesture Raizl has never seen before, like pressing smooth a wrinkle, over and over.

Boyfriend's wrist floating inches above girlfriend's loch before he dips deeply again.

Then girlfriend's thigh comes up, and when boyfriend notices he interrupts his deepening gesture to push her thigh down. So boyfriend isn't completely different from the other video men, putting bodies where they want them, and Raizl, too, wants girlfriend's leg down so she can see in there, between the thighs, where boyfriend's fingers stroke with a particular method, as if he is searching for something lost inside her, finding and smoothly pulling it out, only to have it slip in again. Girlfriend's body making sideways S's on the bed.

Then, abruptly, girlfriend and boyfriend change places. She sits astride him with a knee on either side of his hips.

Raizl stops the video, not understanding. Why did they switch? What signal did she miss?

Raizl goes back to the beginning of this strange video. Again, she watches. Again, the torment of the quilt. To watch and not see! But the video does show how to follow the covered shape of desire to its destination. This time Raizl's fingers travel the path of boyfriend's hidden hand and find the location on her own body. With fingers like his, she pulls what's inside her outside. So she mirrors the couple, matching boyfriend's rhythm with her hand, and girlfriend's with her hips and tush. Her body makes endless silent S's and the laptop tilts and falls to the side; happy birthday boyfriend, happy birthday girlfriend, happy birthday Raizl.

Shmutzvelt

Nearly morning, Raizl wakes with the laptop still resting against her thigh, under the blanket. The humming in her shmundie reminds Raizl there is more still to watch, and she rights the computer on her belly. There's girlfriend sitting with her knees on either side of boyfriend's thighs. The string from the floating birthday balloon slips like a stray hair across her face. Girlfriend swats it away, but it dangles on her head, and boyfriend takes care of it. He tucks the balloon string under the mattress, out of the way. Then he collects girlfriend's hair, the long strands that fall in front of her face, holds the hair in his fist, and she, bowing, licks his shvantz, then swallows it deeply but not greedily. Swallows it not to take it from him but to reveal it—the purpose of her swallow is to pull away and give it to him. As if the shvantz begins not on his body but in her mouth, and each time it emerges more grand.

In the dim light, girlfriend's golden body describes a parallelogram, with the line of her back matching the line of boyfriend's pale thighs on the bed. Her limbs make the diagonals: the line of her thigh from her tuches to her knee on one side, and the line of her arm from her shoulder to her elbow on the other. This is a mathematics Raizl understands. A shape fully discovered. And Raizl feels, for the first time ever in this shmutzvelt, that she knows much more than the people in the video, more than girlfriend and boyfriend—how beautiful they are, the lovely drop of girlfriend's tittes, inverted domes falling from the roof of the parallelogram; and the outline of boyfriend's shvantz as girlfriend rolls her lips along one side of it and back up, down the other side and up—

The video ends, the shtupping unfinished, but Raizl closes the laptop with an odd sense of contentment. Light's coming in around the blinds, so she can't watch the video a third time—the computer must be hidden under the bed before Gitti wakes—but she feels more at home, has a sense of her place in the parallel universe of porn. When night circles back and the second seder is completed according to all the laws, she will watch this again.

Shloimi

Shloimi, Raizl's oldest brother, pious and strict and married, is visiting for Pesach with his wife, Suri, and their baby. Raizl is surprised when he stands in her doorway. Usually he is too busy with his studies to spend time with her. Today, though, one of the intermediate days of the holiday, he is neither in synagogue nor at his studies. He is here, pacing between her bed and Gitti's, his beard so straight it looks like it's been ironed, trailing a scent of cigarettes.

Shloimi goes to Raizl's desk and lifts the cover on her calculus textbook. Shakes his head, clicks his tongue. "Oy, Raizele, farvus?"

Raizl had tried to explain the beauty of math to Shloimi before, and it didn't go well. "Algebra is like gematria," she'd said, back when she was in high school. "Letters represent the values. So instead of numbers we have x and y, and then we find the value."

He'd swept her math book off the table with disdain. "Mamesh kfire!" he'd yelled, accusing her of heresy. "How dare you compare your math to the holy secrets of gematria. Der Bashefer set those values! We don't make up the meanings!"

He went on contemptuously. "You think you're so smart because the numbers jump into your head. Der Bashefer put them there! They're not yours, and don't forget that. Whenever He wants to take them back, take them away from you, He will!"

Raizl had shuddered at the threat. What kind of Creator would take numbers out of her head?

Shloimi shredded the dinner napkin that had doubled as scratch paper, where Raizl had written a simple problem. The equation turned to zero, the x and y got pulped.

"Watch out, Raizl. Don't worship a false idol. Your numbers, your grades, your future—they are nothing without Torah!" Shloimi was so angry, even after the napkin was torn, the tiny bits floating down and landing on his shirt, all around, like the worst possible dandruff. Then he spat. Raizl had gone numb during the tirade, but the spit woke her up. It revolted her, the little jelly-pond of Shloimi germs right there on Mami's floor. Raizl shifted her feet a few inches.

"Watch out," he warned again. Wagging his finger like an old man of seventy, not a teenager. Then he'd stood right in front of her—Raizl shut her eyes tight, praying please don't let him spit, please not that— and what came at her was not spit but a slightly humid hiss. "Math won't give you children."

▼

Raizl understands her brother, his outlook, perfectly. She knows in her heart that he's right. Numbers have no G-d, and she barely has any G-d left. First she traded Torah for math, and then she traded accounting for porn. What's left for her to trade?

For today, though, Shloimi isn't here to lecture her about the value of Torah over math. Shloimi's hand leaves the calc textbook and travels absently to the stack of papers under which her computer is hidden. Raizl reminds herself not to look anxious—and to get to the bottom of his sudden interest in shmoozing.

"So, Shloimi, is everything okay? What about Lazer?" Raizl remembers how puny that baby was, four pounds seven at his bris last year, and he's still small and crying all the time. "And Suri? They're not sick?"

"No, no, they're fine, burech Hashem." He fake-spits over his shoulder, mimicking an old person's superstition. "Don't make me an evil eye, Raizl."

She sighs. "Do you want a cup of tea?"

"No, no," he says again.

She keeps guessing wrong, until finally comes a clue.

"Em, Raizele, nothing is wrong exactly with Lazer, but there are some expenses. A baby isn't cheap!" He gives a hollow laugh. "I thought you might like to make a little gift for your first nephew."

"Yes, I'd like to," Raizl agrees, relieved to be getting closer to the point of Shloimi's visit. "What does he need? Some new clothes?"

"Well, actually, it's a little more than that. A few hundred would be good, Raizl, a thousand even better. If you can." He smiles, and she sees his yellow teeth. He started smoking cigarettes in yeshiva, and Mami couldn't get him to quit. It seems Suri can't get him to quit either.

She should have known he was here for money—what else? Whenever the brothers needed a few dollars, they came to Raizl. Money for the baseball cards Tati forbade, for candy, even for tzedakah—the charity they wanted to give to impress their classmates, their rebbe—Raizl was the good girl with the gelt.

"You know, Raizl," Shloimi continues, "anything I could do to help you, I would. I'm just thinking of it now"—he snaps his fingers to demonstrate how very sudden this idea is—"that Suri has a cousin, very handsome. A little older, divorced, actually, but handsome. His family is on Forty-Seventh Street, you would have a very fine ring from it."

Raizl rests her hip against the side of the desk. She knows all about Forty-Seventh Street. He is peddling something she doesn't want, to get something he wants very badly.

"I don't have a thousand dollars, Shloimi. I can give you thirty, maybe forty I have"—she gets her purse, unclasps the wallet. "Here," she says.

"No, no—" He waves away her wallet. "Put that away, I'm not asking for that."

"You're not?" Raizl says, tossing her purse on the bed.

"You know very well." He sounds offended. "Tati told me your income. You make a very handsome parnussa. For a girl with no responsibilities, no children to support, it's quite a nice salary."

So he thinks she's holding out on him? Very well, let him think. She might as well try to get something out of this. "You and Suri came by the car, right?" She knows, of course, that they did, how else to shlep the stroller and the suitcases and all the little pecklech, plastic shopping bags filled to the brim as if they were staying for a month, not a week.

"Yes. Suri's parents let us borrow it."

"Can you teach me to drive?"

Shloimi's face contorts in resentment. "Suri would never ask such a thing!" he sputters. "Driving is not for women, and certainly not for an unmarried young woman. But you think, because you're studying and working, you should drive, too? This is what it leads to!" Shloimi says, angrily rapping his knuckles on her papers. Suddenly he shuffles them, and the air rushes out of Raizl. If he finds the computer and opens it, if the last frame reloads, if *Bigtit Hottie Nailed by Her Man* opens full screen to Shloimi, then what?

Fortunately, he doesn't notice the aluminum under the papers. Ending the chastisement, he changes tactics. "If you're working in accounting, why don't you have more cash?" he demands.

"Mami takes my paychecks," Raizl says.

"She keeps all of it?" Disbelieving, though it's in his interest, that her check is deposited into an account that pays a portion of his rent. For all she knows it pays his pastry bills, his deli. "What cash do you have?"

Shloimi starts fiddling with a three-ring binder. Raizl, convinced the computer is about to be revealed, lunges for her purse as a distraction. A couple of Ben Franklins live in there, the secret stash that is supposed to buy—what? A lifetime supply of cheeseburgers and non-beige lingerie?

"Here, take this." She puts the two BFs on the desk. As soon as the cash is down, Shloimi lets go of the notebook, and Raizl scoops it up along with all the papers, a ledger, and the laptop, jamming it all in her backpack while he fingers the gift.

He heads to the door with no acknowledgment. The moment the money disappears into his trousers, it has no other source, and he heads for the door right away.

Relief pours through Raizl, and regret. She shouldn't have given him so much. That was a mistake. He'll be back too soon. But paying off Shloimi was worth it, to make sure he didn't uncover her computer.

She's grateful now for all the years she earned money babysitting and never spent it. George Washingtons eventually converted into Ben Franklins. This is history come to life.

And now cash bonuses from the Rebbetzin.

All of it stored in the First Bank of Raizl: In pockets. In her bra. Under the lining in her drawers. In a rotating cache of shoeboxes and socks. Tucked into old prayerbooks with torn covers that will have to be buried because they hold the name of G-d, when eventually they leave the back corner of her drawer. Better than a piggy bank.

Now she worries that Shloimi may come looking for more. She'd never thought of the bank-shoes, the bank-sachets and bank-bras in her underwear drawer, as hiding money. All these years, she's just been keeping it. If it had been out in the open, she'd never have saved it. But it's also not a secret. Her siblings all know she has cash. That's why Shloimi comes to her.

"Take care of Mami," Shloimi says on his way out of the room. "Farshteist?"

As if. In addition to being a breadwinner, she should also be her mother's protector, should guard her against Tati's wrath?

"Yah," Raizl says to him. What does it take for him to leave, cash is not enough, he needs promises, too, that cannot be fulfilled? But she obliges him. "Ich farshtei."

Pausing at the door to kiss the mezuzah, he adds, "Burech Hashem that you use your seichel for the family," the closest he comes to thanks.

The Food Falls Out of His Mouth

On the last day of Pesach, when Zeidy stops talking but all the other parts of him live, the eating/sleeping/pishing parts, Raizl sits next to him at the table and feeds him. She starts with a fork, but Zeidy forgets to shut his lips and the food falls out of his mouth. So Raizl makes tongs with her fingers and places the boiled chicken and the sponge cake right on his tongue—it's like an infant's game—and then immediately uses both hands to bring his lips together. She cups his moving jaw in her hand, so no food and no dreams fall out.

After that he stops coming to the table. In his bedroom, she spoons sips of water and soup into his mouth, she adjusts the fan so it will blow air over him. His eyes hold no recognition, don't follow her when she moves about his room. His ankles are swollen, the flesh ballooned around the knobs of bone, the joints made for mobility now so stiff that even raised on a tower of pillows they cannot move. Every night when she comes home, Raizl massages these ankles, the skin so thick that no matter how hard she presses her fingers into them, she cannot force blood and feeling to circulate.

Until 120

The ugliness of the internet falls on Raizl. On the screen, a girl who could be Gitti's age, or maybe younger. Her chin thrust forward along with her narrow chest, smiling in a way that makes Raizl nauseous. A smile that knows and doesn't know what it's smiling about.

Raizl quickly slams the internet shut. "Nein," she hisses at the laptop lid. "Tumeh!" she admonishes this piece of metal. *Impure!* "You know better," she tells the internet.

The girl's smile is haunting. She smiles the way Gitti smiles when she tries on Mami's shoes with a low heel and successfully navigates from the hall to the front door, and then insists on wearing them all day. The way Gitti smiles when she declares that she is ready to get married *now*, boasts that she will get married sooner than Moishe or Raizl, and no one can stop her.

Raizl's face is hot but she has the chills, knowing that when she opens the laptop again, the girl will still be there. Because she just shut the machine, didn't close out of that window. How to open the lid and not see that smile?

Raizl doesn't click on any shmutz that says "TEEN" on it. But TEENs without the label still catch her by surprise, show up in videos even when Raizl doesn't want to see them. And they accuse her: if Raizl weren't here at all, she wouldn't be seeing them.

She lifts the lid a tiny bit, and of course the girl is still there, like every annoying little sister who won't go away. "Gei aheim!" Raizl whispers to the girl. *Go home!* The girl doesn't budge from her shmutzige bed with her shmutzige toys. For a moment Raizl imagines staying in this eyelock with the girl, not just for a few seconds but forever. Until 120. The girl in the video, with her shiny pink cheeks, will never be 120 years old. She grows down instead of up, she gets younger and younger by the minute. If only Raizl could protect her. If only by staying in the eyelock with her, Raizl could prevent anyone else from seeing her. It doesn't work that way. Raizl knows this much: right now, while she stares down the girl, scolds her again—*Go home!*—there are others also staring at her, men who arrived here deliberately searching for a little girl, not an accident.

Now this little sister's cute smile is laughing at her. Raizl X's out of the internet. The only way to send the girl home.

Sam and Spark

At lunch with Sam and Spark and Kurt, on the first day back to college after spring break, which is also the first day after Pesach, Raizl shares leftover matzo, which everyone agrees has no taste but excellent crunch.

Sam puts a piece of matzo in Spark's mouth. And a minute later kisses Spark deeply.

Raizl's stomach drops. At first she looks away in a hurry, as if she's seen something private that she wasn't supposed to. Kurt doesn't seem to notice what's going on, in his usual private world with eyes closed and headphones on, but Raizl peeks again and then stares at Sam and Spark, captivated by the glimpses of Sam's tongue, the slice of red against their black-lipsticked lips. This can't be happening. This *is* happening.

When Spark goes to buy a Diet Coke, Raizl can't hold back her question.

"You like girls?" she asks Sam.

"Of course," Sam says.

"You don't like boys anymore?"

"Oh, sweetheart." Sam laughs. "You don't have to choose."

Raizl has seen this not-choosing in porn. Two girls are kissing, and rubbing each other there, and then in comes a man and the girls kiss him. They forget about rubbing each other. Instead, they eat his shvantz together. If the man shtups one girl, then the other girl might remember to kiss her friend, or start rubbing her there again. It all depends on what the man does.

But this is different. This is Sam with Spark, when before Sam would sometimes hold hands with Kurt as they left the food court.

Sam's not-choosing is on purpose, not a mistake. Raizl had a mistake, once, the time she brushed against her cousin Esty's titte. The feeling went through her fingers and traveled down her spine, the sensation like warm liquid running through her, as though she'd swallowed a spoon of soup.

It happened one August, when Raizl and Gitti were younger and stayed with their cousins in the Catskills. There were seven girl cousins, all in one room with three sets of bunk beds, and an air mattress on the floor. Raizl was on a bottom bunk, under cousin Esty, a zaftig girl with round cheeks and shiny blond hair. Raizl felt that her own red hair stuck out just a little less next to Esty's golden curls, and she stayed close to her cousin, loved Esty's singing and her giddy laughter provoked by the smallest thing, like the landing of a dragonfly in the sand on the shore when they went to the lake known to all as the Chasidishe lake, with a separate section cordoned off for women. The girls were prohibited from going in too deep, but even with all the rules, even without swimming, their voices rose in excitement. Such pleasure it was to be in water, to be for a few moments cool. When they had to leave, they shoved their sopping socked feet into their shoes and made wet tracks from all the water pouring off their clothes. Back in their bunk room, Esty hummed songs from the morning prayers as she yanked her wet shirt over her head, and Raizl, turning to get her towel, touched Esty's titte. It was an accident, but that didn't take the touch away—the round feeling, the little tight twist of nipple. Raizl didn't say anything, just pretended it didn't happen, but the breath went out of her. Dizzy, she squatted on the floor, praying Esty wouldn't be angry, and pulled her suitcase out from under the bed as if she had to find something in there, even though it was empty.

From her perch on the floor Raizl looked up, sideways, at Esty. At her tittes, a heavy pair.

Esty wasn't angry or breathless. She was hum-singing "Mi Kumoichu?"—*Who is like You, Hashem?*—and getting ready for her shower as if nothing had happened. Finally she wrapped herself in a robe and gathered her tangled, wet hair, a darkened blond, spraying lake water from the tips.

Abruptly, Esty stopped singing. "What are you looking for?" she asked Raizl. "Why don't you change? You're soaking the floor." Esty lifted one foot, then the other, dripping.

There was a puddle around Raizl, her dark skirt trailing water. She hastily shut the suitcase and stood. "My clothes," she mumbled.

"You unpacked everything here," Esty said, laughing, pointing at the bureau.

"Ich hub fargessen," Raizl said. And it wasn't a lie, saying she'd forgotten, because standing beside Esty she forgot where she was, forgot everything in the world beyond Esty.

▼

That was the last summer Raizl bunked with Esty. The next year, Esty went to a seminary, and then she got married. Now she lives in Monsey with her husband. Raizl doesn't think about Esty, only once in a while, when Mami shares family news, a happy announcement each time Esty has a baby. Three, so far.

▼

Spark is back with her soda. Raizl imagines Sam touching Spark's tittes the way she had touched Esty's, but it wouldn't be an accident, and neither one of them would pretend it hadn't happened. Sam whispers something, a soft breath with words just inches from Spark's face; it's almost more private than a kiss and it's right in the middle of the food court, with dozens of people talking and plastic trays crashing on tabletops. Raizl stares at Sam's lips. Raizl's never spoken to anyone close like that, except for praying, when she davens with intention and whispers for Hashem alone to hear. *Who is like You?* She wants Hashem to feel what's in her heart, and she wishes Hashem could answer her. But Hashem doesn't reply.

Watching Sam and Spark hold each other and whisper is like watching porn. Raizl might as well be someplace far away, in another room or another building entirely, watching them through a screen, because they are in their own world; unlike the people in porn, they've forgotten she's there.

What Day It Is

Raizl doesn't know, when she gets up, what day it is. She hasn't really been asleep. Though sometimes she does drift off while the video continues, her eyelids unwilling to respond even when her klitoris still has that tight, pressing feeling; and she knows if she touched herself she'd be wet but her fingers are unwilling, too heavy just like her eyelids. Maybe she sleeps an hour, maybe two. The alarm clock rings, though she doesn't remember setting it. Her feet hit the floor and she thanks Hashem for returning her soul, out of habit, and says the prayer after she goes pish, also habit. The morning prayers she still lip-whispers along with Gitti as soon as they are dressed. Raizl holds herself in a tight hug to manage standing for the Shimenesre, but at the end of prayers she cannot say the psalm of the day because she doesn't know the day.

Gitti tells her she looks terrible.

"I was studying for an exam," Raizl tells her sister, and asks what day it is.

Gitti rolls her eyes. "How do you know you have an exam if you don't know what day it is?"

"I always have an exam. Don't be such a rebbetzin."

▼

Raizl decides she does know the day. This *is* the day. Jamming the jeans into her book bag, riding the subway with the heat of the computer and the heat of the jeans, a full bag of forbidden!

The Au Bon Pain near campus has an au bon bathroom. A place she can feasibly enter as a bas Yisruel—a daughter of Israel getting water, only water—but then leave as a someone else.

It's more like dressing for war than for a party. That's how it feels to put on pants: like putting on battle gear, a kind of camouflage that will let her blend in with the rest of Manhattan women wearing jeans. Even without a mirror she feels her tuches sticking out. Showing, like a pregnancy. When something hidden suddenly becomes public. The jeans are like a skin against her skin, the fabric pressing all the way around her tuches and between her thighs. Is this how it feels for all the girls wearing jeans? They don't act as if they are in pornos, as if their tucheses are being hoisted into the air. Maybe, over time, the sexy-consciousness rubs off. It's strange how something that will make her unnoticeable, make her look just like everyone else, ordinary, feels so extraordinary.

And she likes it, that friction. This is the day the pants don't make her nauseous, just tough and traif. She feels a meanness toward her father—hah!—but her mother's face would crumble if she saw this. Raizl pushes that idea out of her head. She rubs her lips together so they look raw and puffy, the red blooming as if she's just been kissing, as if she's just about to start. Today is the day to be alive, to have two legs and the feeling between her thighs. Today is the day for bacon-cheeseburger and fries.

She practices ordering in the mirror. "Baikncheesebrrggrr," she says. "Friezz," she says. Tries to say it fast, to get any hint of Yiddish out of it.

She has gel. She goops her hair so pieces stick out. From her curls she makes spikes. Big sunglasses. It's April and warm outside, eighty degrees. If she rolls her sleeves up, she will have sun on her arms!

Pants are beged ish, man's clothing, and thus prohibited. Raizl doesn't feel like a man, wearing pants. She feels more woman: legs, hips, the seam going through her tuches and right up into oyse-mukem. The men she knows don't wear jeans anyway. Maybe if she wore a long rekel, the black coat down past her calves, and black pants, that would make her feel like a man.

She takes her new legs in their new skin on a walk. It's amazing, a giddy feeling, the combined exhaustion from being up all night and the fear and excitement of wearing the jeans. She can't go to school. In these clothes that make her feel like a different person, she can't be in a place where people know her. So she walks fast and avoids eye contact. There are always people from Brooklyn walking in midtown, on business or shopping. She pushes that out of her mind, too. If she doesn't look at anyone, they won't see her.

And what if they do see her? Let them see her! Let them kick her out! When they kick her out, that's it, she's leaving.

First F

When Raizl gets her English paper back the next day, she runs her nail over it, and then the pad of her finger. The F is completely smooth. Sometimes the professor, who requires all assignments to be printed, uses a ballpoint pen that leaves an impression. This time, though, he graded with a fine-tip ink pen, and the F is dyed into the paper like a black blood that made no dent but stained the surface forever.

Her first F. Never in elementary or high school did she get an F. Not in secular studies nor in limidei koydesh.

If she doesn't maintain a 3.5, she will get kicked out of the honors program.

"I don't know what happened to you, Ms. . . ." O'Donovan looks down the roster in his old-fashioned grading book.

"Raizl," she reminds him.

"Ms. Raizl," he says, as if it's her last name.

"Nothing happened to me."

"Well, something must have. People don't pivot like that mid-semester unless there is an event, a trigger. Stimulus and response." Teaching science along with English.

"Please can I make up this paper?" she begs. "Can I rewrite it?"

He frowns. "It's too late for that. If you want to do well in the class—"

"And how!" Raizl exclaims, and blushes for the way she sounds just like Mami, full of determination. "Of course I do."

"Don't worry, you still have another paper before the end of the term. You'll be fine." He shuts his grade book. "Just don't fail the last paper."

"But this one? I can write it again?"

O'Donovan reluctantly reopens his black book. "Your quiz was fine," he nods, running his finger across what must be the Raizl row. "And the first two assignments were fine," he adds, though she hasn't asked for an accounting of all her coursework. She knows what her grades are. "But you didn't turn in the last homework assignment. And you could have turned in a draft paper, but you chose not to. So"—he finally looks up at Raizl—"no."

The logic escapes her. If she'd done all the work, she wouldn't need to make up this paper. Only someone missing a few links in the A-chain would bother to ask for this.

▼

"Razor, you look seriously bummed." Sam swats at the long pleats of Raizl's skirt as they sit together. It's lunchtime, but neither of them eats. Raizl has food in her bag but no appetite; Sam's hungry but forgets to ask for leftovers. "Your mum die or something?"

"Chas v'shulem!" Raizl says reflexively, then bites her tongue, embarrassed. When she's upset, she sounds like Zeidy. "No way," she manages.

Though it might kill her mother, if she finds out about the F.

"So what is it, then? Don't act all breezy now, when you were just about to dig a grave and jump in."

Raizl can't help smiling at Sam. "I got an F," she says.

"And?"

"I got an *F*," Raizl repeats. "In English."

"You're upset because of an F?" Sam's pierced and penciled-in eyebrow lifts nearly to her hairline.

"I never got one before." Even as the words leave her mouth Raizl knows they are not going to help her.

"That's why you're so glum?" Sam throws her head back and laughs so loud half the cafeteria stares at them. "She's never got one before!"

Sam holds her stomach, she's laughing so hard. "Well, Razor, now you know how FFFFFFF fuckin' feels," she says. Lingers on the F like spitting.

"Razor, if you never get an F, how can you possibly appreciate an A? I bet you have a thousand A's. I bet you wipe your ass with A's, all your cheapshit toilet paper A's. I bet you can run a mile and not get to the end of your A's."

Sam empties all the napkins out of the dispenser and starts placing them in a row across the table. "A-A-A's up the wazoo." After about ten napkins she gets bored and brushes them aside, leaving a trail of soggy paper.

"Spice it up a little, Razor. F it up!" She puts her hands on Raizl's head and messes up her curls. The way Sam's eyes don't know what her hands are doing clues Raizl in to the idea that Sam must have been smoking.

"Razor? I want you to have some Fuckin' F Fun."

"I am," Raizl says very quietly. "I'm having fun."

"No you're not. You're not having anywhere near enuF Fun. We need to have a celebration. We need to have a picnic. We'll go to the beach, and you'll Forget the F!"

What No One Can Take from You

For so long, Zeidy had called Raizl into his room each evening when she came home. All through her elementary and high school years, he did it. Zeidy had wanted to see her schoolwork, every test, every quiz. Once she got to college, though he still called her into his room, he waved away the pages. He still loved her and was proud of her, but even for Zeidy, this going to college made Raizl a little different. Set her apart.

"Raizl, study for yourself. Not for me," he'd said, when he was still talking.

"All this can go," he added. He'd made a sweeping motion with his arm—a gesture that pointed at his bed and dresser, and took in all that lay beyond his room, the whole apartment, and all material possessions belonging to Jews everywhere. "Your property, someone can steal. What you study, no one can take from you."

Raizl wishes someone *could* take the F away from her. The F burns through her books and papers. The F burns through her skin. No matter that it's zipped into her nylon backpack, that it's tucked into the pages of Shakespeare, that millions of lifetimes separate hers from the life of "the Bard," as O'Donovan calls him. No matter that she could never care as much as her professor about the Torah of Shakespeare. An F is an F that will never die, never be erased. An F is a giant crack in the path she's been on, going to school by day and watching pornography at night, a chasm deeper than the divides of dawn and dusk.

The F means that a choice is facing her, a decision about which of her lives she wants most. The F is undeniable.

She is relieved, walking in the apartment that evening, that Zeidy hasn't ever wanted to see her college papers. Still, she thinks, maybe she can tell Zeidy about the F. If there is anyone at all she could tell, anyone who could console her, find a way out of the chastisement, a way forward, it would be Zeidy. She would shrug off the backpack and massage Zeidy's ankles, a gift of touch for which she did not ask permission, a touch that she didn't mention to anyone but knew beyond any text or teaching that the contact was correct and permitted. More than permitted! It was her commandment to fulfill. After a few minutes, Zeidy's chest would rise higher and release more deeply, the tight purse of his lips would relax a bit, and as she continued, relax further, not all the way into a smile but into a loosening, an opening in the pain. She doesn't want to know his pain; she only wants to take it away.

For the last few nights, he couldn't be freed from the pain. No massage was strong enough, no words. He didn't open his eyes to look at her, just a barely perceptible nod when she took up his feet. The skin was tough and scaling around the heel and on the sides of the pinky toe and the big toe. But the bottoms were surprisingly soft, and she kneaded his arches deeply before steeling herself against the chills as she rubbed the scaly heels and the flesh blanketing his ankles. She tucked a bottle of lotion under the foot of his bed and used it to moisten his skin and ease her own moment of revulsion.

Tonight the light is on in his room, shining on Zeidy's slight snore, and she puts her backpack in the corner, the only place she'd ever leave it unattended, because Zeidy cannot pick it up. She turns off the light and goes to the kitchen. It's a Thursday night, with Mami cooking a special Shabbes meal, a steamy tomato sheen in one pot, the sauce for stuffed cabbage, and in another pot the ground meat seasoned with salt and sugar and pepper and dotted with rice. She does her favorite job in Mami's kitchen, the taste-test, and everything is as it should be. Delicious.

But when she goes back to the bedroom, all is silent. No snore, no breathing.

Zeidy? Zeidy! He will not answer, he refuses to wake up. Mami throws herself on Zeidy, and Raizl screams; the neighbors have to call the chevrah kadisha to come prepare Zeidy's body for burial. Gitti tugs on Raizl's arm but she will not leave the room. She presses herself against the bookcase as the men from the burial society arrive, their psalms and presumption, their right to ritual stronger than her right to grief, and then she must go.

Not until later, weeping in her room, does she remember that her backpack is still in there, her F, if only it could be buried.

She will never have to tell Zeidy about this F, or any other, the F's of the Future. He has died ahead of them, he has left her alone with them. There is no decision, now, whether to keep them a secret or tell him. There is no redeeming herself in his wisdom, his comfort. No, he has entombed them in her without a choice.

Habits

"I'm so sorry for your loss. How are you feeling this week? Is it the shiva now?" Doc Pod says.

"What?"

"Last week, you canceled your session. I assume that was because of your grandfather?"

Podhoretz, so proper, almost austere, without makeup or with makeup that looks like no makeup, her legs crossed modestly below the knee. Won't come right out and accuse Raizl of lying. Only hints at it, to see if Raizl will come clean.

"Yah," Raizl says, more than happy to keep up the charade. "I even missed an exam."

That was true; she had missed an exam. And she wouldn't apologize for missing the appointment with Doc Pod either, even if it was before Zeidy passed away. What was a therapy session but forty-five minutes when anyone who cared wouldn't ask what she was doing, because she had something to do? A class, a therapy session, an exam—these were all places her mother knew her to be and activities of which she approved. Such slots of accounted-for time were her opportunities to sleep, to go in the library and put her head down on the desk, to cover the ulterior hours—the hidden quadrants of porn.

"How often are you watching pornography, Raizl? Has anything changed in your habits?"

Habits. That made it sound like brushing teeth, or praying.

"Every night," Raizl says. She likes this clinical way of speaking.

Nightly, at bedtime. Medicinal, a dose taken at day's end to unwind and prepare for sleep, if only she slept.

"And how's everything else going? School?"

Podhoretz, with her nose for news.

"Fine," Raizl says. F is for Fine. She doesn't mention the first F on the English paper. Instead, she offers a diversion.

"When I was sitting in the food court with the goths, a bunch of Hillel girls passed right by me and stared. It was so awkward, most of all because they didn't even know it was awkward." Raizl rolls her eyes.

"Why were they staring at you?" Podhoretz asks.

"They don't want any members of the tribe skipping out. And that's what they assume, when they see me sitting there with the freaks—that I've skipped out, and I'm not coming back. As if I don't go home every night to Brooklyn!"

Dr. Podhoretz scribbles across her tablet without looking down, something she must not want to forget.

"Why not thank me?" Raizl continues. "Without me, the ratio is that much better for them, no? When you consider the number of Hillel guys? But they looked at me as if I'd insulted them. Like I owe them something. I'm supposed to reject my Chasidus and see the light and be the better brand of Jew, their brand, when they don't know anything. They're worse than the goyim, they know so little."

"You sound angry," Podhoretz says.

Raizl says nothing.

"The Hillel girls don't sound like your cup of tea. But it is curious that you hang out with the goths. Why *do* you like the goths so much?" Podhoretz asks.

Raizl takes a strand of hair from behind her ear, loops it around to her mouth, and chews the end.

Instantly, even before the straw-salt flavor of the hair is on her tongue, Raizl sees the flicker across Podhoretz's face: New habit, when did that start, what does it mean?

It's tiresome, being the object of someone's fascination. *It doesn't mean anything*, Raizl wants to say. It's not new, she's done it before, only Podhoretz watching is new.

"Like them? No," she says. "But they don't bore me. I can ask them anything. Sam has twenty-nine piercings. I mean, she told me that, you can't see them all from the outside."

Raizl blushes, and then is doubly embarrassed and furious at herself for blushing in front of Dr. P, who's going to take that and run with it. *What do you mean, from the outside? Do you want to be on the inside? Isn't that why you're here, Raizl, to find the passage from outside to inside?*

But Dr. P doesn't say any of that.

"Twenty-nine? That's a lot. And doesn't that hurt?" Dr. P's practical side.

"Exactly!" Raizl says. "That's what I thought, too. So I asked her, does that hurt?"

"What did Sam say?"

Is Raizl imagining it, or is Dr. P sitting slightly forward in her chair?

"She said no and offered to pierce me."

But that isn't true. Sam didn't really answer her question. And even if it was just a pinch for Sam, it might be excruciating for Raizl. The only part of what Sam said that Raizl could count on was, life hurts.

The goths know something true and they aren't hiding from it. Whatever they're feeling, it's not under any long sleeves. Raizl wants that. She wants the truth on the surface, the way they have it. But does that make her a goth? In the end the goths are not her people, no more than a group of Asian straight-A students were her people back when she got A's. The geeks into anime? An internet porn habit doesn't turn her into their cousin. No matter what grades she gets or who she hangs out with, she is still Raizl from Brooklyn. She is still working to support her brothers so they can learn Torah all day and she can study porn all night. Still working to help pay for a wedding she may never have.

"I got an F on my English paper," Raizl says. "I tried to peel it off the paper, scratch it off with my nail."

"Did you really try to peel it?" the doc asks. Raizl knows Podhoretz doesn't believe that. Just as she knows—they both know—Raizl understood she would get an F before the professor marked the assignment. But knowing something is on the way doesn't mean you can't be shocked when it arrives.

"That must have been devastating. You've been an A student your entire life, haven't you?" Podhoretz says.

Raizl shrugs. "It's not such a big deal," she says. "English is not my major, who cares about *King Lear*?" She laughs suddenly, bravado bolstered by actual levity. Her copy of the play is a small paperback edition, secondhand, and someone had carefully penned the missing curves to transform the *L* into an *R*. A porn version of the classic, the delirious senile king barebottoming his daughters before he gets offed.

"What's so funny?" Doc Pod asks.

"*King Rear*," Raizl says, laughing so hard she gives herself hiccups.

The serious Pod waits until Raizl's laughter dies out. "You don't care about your grades anymore?"

"Yah, I do," Raizl says. "I'm going to do fine." She hiccups. "In the things that matter. Accounting. Math. Econ."

"All right," the Pod says in her soothing tone. "I'm sure that if you decide to do well, you will. But what happened with the paper? Did you decide to get an F?"

Raizl's hiccup is so explosive it echoes. "What are you talking? Why would anyone *decide* to get an F?"

"If you can get A's when you want to, why didn't you try to get an A in English?"

Raizl remembers writing the paper. The way the words swam together, in proximity but not in harmony in her exhausted brain. She had tried. But she was so tired.

Zeidy's Bed

Raizl creeps away from the visitors and takes a folding shiva chair to Zeidy's room. All those people parading into the apartment, crowding around Zeidy's memory when all she wants to do is be alone with him.

But they are supposed to crowd out the grief, and she's glad for Mami's sake that so many cousins are here, Meema Freidy sitting shiva next to Mami.

"What, are you in here?" Moishe discovers Raizl.

"Why wouldn't I be in here?"

Moishe flips up the back of his long coat and sits on Zeidy's bed. Raizl doesn't like this. Moishe should be more respectful. Zeidy is practically still lying there.

"What's wrong, Raizy? What is it?"

How can he even ask such a question?

"I'm not speaking of Zeidy, may his memory be for a blessing. Even before this, things were not right with you."

"It's nothing," Raizl says. "I'm just sad."

▼

On the night after the shiva ends, Raizl slides into Zeidy's bed and pulls his covers over her head to breathe in the Zeidy smell: long-ago tobacco, slivovitz, pish. "Zeidy," she whispers, "tell me the dream I'm dreaming right now." Shutting her eyes ferociously and imagining Zeidy against the orange insides of her eyelids.

Later, Raizl tells Mami not to worry. She takes all of Zeidy's clothes to the charity, throws away the bed linens and the plastic mattress cover, cleans the closet and the drawers as best she can.

Before any other plans can be made, she fills Zeidy's furniture with her own clothes, and moves into his room.

The Boats Are Not Here

The third date. The third maybe-chussen. Like the third question or the third cup of Pesach wine, the taste of a date with Avrum is something Raizl can anticipate even before it's in her mouth. But he surprises her. "I want to show you a boat," Avrum says when they leave her apartment and get on the subway, keeping an empty seat between them. "A giant boat, like a cruise ship, but not for hundreds of people," he explains. "A ship for just a few people. Or maybe one person only, a rich man."

They head north from the Holocaust Memorial, walking on the promenade in Battery Park with meshiggeneh Rollerbladers whizzing right between them, and people jogging with dogs, everyone out in tank tops and shorts, clothes that look to Raizl almost like porn outfits except for the colors, neon orange and purple and blue. It's a sunny spring day at the end of April, on the minor holiday of Lag B'Omer, partway between Pesach and Shvi'es. It's hard for Raizl to stay entirely focused on Avrum when there are so many people almost naked around them.

But he's very animated, talking about radar that looks like weapons, the strange blades and white spheres they will see on top of giant boats in the marina, the sophisticated navigation and weather information systems. This equipment absorbs signals transmitted from above, the heavens filled not only with the Creator but also with satellites. Avrum explains how the magnetron radar sends out a pulse and receives its own echo, in order to know what's around it.

At first this seems an odd conversation for a date, but Avrum has a cute smile, and he semi-demonstrates with his hands—a pulse somehow being a thing he can throw into the air and then catch again in his palms, as if his echo were bouncing back to him from Raizl.

No one has ever taken her to see a giant boat.

When they get to the marina, Raizl recognizes it from his description: the wall sticking out into the river to create a square of water, almost like a cage for boats—

"Is this it?" she interrupts Avrum, who is waving his arm overhead, imitating the spinning blade of the radar.

He pivots, his fingers still pointing at the sky. "Where are they?" he says. "They're not here." As if he's made an appointment with the giant boats, and someone owes him an explanation. They stand at the railing and he takes his hat off and repositions his yarmulke and replaces his hat on top of it, so now instead of a semicircle of black velvet only a quarter-moon shows against the sideways-matted hair at the back of his head.

"The boats are not here," he says definitively, as though he's deciding, rather than observing the fact.

Raizl holds the metal railing, looking out at the empty marina, smelling Avrum's aftershave. She's sure someone had told him to put it on. Someone said, *Avrum, when you go on a shidduch-date, two slaps of aftershave across your face. Girls don't want to smell you sweaty.*

And she knows with certainty, an intuition anchored in her gut, that she's not the first girl to stand at the railing by the boat marina with Avrum. He's been there on another date, with another girl.

Or dates; girls.

His aftershave is so strong that the cloud of fragrance envelops her, but she still smells sweat. Not sweat like the gym on campus, the sweat of so many athletes. This is a doughy, yeshiva sweat, of poring over books for many hours, and her brothers have it, too.

They stand in silence before the empty marina. The late-afternoon sun hangs low over Ellis Island, over New Jersey.

"Do you want to go back to the Holocaust?" he asks.

"The museum's closed already."

Avrum looks at his watch. Out of reflex, shaking his wrist so the metal links shift. Somehow he doesn't notice, right across the river, the giant clock of New Jersey telling Manhattan the time.

"Oy, you're right," he says. "We should go home."

The front of her face is frozen in a smile, will stay like that all the way back to Brooklyn. Because the same matchmakers who give dating advice to the Avrums, who tell the Avrums to wear aftershave, they tell the Raizls to smile. Whatever he says, you have to smile, to show you have a good disposition, only sometimes also you should laugh, to show you have a sense of humor. Because if you look happy, your date will know you are happy, and then he'll want to get married. And then you'll be happy.

And she does it, she smiles like that for Avrum. She does her part. Smiling even when she feels humiliated because who knows how many girls he's already brought to see the giant boats? The empty marina isn't her fault, of course; yet somehow also it is. She hates him for bringing her here, for leaving her with the mark of a failed date.

Seventy Percent

"You tricked me," Raizl says.

Podhoretz wears an expression of smooth, blameless curiosity. "How so?"

"You know you did. You told me to go on another date. Convinced me."

"And you went! Congratulations," says Podhoretz. "Mazel toff," she says. Pronouncing it like "toffee," not like Yiddish.

"It was terrible!"

"Yes, but you went. That's what's important. You didn't let your worry stop you."

Raizl has the urge to slap her. The smooth, powdered cheeks. The doctor wears librarian's glasses, with her hair in a tight bun, and a peach blouse with a bow at the collar. She could be in a porn video. Right now, even. All they'd need is for some man to burst into the office, without any reason or explanation, and for Dr. P to look flustered, to put her hand to her collar. The man would brush her hand aside and tear her blouse off. Bye-bye, little bow at the collar. He would have sex with her on the sofa across from Raizl, the biggest, leatheriest sofa Raizl has ever seen that's not in a video. Where Raizl never sits.

"I'm supposed to meet my ziveg! My match! I'm supposed to get married! Going on a date doesn't matter if nothing comes out of it."

A tear drips off Raizl's nose, and she hates herself for crying, for falling stupidly into Podhoretz's trap. To every session, Raizl arrives filled with dread and hope, certain that the doctor won't be able to help, yet praying that she will. Duped again, Raizl sprawls helplessly against the chair with her arms flung over the sides, the weight of her torso and legs sinking against the cushion, but the cushion does not yield. The giant armchair, for all its size, is not comfortable.

Podhoretz closes her notebook. She picks up the box of tissues from her desk and brings it to Raizl, though there is already a box on the small side table beside the armchair. She stands there while Raizl blows her nose.

For a moment, when the noseblowing is done, there is silence.

"So tell me about the date," Podhoretz says.

Raizl has to hand it to her. She's purposeful, no monkeying around.

But Raizl doesn't know what to say. This isn't her mother asking. Her mother, in fact, asked her the same question the minute she came home from the shidduch-date. *So how was it?* Raizl understood what her mother meant. Did Avrum like you? Is he going to marry you? Her mother had wanted Raizl's assessment of the date's assessment of her.

But what does Dr. P want to know? Surely not that. So much of this room is a mystery to Raizl. It doesn't have rules like yeshiva, rules like college. It's more like the Torah sh'bal peh, the Oral Torah, before it got written down. Someone has to know it, and tell it to you, before you can know it. You can't read it or google it, it's too personal; you need to have the wise one right in front of you, the one who knows this Torah, and then it can be revealed to you.

Only Dr. P doesn't tell when she knows something. She doesn't tell Raizl any rules, and she doesn't say what she knows, or even what she wants to know.

If Raizl thinks about it, she might not like Podhoretz.

But the doctor is patient, waiting for the story of the date. Luring her with listening.

And Raizl tells her: the path by the river full of runners and skaters, the promise of giant boats. The empty marina.

"Do you think someone who knows about boats also knows about sex?"

That's what Podhoretz says about the date. And what Podhoretz does, when she's pleased with herself, is twiddle her pen between her index and middle fingers for a few seconds.

With her twiddling pen and her certainty that she is doing good, Podhoretz reminds Raizl of a rebbe plunging his thumb through the air and pulling out the perfect Torah citation for whatever point he is making.

Podhoretz, too, presses her point. "It's quite likely that your date looks at porn," she says. "More than seventy percent of men do."

"Seventy percent of yeshivish men?"

"I haven't seen any statistics about yeshiva in particular," Podhoretz says. "But they do fall under the category of men."

Raizl considers the possibility of Avrum watching porn. It's true that he must have gotten his boat information online, since that topic would never be covered in the yeshiva curriculum. Perhaps, as Podhoretz is implying, for anyone with internet access it's only a matter of time until porn is ingested.

"At least you'd have something in common with him," Podhoretz says, "if he did watch porn."

No, Raizl thinks. *No no no.* And yet the image of Avrum is conjured in her mind, Avrum with his black coat on but no pants, Avrum peering nearsightedly into a video and holding himself, watching porn but also trying not to spill his seed, according to the strenuous prohibition of his rebbe . . . Raizl doesn't explain this to Podhoretz, the way porn would be wasted on Avrum, a torture for him even worse than it is for her. He might see what pleased him, and then be required to stifle his pleasure. Better to believe that he doesn't watch, doesn't know.

"When's your next date?" Podhoretz asks.

"With Avrum? No more dates."

"With someone else, then."

"If there is someone else," Raizl says.

Who's in There

It's a late-spring afternoon. The sound of voices comes from inside Tati and Mami's bedroom. Raizl stands in front of the closed door for a moment, listening. Sometimes Tati dials in to a Gemureh hotline, for Talmud study over the phone. But he sits at the dining table for that, with the huge book open and the silver wing of the flip phone open beside it, emitting a tinny lilt. The muffled sounds coming through the door don't land in her ear as Yiddish or Aramaic or lushen koydesh. It's another language, like English but more raucous.

Mami is in the kitchen, getting a start on the Shabbes baking. "Who's in there with Tati?" Raizl asks her.

"Shah! What are you saying? No one is in there!" she huffs. "His back is bad today, very bad, even with the medicine. Leave him alone." Mami keeps track of Raizl with half an eye while she kneads the dough. "Don't make for him any more tzuris," she adds, nodding at Raizl. The you-know-what-I'm-talking-about nod. Which hurts Raizl's feelings. And no, she doesn't know what troubles Mami's talking about. Other than the ongoing tzuris of two adult children who've made no progress on getting married, the tzuris of only one grandchild (so far), the tzuris of a thrown-out back, the tzuris of no Moshiach coming—the elusive messiah determined to disappoint this generation as all the others. Tati doesn't know about her tzuris of secrets, of English class and internet porn. His tzuris are out in the world for all to say oy, while hers are hidden, heavier to bear because borne alone. And why does Mami suspect her of wanting to lay more worries at Tati's feet? All she wants is to know who's in the bedroom with Tati.

Raizl goes back to the doorway. Dim as they are through the door, the sounds still have the sharp, barking edges of English. There is a rhythm to it, a single man's voice at a leisurely pace, occasionally bursting into rapid speech. And then the huge roar of a crowd. "Aaaaand the Mets are up by one!"

Raizl knows the Mets. They play baseball at the field where the rabbis banned the internet. She doesn't dare open the door. Baseball is tumeh. But she can imagine it: Tati listening—or perhaps watching? Distracting himself from his pain with a little bit of pleasure.

Exception to the Rule

Today at lunch there's a new boy at the table. He has black hair, which might be his normal hair, not dyed. He has dark eyes and brows, so who knows? And a strange beard that no Chasidishe man would have, where below his shaved cheeks a patch of hair points down from his chin. He wears a white shirt with long sleeves and a collar that has strange little buttons attaching it to the shirt, as though the shirt is afraid the collar will float away unless it's fastened. And something Raizl has never seen at this table: he wears a tie.

Raizl waits for Sam to tell the boy to leave, this Solo. But she never does. She gives him her Diet Coke, and Spark passes him some fries and hot sauce. He graduated in December, and he's on campus to meet with recruiters, wearing white-shirt camouflage. "I can't stand these interviews," he says. He yanks off the tie. He rolls up his sleeves and a few beads of color show—a strange trail of red drops inked along the inside of his left arm. A row of feathers on the outside of his right arm, perhaps to draw himself into flight.

He has to move out of his parents' house, but he dreads the jobs that await. "It's like they can see through me, they know I don't want to work at their company. And they don't want me either."

Raizl has never seen all the toughness melt out of Sam's face the way it does now. "You don't have to do this, Solo."

But he has his own hardness. "Don't tell me what I don't have to do," he says, pushing away the Coke and the cheer-up fries.

"This is the way to escape, remember?" he says. "And you're going to do it, too. Earn enough to get out of your father's house. Why else would you be in college, put up with all this bullshit?" With a flick of his hand he dismisses the line of students waiting to buy burgers, their backpacks hanging heavily from one shoulder, the campus beyond them.

Sam nods, but she doesn't agree. "You can make money without working at a big-four accounting firm," she says. "You can escape from your parents without enslaving yourself."

"I'm going to have an apartment in a year. Talk to me then. Tell me what I need then, when you call asking to stay with me."

Raizl knows that Sam's left home a few times, "when things got bad." And that she doesn't really like school. Will going to work let Sam escape as she wishes? Or will it be like working for the Rebbetzin, a path toward what Raizl wants, that also puts her in a bind?

Sam puts her index finger to her mouth and licks it, the way Raizl has seen women lick their finger before turning a page of the prayerbook when the pages stick together, only Sam isn't turning any pages. She runs her moistened finger across the blood drops inked on Solo's arm. A gesture that might be wiping them away but also seems to pull the skin toward herself.

Sam doesn't care that Raizl is watching. And Spark, too, watching quietly, now with an unmistakable look of hurt.

"Cut it out," Solo says. He shakes Sam's finger off his arm. "That's not happening, and you know it."

He gets up to go, saying, "I'll talk to you later," but Sam's face tells Raizl otherwise, that there won't be a later.

They sit in silence for a minute after he leaves, then Sam suddenly snaps her fingers right in front of Raizl's eyes. "What's the matter, Ray-Ray?"

Raizl can't snap. She'd been practicing once, trying to learn, and Mami told her to stop because it wasn't nice for girls to snap.

Sam makes it look easy. The snap like a tiny thunder, or like a raw carrot cracking in two. The sound hangs in the air while Sam's hand arcs back down to her side.

"That F still gotcha down?"

Raizl nods.

"I'm sorry I was so mean about that." Sam pauses. "I *was* mean, right?"

Raizl doesn't nod this time, doesn't shake her head either. What's the right answer to this question?

"I was just a tiny bit wasted," Sam says. "But I'm much better today, and you're still a soggy pair of tights." She pinches Raizl, lifting a little fabric off Raizl's leg and letting it pop back into place. "Still moaning about that F."

Spark leans across the table. "Sam has a four-oh," she says in a low voice, as if Sam might not want to hear it, might not want to know this about herself.

"Yah?" Raizl says with too much amazement, and Sam winks at her.

"Stick with me, and you could have A's without studying, too."

"I have to study. I can't make A's without."

"You'd make more A's with more play," Sam contradicts her.

Sam takes a strand of hair—from the long side of her head, not the shaved side—and chews the end. The unconscious gesture surprises Raizl, who has done this and seen Chasidish girls do it hundreds of times. But Sam? Never.

"Seriously, you're too smart to fail. What's going on?"

In certain light Sam's eyes are more green than brown. The thick fringe of black lashes and the black liner emphasizing how not-black the irises are. For once, Sam's eyes hold no judgment, and she seems curious, even kind, in asking this.

Raizl considers telling her the truth. What she can never tell Mami or anyone in her family. Pod knows she watches porn but doesn't know she's failing. Sam knows she's failing but doesn't know about the porn. Can she tell Sam? Can Sam be the one person in the world who knows both sides of her?

It's tempting to confide. There's no question Sam has seen all the internet has to offer. But Raizl can't say it.

"Anyway, why is one F such a big deal? I mean, everyone fails *once*."

This might be true. Certainly Raizl is no longer the exception to the rule, and so she has no proof to bring against Sam's claim.

"What about twice?" Raizl says glumly.

"What else are you failing? And you can't know the future in advance! Just cram. Crammit, dammit—"

"Not statistics, it's too hard."

"Oh, stats? Aren't there two hundred students in that class? Not a problem, Ray-Ray. I'll take it for you. I got an A in that class, I'll get one for you."

Cheating? "Nein!" Raizl's guard drops, the *No!* leaping out in Yiddish.

"Don't act so innocent, Raizl. You know what goes on here. You've seen it."

This is true. Raizl has seen students in the large proctored exams flash another student's ID and take their seat.

Raizl's also seen students get caught.

"No," she insists. "They'll kick us out!"

Sam puts her hand on Raizl's back. "Calm down, girl. You're hyperventilating, look at you! Just breathe. No one's going anywhere."

And it's true, a soothing weight comes through Raizl's vest and blouse all the way to her spine, and air fills her chest as if to meet Sam's palm. She exhales slowly, not wanting that hand to go. This is the nicest thing Sam has ever done for her, sweeter than helping her try on jeans. She's been waiting for this, a sign of their friendship. Here it is. Sam would do this thing to relieve Raizl, to free her from the torture of studying for an exam she can't possibly pass, to free her from another F. This is friendship, this is love. This is all that Raizl hoped for. And now she has to say no. It cannot be. She can't take this frightening gift.

"No one'll know, you'll see. This will be fine." Sam pats her on the back now, once, twice; Raizl feels in each gentle touch the warmth of Sam's fingers, the option to give in and accept, the option to say yes.

And then Sam's moving, her arm no longer encircling Raizl. "It'll be fine," she says again. "Listen to me. Everyone cheats."

Raizl shakes her head. "Everyone—no. You—no."

How sad she is, to turn Sam down. When she wants to be tied to Sam this way. To have this bond of dishonor between them. "We can't do this."

"You don't have to do anything," Sam says. "I'm the one doing it. I want to do it."

Raizl says nothing.

"Suit yourself." Sam shrugs. "It's no skin off my tits if you fail." She jams the straw in her Diet Coke, stabbing what's left, ice in the bottom of the cup. And just like that the kindness is extinguished from her eyes, the black shutters are closed.

My Eyes to the Mountains

Tomorrow is the stats exam. It should be easy, just as Sam said. Raizl's too smart to fail, but the shmutz is even smarter. Tonight Raizl is lost. She can't study, can't absorb anything. The words of the textbook and even the numbers swim away.

Raizl clicks out of three screens of notes and study guides and clicks into porn. But exhausted even beyond porn—eyes watering, head aching—she clicks out of that, too. Shuts the computer, shuts the textbook. In the dark despair of her mind she hears the tehillim, psalms where math won't go. *Esu einei el hehurim . . . I raise my eyes to the mountains, from where will my help come?*

She leans back, stretches her neck, looks out the window of Zeidy's room, now her room. She's replaced his clothes with hers in the drawers and closet. But changing rooms just gives her a different air shaft out the window, and the yellow bricks of another facing wall. No mountains and no help coming.

My help comes from Hashem, Raizl finishes the verse. *Maker of the sky and the land, the heavens and the earth.*

A large, embarrassing burp follows the psalm. A memory of lunch, baconcheeseburger reflux. She blushes, though no one is with her to hear the burp, and quickly turns out the light. She lies on the bed, too tired even to undress. With eyes shut, Raizl silently mind-sings the psalm again. Who is this Hashem she prays to, now that she has also defied Hashem? Hashem who knows all about the bacon and the porn and the pants. Hashem who *made* the bacon and the porn and the pants. And here she is praying, a mini-repentance, an antidote. Like a girl she knew in high school, dieting on a spear of broccoli after eating a cheesecake.

Useless as repentance, the psalm still brings relief. She chants *I raise my eyes I raise my eyes I raise my eyes.* A rumble of words and the smoothing out of her mind, a kind of mind-stop, a song that does not require consciousness. The murmur of wordflow is a transport. A path out of her thoughts.

The psalm is a heart-cry.

Hashem is listening. Hashem is watching her. Even if Hashem knows what will happen, still Hashem watches. She is naked before Hashem, her clothes are nothing. The shadow of her skull in no way obscures her thoughts. And since Hashem already knows, why should she feel shame?

I raise my eyes I raise my eyes—in the psalmic moment Hashem still loves her. Independent of her willingness or ability to follow commandments. Hashem a force separate from her sins and not diminished by them. Hashem abiding as the pleasure that lives in the universe, waiting only for the spark of her attention. A force that is known if you make yourself known to it. The porn is out there, waiting. Hashem is out there, too, the whole time.

All her life she has prayed to Hashem for things, prayed for Hashem to set her world right. In the past she prayed, *Please, Hashem, heal Tati's back. Please, Hashem, don't let Zeidy die. Please, Hashem, send Moshiach.* Calling on Hashem as Maker to fix the things that are broken.

This is the first time she is praying to listen. Praying to hear. *Hashem, please, give me an answer. How can I get married? How can I stay in school? Let me be as naked to myself as I am to You.*

Statistically Speaking

"Raizl, it looks like you're failing three classes this semester." The dean pauses and taps his keyboard. While his eyes are on the screen, Raizl studies the books behind his desk. She is surprised to see that in addition to economics texts, the ones he's written and the ones that, presumably, he has read, there are books about African art, French cinema, the Holocaust. *While Six Million Died* and *Denying the Holocaust*. She'd assumed the dean was Jewish, but she didn't know, yet, if that would make him more or less sympathetic to her. One time, a professor had stared at her all through class and told her afterward that she reminded him of his grandmother—looked just like the only photo his family had of this matriarch, taken when she was a girl in Lodz. She died in a concentration camp. Auschwitz. Her parents, he'd said, died at the other one, what was the name? Treblinka? Raizl dropped the class.

But there is no escaping this encounter with the dean. The semester is almost over. If she's failing now, statistically speaking, she has failed the semester.

Books rise on shelves over the dean's head. An entire wall of books, to the ceiling. There's no ladder in sight. He has two monitors, side by side, on his desk, and a laptop open on the side desk over his files. How many monitors does one dean need? His beard is streaked with gray, or white, really, right at the middle, and red on the sides. The pattern is reversed on his head: white on the sides, a patch of red at the center of his receding hairline. His eye pouches have pouches, the folds magnified and blued by his glasses. Why doesn't the dean get any sleep? Writing books about economics all night, or maybe, as Podhoretz says, he is 70 percent of men. Online. Watching.

"Why on earth are you taking six classes?" he says, still facing the computer. "Who approved that?

"Well," he says, without pausing for an answer. "You're barely passing the others."

A few more taps and then, when the screens have no more bad news to give him, he swivels away from them to look at Raizl. Sighs. His head tilts slightly to the left. "Is everything okay? Anything going on at home? You had straight A's last semester and now . . ."

Raizl wants to reassure him but can't think of what to say. Sometimes, with men, especially men who are disappointed, it's best to say nothing.

"You're going to be put on academic probation immediately. And if you do fail the classes, you'll have to take a leave. Or, it would be unfortunate, but you could withdraw from college. Perhaps there is something else you'd like to do?"

Something else she'd like to do, other than have freedom to travel to the city every day, to have her own computer? No, there is nothing else she'd like.

"Please don't make me leave," she begs the dean. "I have to finish my degree. I'm going to support my family. I *am* supporting them."

The dean nods. "I understand," he says. Raizl nods, too, as if he does.

"You've got two weeks left in the semester. You have to turn in your work. Get your grades up."

She nods again, as if she will do it. As if she can.

Killed Her

How could Gitti enter the room without a sound? Without, it seems, opening the door?

But here she is, materialized beside Raizl, peering at the computer.

"What is this?" Gitti sticks her face right up to the screen the way Mami looks into their throats for strep. A man, naked except for a mask over his face, is slapping a woman's tuches. The volume is turned off, so the slap is silent, but the motion is exact and harsh. In his hand that is not slapping, the man holds a leash that attaches to a leather collar around the woman's neck. On her hands and knees, the woman faces away from the man. Her hair hangs forward, covering her features. Below that her tittes hang down, too.

"Vus iz dus?" Gitti asks again.

Raizl reaches out to shut the computer, but Gitti quickly puts her hand on it, her fingers on the screen, as if testing whether she could actually touch the bodies there.

"Tumeh," Gitti says, very low and firm. *Impure*.

Heat rushes up from Raizl's shoulders into her neck and face. If she slams the lid shut the way she wants to, she'll crush Gitti's fingers against the keyboard. So she restrains herself, a hot shame in her cheeks.

Gitti points with authority at the screen. "Change it, now. Make it your homework."

Again Raizl tries to close the laptop, but Gitti keeps her hand decisively in the way.

"No," she says. "Don't close it. You have homework." Gitti's lip trembles. "I want to see numbers on the screen. Do it," she insists, her voice firm though there are tears in her eyes.

Raizl nearly tells Gitti to get out of her room—it *is* her room now. But something in Gitti's tone makes her comply. She pulls up a spreadsheet and begins working. It's good, actually, to get some work done. But it's odd to do the problems under Gitti's stern supervision.

And Gitti doesn't leave. When the assignment is done, she's still there. Waiting to see what Raizl will do, guarding Raizl, as if she is the big sister and Raizl the misbehaving little one.

If Gitti wants to see, then fine! Let her see! A rebellious despair surges through Raizl—a sudden certainty that she will fail college, no matter that she's completed one assignment tonight as Gitti demanded. Even if Gitti stays there all night and Raizl finishes more work, it won't be enough. Raizl switches screens again. Back to the video. The woman is still there, on her knees, and the man slaps her again, then pushes himself against her tuches, over and over. Surely Gitti will leave now, rather than watch. But then the man yanks on the leash and the woman's head twists around sharply, suddenly revealing her gaunt, pale face. Her eyes round with pain. Her mouth open in a shout or a sigh—a pain or a pleasure Raizl and Gitti cannot hear.

Gitti gasps, for the woman and for herself. But instead of leaving, Gitti hunches toward the computer, squinting, as if she recognizes someone. Moving closer still, beyond the point where moving closer can help her see better, or help her comprehend what she sees. She cries, silently, and when the tears drip from her chin, she doesn't wipe them. She is transfixed by the video, rapt, as unable to move away as the woman held by the leash.

And Raizl, watching, too, flinches each time the man hits the woman. But after she blinks, Raizl looks again, more intently, searching for signs of the woman's desire even if it's masked—heightened?—by hurt. Watching to discover the moment when pain turns to pleasure.

But Raizl can't find the pleasure in it, not the woman's and not her own. It's impossible to focus with Gitti there, and her own yearning to understand what's going on in the video is split-screened by anxiety, watching Gitti's watching. Raizl X's out of the scene, and Gitti straightens up, her damp cheeks terribly pale, with a bluish tint, as if she's taken the sheen of the computer light inside her, the high-energy waves contagious.

Then, with a glint in her teary eyes, Gitti makes Raizl swear. "Never watch this again," she says, her fingers again touching the laptop screen. "Swear it."

"B'li neder," Raizl says, making a promise without a vow because it's forbidden to take an oath, and surely Gitti doesn't want her to sin.

But Gitti shakes her head like an animal, whipping her hair around her head, and yells, "Nein! Nein! Promise me you won't do this!"

Gitti looks meshigge, her eyes almost popping out. "Swear it, swear it on your life! Never to watch this again!" Her body shakes, and she stabs at the screen with her index finger.

Frightened by the force that possesses Gitti, Raizl is shaking, too. "I swear!"

She says it so fast the sound of the words comes around to her ears from the outside, as if someone else had said them. Did she just promise no more porn? Her lips are numb even as they move.

Finally Gitti calms down. Her hand drops to her side, and Raizl can shut the laptop.

▼

The next day, Podhoretz asks, "So you watched the video together? Did you like that?" And answers herself: "You weren't alone, then."

A wave of shame washes over Raizl. The selfishness of bringing Gitti into it! She is supposed to protect her little sister.

"Yah," Raizl says. "I wasn't alone. Gitti was with me, and I killed her."

"You didn't *kill* her," Podhoretz admonishes. "Watching porn isn't deadly. You're not dead, are you?"

"I can't say if I'm dead. A part of me, maybe. And part of Gitti, now, because of me."

"How do you know she's dead? How can you tell?"

Raizl has seen a frozen almost-smile before, on Zeidy's face when she walked into his room and he was dead. Yesterday it was Gitti, with lips tipped up, her cheeks stiff. Gitti didn't make any noise, didn't say anything while the man was in the woman's tush, while he pulled the leash. Gitti, crying and smiling, silent until it was over. The smile a reflex, the last bit of joy left on her face from the person she was before she saw the porn.

"I ruined her."

"She doesn't sound ruined," Podhoretz says. "I disagree. Gitti sounds quite strong, actually."

Raizl remembers the hard look in Gitti's eyes, shiny from tears but also determined. Podhoretz is right. Gitti is strong.

"At the end of the video, Gitti was so upset, she made me swear not to watch anymore. I was afraid she would yell even louder, or go right then to tell Mami, to get Tati."

"What did you do?"

"I swore."

"Never to watch porn? You took an oath?"

"Yes, just like Gitti wanted. A real vow. Chanting Kol Nidre on Yom Kippur cannot wash it away. Like a nazir, a man promised to Hashem who swears not to cut his hair or drink for the rest of his life, I swore like that."

After she swore, Gitti had finally left, and Raizl was alone with her promise. It filled the room, the weight of the vow as heavy as a body lying on top of hers, preventing her from reaching for the computer and turning the video back on. She could not sleep. Each time she shifted to find a more comfortable position, she told herself that if she took the laptop in her arms it would be for just one video, and surely that would not break the promise; the vow was not against watching a single video, it was against watching all of them, over and over, as she had been doing. And wasn't the vow even narrower, a vow against watching *that* video, that terrible tuches-potching and leash-yanking? She could keep the promise not to watch that. She didn't want to see the woman choking anyway. Well, she did want to, because why would the woman do it if she didn't like it? Maybe it didn't feel so awful as it looked? The only way to know was to watch it again. But every time Raizl swung her feet to the floor and sat up, ready to get the computer, she stopped herself and got back in bed. *Keep the promise*, a voice said in her head. *For one night, keep the promise.*

Now Podhoretz struggles with her face. She tries to sew her lips into place but they are gaping open. Her skin is paler than usual. "You swore never to watch porn?" she asks again.

"Yes," Raizl says, impatient. "What Gitti asked me, I swore."

"Will you stop watching, then?"

"I swore it. I have to."

"That's not what I'm asking you, Raizl. I understand that you promised, but you've tried to stop before. What will you do this time, what'll be different?"

She looks at Podhoretz's shoes. Plain brown flats. Why doesn't Podhoretz wear high heels, since she can?

"I'll stop," Raizl says. "I can stop."

"Can you?" says Podhoretz.

Meema Shprintza

When Raizl gets home that night, Gitti is in her room, already in bed. Even though it's a warm spring night, she has the covers pulled up to her chin.

"Shprintza," Gitti mumbles as Raizl sits on the blanket beside her. "Meema Shprintza oyf de komputer."

Gitti looks like she's seen a ghost, with her eyes focused on some faraway point, not in the room. A look Zeidy used to get sometimes when he saw other people's dreams.

"What are you talking?" Raizl says, annoyed.

"Meema Shprintza," Gitti repeats. "On your computer, she is there! Shprintza! Shprintza! Shprintza!" Gitti chants.

"Shah!" Raizl says, nauseated and a little frightened. Meema Shprintza, the sister from Tati's grandfather, Shmiel, was deported with him to Auschwitz in 1944.

The noise brings Mami to the door. "You're shmoozing in bed while I'm making dinner?" Exasperated, she signals them to follow her. "Come, both of you, set the table."

"Gitti's tired," Raizl says, as lightly as possible, but Mami squints at her.

"What's wrong? From what is she so tired?"

Gitti repeats her meshiggeneh talk. "Mami, look on the computer!" Gitti says. "Meema Shprintza is in there."

"Vus?" Mami comes in and shuts the door behind her. "The komputer is none of your business! It's for Raizl to do her studies and help the family, that's all. Nothing to talk about. I don't want to hear it. And Tati? Not one word to Tati!"

Gitti's chin trembles and her eyes shine with hurt. In a softer tone, Mami says, "And I don't need to see it. Do you want to know why?"

Gitti nods.

"First, Meema Shprintza, may her memory be a blessing, is not in any komputer. She's in my heart." Mami puts her hand on top of her chest, which rises a half inch, as if Meema Shprintza really is in there, puffing up Mami's dress to prove it.

"Second, I have better things to do with my time than go looking for the dead where they don't belong." She spits over her shoulder like an old woman. "Let Shprintza rest in peace."

Then she takes her hand from her chest and pulls Gitti's blanket aside. "Such a strong girl like you needs to come eat." She pinches Gitti's cheeks, putting a little color back in them. "I have soup for you." She takes Gitti's hand with a gentle-firm grip and draws her out of bed, loving her and giving her no choice.

Gitti stands. She walks slowly, her legs moving but her eyes still vacant, as if having seen time unravel, they cannot resume the present.

Raizl follows Mami and Gitti to the dining table. Gitti pushes the food around on her plate, refusing to eat. Not Raizl. The smell of chicken paprika makes her mouth water. She is disgusted by her own hunger. How can she be hungry? Why doesn't the video make her sick, knock the life out of her the way it does to Gitti? Is it just that she's older, or—truth—is she hardened from all she's seen? She craves the golden-orange pulkes.

There's not time to eat her sister's extras, though. Mami motions for her to come into the kitchen.

Mami's eyes are pinched, angry. "You showed Gitti the komputer, farvus? Why would you?"

But before Raizl can answer, Mami slices one index finger through the air until it points at Raizl's nose. "Nein!" she hisses. "Don't speak to me! If she ever sees it again, aroas fin fenster! Out the window! Farshteist?"

Raizl nods. She understands. But Mami need not have warned her to hide the computer away because her little sister keeps her distance. When Raizl tells her jokes as they clean up from dinner, Gitti doesn't laugh. When Raizl offers to help with homework, Gitti declines. She doesn't go into Raizl's room. Gitti seems, if not sad, then distracted.

As Raizl knows herself, what is seen cannot be unseen.

But that video meant something different to Gitti than it did to Raizl. The computer is a fire that Gitti would never touch again. Raizl, burnt once, still seeks the heat. For her, sensation is more necessary than comfort.

That night, after dinner, Raizl closes the door to her room and pulls out the laptop, hurriedly searching to find the video again. The woman in the video isn't Meema Shprintza—Of course not! It's impossible!—but Gitti's certainty is still unnerving. Now it's Raizl who peers at the screen, hunching close the way Gitti had.

Surely it's permitted to put aside her promise, just this once.

And yes, there is a flicker of resemblance. Shprintza and the woman in the video both with dark hair and enormous eyes. In the video, the woman's hair hangs down, lank and shapeless, while Shprintza, in the photo that Tati keeps on his dresser, wears hers pinned up, a dark crown over her forehead, stylish. This picture all that remains of her, a photo hidden in a pocket of her brother's coat when he was selected to work, and she was not. Shprintza, Shprintza.

Raizl watches the woman in the video closely, her hollow cheeks and thin neck like so many in the Holocaust photos Raizl has seen since childhood. Raizl can't remember a time when she didn't have these images in her head, of women stripped and shivering, women and men naked and dead in pits, disjointed limbs, eyes enormous and inert. The eyes! Daring the camera to see. That's what hooked Gitti, what made her find Shprintza in the porn video.

It's clear the porn woman isn't actually Shprintza. "Nein," Raizl says to herself, settling the matter. But now that her promise is abandoned—crushed—a reckless curiosity takes over Raizl's finger-tips, scrolling past tiny images of torture—a mask, a gag, a chain—that hint at larger scenes.

One tiny image shows a woman with a large black collar around her neck. The thick metal chain linking the collar to a tall post is like nothing Raizl has ever seen on a living human being, only on cartoonish depictions of Israelites as slaves in ancient Egypt. This thumbnail makes her pause. Makes her click.

With the video expanded to full screen, Raizl sees that the woman lies on a bare wooden platform on her belly. The chain to her neck has no slack, so her back is arched and her head upright. Her wrists and ankles are also bound behind her and linked by the same chain to the post behind the platform.

So thin, this woman! Her collarbone is prominent above her meager tittes, and her shoulders are narrow as a child's. Another woman, more zaftig, stands tall in high-heeled black boots and a tight black suit like a second skin around her large tittes, her round hips. She marches around the platform and whips the tuches of the slave-woman, whose body registers each slash with a jerk against the chain. But the slave-woman smiles, sometimes, when the whip-woman leaves off whipping and runs a gloved finger so gently over the skin she has just lashed. This seems important; Raizl searches the woman's face for the mechanism of this smile, for the hook that might connect the upward curve of her lips to willingness or want.

Then the whip-woman stops and unhooks the other one from the post, helping her up from the platform and leading her by the chain to the back wall of the room. Where are they? Where is this wall? There is no furniture, nothing for bedroom, kitchen, office. They exist in no place, in no time. Without the usual markers of porn place, porn time, Raizl feels anxious. What will make this end? What if it doesn't end? When the whip-woman clips the slave's bound wrists to a new hook over her head, so that she dangles with the length of her thin body exposed, Raizl's gut tightens with fear. This woman is not Shprintza. Before Auschwitz, Shprintza had a round face, a full body. This woman's eyes are huge in her cavernous face, but the gaze is not focused. What little tittes she has left! Two flattened outlines with dark smears for nipples. A hollow pupik. Her hipbones stick out, and just below them the raw skin is crossed with red welts.

Whatever is coming will be awful. Whatever is coming is so awful that Raizl cannot guess at it, and she watches to know what the awfulness is.

The whip cuts across the slave-woman's tittes, and Raizl shuts her eyes. Reflexively she clutches herself, folding her arms across her own tittes.

Now she understands the promise that she made. This is what will take her life, if she keeps watching. Looking down at the keyboard, trying not to see the screen at all, Raizl clicks out of the video. No more torture! In the internet, there can be walls. Some videos she will keep outside her insidernet. She types a word for what she wants, gentle shmutz, and there it is, a woman with long brown hair and dark eyes in a flowery gauzy blouse, her tittes visible like more flowers underneath, and a man lifts her shirt and holds her tittes as if they are precious, made of glass. He kisses them, and the woman closes her eyes, and Raizl eases onto her bed, letting go of her computer. It plays beside her unattended so she keeps her promise fully, not watching anything, her eyes closed now, too, her hands at the source, right middle finger circling and pressing down as if she could rub her klit flat but it is a stubborn little shteindele, asking for more asking for faster and sending pulses out along her lippen to make the shape of O, long O, oval O, which is oy oy oy she enters oyse-mukem with her left middle finger deep in the loch burrowing the soft map of ridges mit finger outside mit finger inside pushing shtupping together as if they could loop through bone and flesh to connect in one more tsunoyfshtoys oyyyyyyyy.

Dean Zeidy

Another sweaty night, and Raizl dreams she goes to see the dean again. She knocks timidly at the door, for what can she possibly say this time that will change the outcome? That will persuade him to rescind the F, restore her academic standing? There is nothing she can say. Still, desperate, she wants more than anything to be restored, to have her sense of self back. Her place as a student in college, which is her place in the world. He has to let her back in.

Raizl pushes the door—it's slightly ajar, a sign that he must be inside, must be waiting to see students—and walks in. Sitting in the dean's chair is Zeidy. He appears to be startled from sleep—and she immediately apologizes, stepping back because she has woken Zeidy from his nap! But he waves her in; he's too old, too close to death for such politeness. He smiles, so happy to see her! Behind his head rise shelves upon shelves of sfurim, with two complete sets of Talmud, the Bavli and the Yerushalmi, and all the books of commentary. To accommodate all the holy books, the shelves not only start at the floor and go all the way up the wall, now books cover the ceiling, too, their spines facing down for Zeidy to pull from on high. (*What keeps them on the ceiling and holds them to the shelves?* This is the unspoken question in Raizl's mind. *Emineh*, Zeidy answers without talking, his mind to hers. *Faith.*)

Raizl feels the books multiplying as she sits there, extra rows forming overhead, new shelves sprouting from the wall behind her. The books consume a great deal of oxygen and make the office very warm and dusty. She has no fear they will fall on her but they do make her nose itch.

"Asisa," Zeidy says.

Relief surges through Raizl: Dean Zeidy will be the one to right this wrong, this misunderstanding that has reduced her status to F. Zeidy will take her off probation, of course! But her confidence wavers as he looks at her, his hands shaking, and she is afraid, seeing the palsy of his fingers. How can he help her? He is the one who needs help. He's the one who needs her to take care of him, to put aside her schoolwork for once and look after him, tend to him. He needs her to stop with the shmutz. This is what's needed to prevent his hands from shaking, to keep him alive!

"So, Raizele?" Zeidy says. He doesn't have time to waste. Suddenly Raizl wonders if he even knows her academic status. If Dean Zeidy missed this piece of news. Will she have to tell him the whole sordid tale, the F, the near-F's? Will she have to tell him she's on probation *and* ask him to get her off probation? Will she have to promise him, as she did with Gitti, that she will give up porn? And fail him, as she has failed Gitti, failed school? She loses heart.

"Sheyfele," Dean Zeidy says. Looking at her with love beyond love. His little lamb.

Gonif

Raizl comes home one evening at the time she'd be home if she'd gone to class instead of finding a place in the library to sleep.

"Riyyyyzl!" Tati is waving a letter in the air, the torn envelope on the dining table in front of him. This is unusual, a bad sign. Tati doesn't read the mail. Her mother collects it from the lobby, jamming a bent key in the almost-broken lock so she can sort the requests for charity, the government letters, the letters from synagogues, yeshivas, and modesty committees, the true government. Invitations to benefit dinners and simchas. Her mother the one to pay, throw out, worry, defend, contest. If a letter is bad enough for her mother to give it to her father, it must be very bad.

"You didn't go to kollej? You failed your classes?" Dubious, and then, when she doesn't answer, doesn't dispute the accusation, he becomes enraged.

"Thief!" he shouts. "Gonif!"

The letter is an evil pigeon, flapping white wings. If only it would fly away, out the air shaft window and up to the sky! But Tati has it in a deathly pinch.

"Stealing our money, our time. You think days of school are yours to skip, yours to do as you please?"

He stabs the letter with his finger. "You will pay us back. You will pay back the days." He leans close, his breath hot on her face. "Show me how good you are with figures. Tell me what you owe me for half a year of lost wages, when you could have been working the whole time."

He waits for an answer, and that's when Raizl understands he is serious. "I'll have to do the calculations," she says.

"Be my guest." He stretches out his arm, as if welcoming her into her own home. "But first"—he points at her backpack—"before you go inside, you leave that here. The calculations you'll do in your head from now on."

Raizl has no intention of taking off her backpack and does not move an inch, but Tati stands and pulls the straps off her shoulders. She keeps perfectly still, not helping him, not fighting him. He puts the laptop on the table, smacks the lid. "Mine now!"

Raizl hopes desperately that Mami will emerge from the kitchen to help her, to take her side and win the computer back from Tati. But after the trouble with Gitti, why would Mami want the computer in Raizl's hands? Mami hums to herself, busily cooking, her back to Raizl.

Why

For a week, Raizl lives with the constant itch of no computer. At work, she says the laptop has a virus and is being cleaned. The Rebbetzin gives her a laptop to use at the office but refuses to let her take it home. At home, Raizl searches. In the closet with the winter coats. In the cardboard boxes that hold the Pesach dishes. In the bathroom, behind the stacked packages of toilet tissue squares for Shabbes. She looks furtively. She looks while pretending she isn't looking.

She's certain it's still in the house. If her father sold it, or even simply threw it away, someone else would know he'd had a computer. Worse, they might somehow find out *his tochter had a komputer*. No, it's hidden in the apartment, she's certain.

"I'm just wondering," Dr. P says, "if your father asked why you stopped doing your schoolwork?"

The question doesn't compute for Raizl. As if her father were even remotely like Dr. P, interested in Raizl's whys and why nots. Dr. P's ignorance, to think her father would care. Raizl is to do things because G-d says so, or the Rebbe says so, or her father says so. That is the complete list of why.

"Could your father find the porn on your computer?"

Raizl shivers. Father, porn, same sentence. "No!" she shouts. Driving away the vision that Dr. P has conjured. Never let a shrink imagine. Raizl sees, thanks to Dr. P's horrible idea, how much worse things could be. For now, though, her secret is still her secret. Hers and Dr. P's. Their secret.

"But what would happen if he found it?" Dr. P presses her. "What would he say?"

Raizl imagines the thunder of Tati's voice. She lifts a threatening index finger and stabs the air the way he does, shouting, "'Riyyyyzl! Tumeh!'" Spitting out her name, and the judgment. Not just kollej that's tumeh, and not just the komputer, but Raizl herself.

Dr. P looks confused. "He calls you Riy-zl? Like rye bread?"

Raizl nods. She hears her name with new ears, with the doctor's ears.

"Is that your name? Not Ray-zel?"

Raizl shrugs. "It's also my name." The Chasidish *Riy-zl* and the college *Rai-zl* and all of them her.

"But how do you like to say it?" Dr. P insists.

"Raizl," she answers. "How you always say it." She likes Raizy, too, but she can't imagine Dr. P calling her that, the sweet, singsong way Gitti does.

"Okay." Dr. P nods, though it takes her a moment to continue. "So, Raizl. If your father discovered the porn, he would yell. And threaten you? But what would he actually *do*?"

"Take it. Take the laptop away . . ." She sees where this is going. "Which he already did."

"That's right," Dr. P snaps back. "Is there anything he could do, that he hasn't already done?"

He might threaten to kick her out, might want to, but Mami would never let him. Besides, that would be too public, and then how would Moishe and Gitti find their marriage matches? No, Tati isn't sending her away. But he isn't returning the computer, either. How is she going to get it back?

Raizl already knows how difficult it is to find time when she has the apartment to herself; that was her chief problem when she had the computer, and now that she is bereft, computerless and in pursuit of it, the constant presence of her family again thwarts her.

Her only time alone is on a Friday, erev Shabbes—her mother grocery shopping, her father at the mikveh for his ritual bath, her brother off learning at a shiur, her sister visiting a friend—she has a chance to search. She ransacks her parents' dresser, Mami's side on the right and Tati's on the left. No risk that the panties would mingle with the undershirts. And no computer.

The laptop is like something alive, something that was part of her body, now removed. It's not her baby, but she worries about the computer even when she's not with it. She's more obsessed than when she had it with her all the time.

"You know," Raizl tells Dr. P, "I actually thought it would help me if they took the computer away."

A twitch passes across Dr. P's lips, which is reshaped into a smile.

It's shocking, the speed at which a question dissolves in the bath of understanding. Because the minute Raizl wonders why, why would Dr. P be smiling to hear this, Raizl knows the reason: Dr. P *wants* her to be addicted.

"You're sick," Raizl says. "The only thing sicker than someone being meshiggeneh and addicted to things they can't help is a doctor wanting them to be addicted. You don't want me to get better. You want me to keep coming back here each week, more sick than the week before.

"I hate you," Raizl says. "You're the gonif! You're stealing my mother's money, stealing double time, mine and my mother's."

"I can see why you might feel that way," Dr. P says, impassive. "But let me ask you: Since your father has taken the computer away—did that cure you? Are you free of your desire because the medium of your desire was removed by force?"

Doc answers her own question. "No. The only way to change is from the inside. Only when you *choose* not to watch will you be free. If you open the laptop and watch a movie, or even look at Jdate—a full life, instead of the one compulsive thing—that's when you'll know you're better.

"I'm sure you'll find the computer, you'll get it back somehow. Or get another one. As long as you want a computer, you'll find one. It will find *you*. But I'm also convinced"—the pen is twiddling faster and faster now, like the rotor blade of a helicopter, going so fast it could take off, Raizl thinks, it could launch right up to the ceiling—"that you could make a conscious decision not to watch porn. You can grow. And you can make choices.

"You're angry at your father, you're angry at me. But not having a computer—your father taking the computer—does not free you from addiction."

"Time's up," Raizl says.

Dr. P looks at the clock, the one on the end table next to her chair, and then at the other clock, on the wall to the left of Raizl, and says, "Yes, it is. Okay." She gives a wan smile and then, strangely, lifts her hand in an elegant little wave, like a queen. As if she'll be the one leaving today.

Silly Poddy, Raizl thinks, and sadness plows through her, so sudden and heavy she can't get out of the chair. Having called the clock on the session, Raizl now has the urge to pour her heart out. On her digital watch there are still thirty seconds left of the forty-five-minute session, now twenty-nine, twenty-eight. She wants to have sex with a man, and maybe also a woman. She also wants to be Chasidish to her core and without even the flash of a doubt, like her cousins, who will never, ever be troubled by porn, whose pious lives seem gorgeous in their purity and also unobtainable. She wants to cry, in the twelve seconds that are left. She wants the doctor to hold her, to abandon the project of navigating her mind in order to comfort her body, suddenly weary; she wants the doctor to hold her so she can cry into the structured shoulder of the doctor's suit; she wants to cry like a baby and be released if not from the addiction then from the prison of her brain. *Can you give me a hug?* Three seconds are left, and she's not sure if she's said it aloud or her mind is fooling her, with only one. Second. Left.

"Raizl, I'm sorry, we do have to end now."

"But can you?"

"Can I what?"

"Hug me."

"You want me to hug you?"

The corners of Podhoretz's lips pull down. Beyond frown or saying no. Of course she's going to say no, but something has stopped Podhoretz from twittering her pen. She looks, briefly, at the wall, and Raizl looks, too, at the wall of Podhoretz evidence. Framed degrees from City College and New York University.

"Of course, we can do anything, Raizl, anything at all, in words. But it wouldn't be ethical for us to have physical contact."

Raizl is familiar with this kind of closeness. It's just like a date with a man before you're married: no contact allowed.

Raizl stands and instead of walking to the door, she heads to Podhoretz's chair.

"The session is over now," Dr. P repeats. "I'm sorry," she says, but it sounds false. Her lip trembles slightly, a moment of Podhian anxiety.

Raizl sits on the floor and lays her head on Dr. P's knees. She snuffles in the deep smell of lavender, the musty smell of wool that has gotten wet and then dried, the smell of bread, and wedges her forehead between the doctor's thighs, and the doctor, oh doctor, presses her thighs together, perhaps intending to shut Raizl out, but in effect locking her in.

"Raizl!" she says sharply. "Get up this instant."

That's what Dr. P says. But the shake-off Raizl expects doesn't come, so she nuzzles her face more deeply into the wool of Dr. P's skirt, into the scent of herbal sachets and velvet hangers, Dr. P's closet full of suit jackets and fancy blouses and skirts, which must be roll-taped to get the lint off because there's not a whisper of dust. Dr. P's thightops more cushiony than Raizl would have guessed, deep breath, another, her inhale in sync with the slight rise of Doc's belly because the Doc is leaning forward now, and still no hands pressing against her, nothing, a resistance in word alone and not in action.

Then Dr. P leans away and loosens her thighs. Raizl looks up and finds Doc's arms dangling at the sides of the chair, limp, almost dissociated from her body, even her legs don't seem part of her, some weird passive trick the Doc's conjured to give the illusion that her head and torso aren't connected to any limbs—that it's not really her lap under Raizl's smeary face.

Dr. P's propriety makes Raizl even sadder. She can't stop crying. She's left a little snot on Dr. P's skirt. Instinctively Raizl brushes at it, trying to clean off her sad goo, and Dr. P can't help it, reaches out to comfort her, and there it is, the hug after all.

Dr. P tries to disguise it by standing and pulling Raizl to her feet, almost tugging on her shoulders.

"Therapists don't hug their patients, Raizl. It's just not done." Then Dr. P walks to the entry hall and goes into the bathroom. Raizl hears the lock, a lock Raizl has turned many times in those few moments before her appointments, staving off the conversation with Dr. P, and after appointments to delay just a bit her reentry into the world where she must keep all her secrets secreted, packing them up after they've been aired out in this little office. Never before has Raizl been the one in the office, alone. She doesn't like it. In the hall, she can hear the sound of water running, or maybe it's Dr. P pishing, a terrible sound. Raizl hums Adoin Oilom in her head, and when the prayer doesn't drown out the pish she hurries into her coat, leaves as fast as she can.

Every Night Is a Fight

Every night is a fight. Her mother's face is drawn, her father spits each time he sees Raizl. When Mami tries to serve her dinner, Tati takes the plate and scrapes Raizl's food onto his own plate. When Mami leaves the table to get water, Raizl reaches to take her plate back, but Tati grabs it and doesn't let go; one moment they are both holding it, the next it is shattered on the floor.

"Vilde chaye!" her father yells. "Kicked out of school and destroying the house!"

"I didn't break it, you did!" Raizl yells. "And I didn't get kicked out," Raizl corrects him. "It's a suspension. A warning. I can go back next semester."

"Nein," says her father.

"Nein," says her mother.

On this, they are united: no more school.

"Send her to work full-time," thunders her father.

"Let her get married," pleads her mother.

"Fine," her father decides, "she will go to work full-time for now, and tell the matchmaker we want a fast wedding."

Working Girl

The Rebbetzin's wooden desk is so enormous, it's impossible to reach the front two corners from a seated position at the center. The Rebbetzin doesn't need to reach, however; she has Raizl the reacher, now working full-time. The other girl, Basya, was never replaced. The Rebbetzin says with an awful smile that Raizl is such a good worker, she doesn't need a second girl.

"Raizele, bring me last month's bank statements." The Rebbetzin doesn't keep much on top of the desk, which is covered in a giant sheet of glass; below the glass protector are dozens of black-and-white photos. They capture an era that is long past, when the Rabbi was still alive and the Rebbetzin stood beside him, smiling stiffly at one charity event after another. The Rebbetzin, in most of the photos, wears some shade of white, with her strands of pearls larger than marbles, only her sheitel brown or black.

▼

Desk Games

1. Reach-for-It-Raizl.

The Rebbetzin places a stack of invoices on the very-far-right side of the desk and asks Raizl to review them. The Rebbetzin does not move her chair, does not allow Raizl to pass behind her or walk around the desk. No, Raizl must reach across the Rebbetzin, with her tittes hovering near the Rebbetzin's arm, to retrieve the papers. In the extra seconds she spends in this posture because this, after all, is her job, Raizl thinks of the QuickBooks program that would render paper invoices obsolete. No more copying from paper into Excel.

2. Pick-It-Up-Raizl.

"Ein minit." The Rebbetzin stops Raizl as she straightens a pile of paper, shifting the many edges in her hands to make them all line up. "Ich hub fargessen . . ." The Rebbetzin fumbles through the bills to find the one she forgot, an invoice that, if only it were paid now, would end all suffering; if only it had been paid generations ago, lives would have been spared. The Rebbetzin searches as no one else has, fervently, licking her index finger to separate the pages more quickly, picking and pulling at the sheets until, inevitably, the entire pile falls out of Raizl's hands and scatters on the floor, and Raizl must bend over to pick up the papers.

3. Hands-and-Knees-Raizl.

Now Raizl is on all fours behind the desk, hidden from view even if one of the jewelers or a messenger opens the office door. The papers have flown in every direction—where did the laws of gravity go that could have sent them all to one side or the other? Why is she subject only to the physics dictated by the Rebbetzin, whose cane suddenly finds the indentation of Raizl's tuches even through her skirt and presses against the woolen barrier. What is the Rebbetzin doing? Raizl stops moving, drops the papers she's already gathered, is perfectly still, registering this backside touch.

4. Get-Up-Raizl.

The cane falls to the ground. "Ach," the Rebbetzin snorts, smacking her hand against the desk. "Klotz!" the Rebbetzin says. "So clumsy! Get off the floor, Raizl, and help me for once. Give me the cane."

Favorite Brother

There are footsteps in the hall. Raizl's door swings open, and Moishe breezes into the room. Flipping up the tails of his long black coat so they sail out around him, he plunks himself as usual on Zeidy's, now her, bed. "So how's the college girl?"

Raizl sits in the room's one chair, biting her nails. Not even Moishe can lift her spirits. He laughs easily at his own foibles, and normally he makes Raizl laugh, too, but his question immediately darkens her mood. Raizl admits to Moishe that she is not, anymore, a college girl.

"I dropped out," she says. At least half true. "Tati wants me to work full-time."

"Oy yoy yoy!" Moishe slaps the bed. "Why do you have to?" His beard, getting fuller now, shakes along with his head. "I know, I know," he says, ruefully. "So *we* can learn . . ."

Raizl feels guilty for his guilt. Moishe imagines that Raizl's future has been sacrificed so her brothers can study Torah all day, her intellectual growth confined as theirs broadens. When in fact her future has been hijacked by porn, her intelligence pinned by so many naked bodies.

"I'm going to speak to Tati. It's not right."

"Don't worry," Raizl says lamely. "It's better like this."

"What are you talking?" he replies sharply. His glasses, always thick, seem even thicker now, with magnifying power. He might see through her. "Why are you giving up? You can't!"

"It's just for a little while. I'll go back to school. I'm taking a break, that's all," she explains, but Moishe looks unconvinced. She gambles on what will put him off the scent. "This way I can work more, and save for my wedding. Maybe I'm going to get married," she mumbles.

"Ah." He grins. "Mazel tov! Who is he?"

"Well, not yet." Raizl backpedals. "I mean, I haven't found anyone yet. Just a couple of shidduch-dates."

"That's good," he says. "It will happen . . ." He stands abruptly and paces, having to turn every three steps in the small room.

"Do you think I should try again?" he asks. "Or is it too soon after . . . ?" He trails off, but Raizl understands. Too soon after the broken engagement to start again, to ask for a b'show. What kalleh will believe he's ready? "I was maybe going to wait until I get smicha. So I can stay focused on studying."

"Yes," Raizl says, "it's too soon. Wait till you're a rabbi, then you'll be ready, and you'll get the best match, too. A serious girl who wants a scholar."

Raizl smiles at him, knowing this to be true for the girls in her high school circle except, now, herself; she has a secret list of qualifications that are not of a spiritual or intellectual nature. If a man with smicha wants to put his tongue all over her body, then fine, let him have smicha. For a moment she indulges in the fantasy of such a man, pleasing to her parents and pleasuring to her, the perfect man. An impossible man.

A sigh escapes from Raizl that she immediately regrets. Moishe drops the topic of his dating and resumes his investigation of Raizl's. "I don't see," he says, "why you can't go to college until you get married. I am going to speak to Tati."

"Please, Moishe, don't," Raizl begs. "I don't want to go to school now."

"You *always* wanted to go to college! When you were ten years old, you wanted to study!" Moishe scrutinizes her as if he doesn't recognize her. "Why not now?"

A chasm opens before Raizl, and all that she has given up falls into it. Itzik and Duvid, Avrum and his yachts, the Holocaust Museum and the photos of Anne Frank's hiding place and Anne Frank herself, the corpses plowed into the cold ground, Professor O'Donovan and the Dean of Students, Tati and Mami and Gitti and now Moishe all swallowed into the open pit containing everything she has abandoned, and on top of them all her own body—her old body. The Raizl-body that was previously transport for her mind and home of her soul, a way to get to class and soak in the knowledge and give back answers on tests and advance to the next level and the next, a way to bow while she prayed to G-d above. Old Raizl wants to tell Moishe he's right; tears start in her eyes because she wants to go to college, it's true.

But without the computer, she cannot study. And with the computer, she failed her classes.

What she cannot tell Moishe: if she had the computer in her hands right now, she would be online! Watching a video. A porn image flashes on the big screen of Raizl's mind, of a woman wearing nothing but a black fishnet over her whole body, and the camera is angled for the view between her legs, the dark, slick pink of her shmundie caught between the black diamonds of the net. Fingers are pulling the weave apart, making the diamond spaces wider until the loose fabric tears and there is a hole as wide and long as the shmundie, but whose fingers—the woman's, or a man's?—the camera of Raizl's memory doesn't say. She wishes she had the computer, wishes she could watch again. Watch how that woman caught in the net also gets caught in pleasure.

"Yes," she tells Moishe, "I wanted to go to college, and I will again. In a mazeldige sho'o," she says, in an auspicious hour. Wishing upon herself the same good luck she'd wish on a pregnant woman about to give birth. "But I don't want it now. You need to stop worrying about it, and you need to go."

As robotic as she sounds to herself, the cold talk works. Moishe gets off the bed and walks to the bedroom door, the hurt hanging off him like tzitzis strings. "I don't understand," he says.

"You don't have to," Raizl says. "It's my life."

"Is Tati forcing you?" he asks. "You need to tell me."

He gives her a look more fierce than any touch. He's not allowed to hold her, or hug her. The way they used to when they were kids:

hide-and-go-seek, he'd grab her and tickle her when she hid behind the winter coats—no matter the season, that's where she hid. She remembers the time he tickled her so hard, she laughed until she had the hiccups. Then Tati had said, "Enough! You're too old for that," to Moishe. "Soon you'll be bar mitzvah!" he said, though Moishe was only ten. The flush of shame over both of them. They were so embarrassed by their father's admonition, making them think about the touch in a way they had not before, that they didn't speak to each other again that night, and for weeks afterward.

But tonight Moishe does not hold his tongue. "It's not right, Raizy. You put so much into your studies," he says. "I want you to finish. What you started, I won't let you throw it away."

Moishe's blunt words have the force of prophecy—as if Zeidy were speaking, telling her what had already been in her mind, but she hadn't yet said to herself. She *has* thrown away what she started. But the shame of it takes her to a new, hard place. She is beyond Moishe's protection, beyond any conversation her big brother could have with her father. She is on her own now.

"Go," Raizl says. "Go back to yeshiva, study more, smoke a little less, get your smicha. You need to *go*."

Topless

The next day, a Friday, erev Shabbes—also the summer solstice, Sam says, the longest day to be at the beach—Raizl packs her bag. She puts in more underwear than Sam said to because she has them, the laundry is clean. Mami does the wash on Thursday nights, so everything is fresh for Shabbes, and Gitti folds the clothes, that is her job. So Raizl has eight pairs of underwear, and her secret jeans, and the secret black V-neck. She's heard—Sam's told her—that her tush is sexy in jeans. She has no lipstick, but Sam's also said she can bite her lips to make them red. Redder. She fits everything she can in the backpack. She grabs the cash out of the various shoe-banks and bra-banks, scoops up two oven-hot challah rolls from the cooling rack by the window, and leaves the house as if she's going to work but goes instead to the library, where it's not uncommon to see people with stuffed bags sitting for hours at the computers. She can't access porn videos, but there is still a world waiting for her: she finds pictures of the beach she is going to in the afternoon with Sam—she's never been to that beach part of Queens, or to any beach at all, only the lake upstate—and then she finds an online accounting course that will give her a degree without requiring her to attend any physical school. No class participation.

At four o'clock Sam's waiting for her, and they take the subway to the bus to the walk to the beach, and then Kurt and Solo join them, too. Solo's beard is longer, and today both boys—men?—wear big black knobs in their earlobes. Sam and Kurt share a beer and when the can is empty, they stop in the middle of the sidewalk to kiss, so it seems that today is a shvantz day for Sam, not a shmundie day. Kurt and Solo have towels slung over their shoulders and Sam has a bikini top on and Raizl realizes she's even more overdressed than usual, no bathing suit and no towel.

"Don't worry, Ray-Ray," Sam says, loud and laughing, "it's topless here! Panties and you're good. I brought a towel we can share, and I brought vodka, so we're really good."

Sam unscrews the red top and drinks and passes it to Raizl, the smell of it awful like the smell of rubbing alcohol on the washcloth that she dabs against Yossi's chest and forehead when he has a fever. Worse than the Rebbetzin's schnapps it smells, but Raizl stops breathing and just drinks, drinks, drinks.

"Whoa, Raizl, leave some for us," Kurt says, grabbing the bottle.

The vodka hit goes in two directions from Raizl's throat: up to her skull and down to the pit of her belly. She wishes she could take a bite out of a challah roll, get rid of the vodka breath that fills her mouth, but she's too embarrassed to take the bread out of her backpack. What the others will say about challah-and-vodka. The vodka slosh makes her want to sit down, the backpack feels heavier and heavier, but Sam points out poison ivy at the side of the path so Raizl keeps moving forward in her flat-soled black shoes. The sand makes the path grainy and slippery and she feels like she's walking on crushed glass, and her head feels like it's already in the ocean, the way she has to balance it on top of her neck. Is that from three swallows of the bottle? Or is it just the effect of being at the beach? Somehow the four of them out here are different from the four of them anywhere else in the city. Certainly she's not Raizl-who-she-used-to-be because the semester is over, and though Raizl didn't tell Sam that she's not coming back to college, she figures Sam must know, and anyway that's not all that's different; what's changed is that the bag on her back has in it all she needs to be free. Her bag is now her house. After the beach, Sam is taking her someplace she can stay for a while, stay as long as she wants, Sam says, at Sam's brother's girlfriend's place in Bushwick. Her backpack is her tent, her refrigerator, her closet, her desk. And her last, tiny bit of Shabbes, those challah rolls she stole while Mami wasn't looking, just before she left the apartment. Didn't kiss the mezuzah. Shut the door and locked that life behind her.

At the end of the path, Sam and Kurt and Solo ditch their shoes and march off across the sand. Raizl kicks her shoes off, too—the only pair like it in the litter of slides and sandals and boots, hers black leather and leaving no toe exposed, shoes for Eastern Europe in the eighteenth century, and even after she's gotten them off she has the problem of tights. She heaves the backpack onto the ground but still it's so awkward to take the tights off, rolling the fabric down one leg and then the other while the wind flattens her long skirt against her, trying to keep her balance and not fall while she finally grabs the toe of the tights off one foot, the other, hopping out. They land in the sand, two peachy-beige circles of fabric connected to each other, somehow like handcuffs but for her feet and legs, and she steps over them, leaves them for the sand to swallow, grabbing her pack and running to catch up with the others.

"Hey, over here," calls Sam, waving, and Raizl stumbles, her feet not quite understanding how to move themselves in the sand unless she's looking down at them, but look up she must, focusing on the face that is calling to her and Sam's tittes waving, too, their fullness moving in rhythm with her arm. There, in a space that Raizl had never thought of as its own definitive location, under Sam's tittes and above her belly button, a tattooed skull stares at Raizl, with inked beads of black and ruby hanging below it like a necklace, dipping down into Sam's black lace panties. If she'd thought about it, of course Sam has tittes, and for sure she has tattoos, and now here they are, as bright and present as Sam's face, a new kind of face Raizl can't stop staring at.

"Come on, girl," Sam says, and throws her arms around Raizl. She almost falls over as Sam hugs her, the combined weight of her heavy backpack and vodka-heavy body pulled off balance, and as soon as Sam releases her she takes off the pack and sets it at the corner of Sam's towel.

"Get rid of this, too." Sam tugs at her sweater. "We want boobage, we want it all!"

"Boo-bage! Boo-bage!" The boys laugh and chant. They, too, are topless. Raizl understands that men without shirts, here at the beach, are not considered "topless," but she has never seen men's chests that aren't covered by many layers, undershirts and white collared shirts and the sleeveless shirt with tzitzis fringes, all beneath long jackets. The modesty of men in her family. Here skin is clothed only in tattoos, a way of being dressed even when naked. Kurt with his long golden hair streaming over a thin, mostly hairless chest, his paleness accentuated by a sleeve of blue-green knots tattooed over his left biceps and shoulder and onto the left half of his chest, like a shield for his heart. And Solo with a huge falcon spreading its black wings across his chest, the tips of its feathers marking the line of his collarbone. A key in the falcon's talons pointing down to Solo's little extra bit of belly.

Raizl unbuttons her sweater, wanting to do it quickly but instead it's slow motion; her fingers take forever fumbling with each mother-of-pearl button on the cardigan, and then the little white buttons on her white blouse underneath. For a moment she's still wearing them both even though they are open—they hang useless, like sheets untucked from a bed—and then she shrugs her shoulders back and shakes herself and the clothes drop off, the sun and the sea breeze hitting her skin simultaneously, a delicious mix-up of hot and cool, a shiver up her spine that is prickling alive. And fast, before the feeling changes, she twists her arms around her back, the ordinary hunched gesture of unhooking the bra that is now a dramatic bow to the chorus of Sam and Kurt and Solo cheering her on—"Go, Raizl!"—and whistling. As she bends over, the cream-colored underwire cups fall away from her tittes, and then she stands as straight as ever she has and swings the bra in a circle overhead like Tati shlugging kapures, waving the chicken over his head to take away their sins on the eve of Yom Kippur. But she doesn't slaughter the bra, she lets it fly free, and it lands somewhere in the sand behind them. "Keep going! "Don't stop!" they shout at her now that she is naked on top and dressed on the bottom. She repeats in her mind *don't stop don't stop don't* while she unzips her skirt, and then she panics, remembering what underwear she has, not black like Sam's, not sexy. Thank G-d it's not her period so she has no period-pad today, but the panties are a dull white, with a thick elastic waistband and plain trim at the thighs, no lace, and they cover her tush, not like Sam's where the back is open except for one black string dividing her tuches in two. The three of them burst out laughing and Raizl blushes, why didn't she ever think to buy other underwear, but it would just be one more thing to hide, it's easier to wear what Mami buys for her and Gitti, just to wear it and be done. But now she won't be getting underwear from Mami anymore, she will have these tsniusdik modesty panties only as long as the heavy fabric holds up. She will replace them herself, which makes her happy but queasy, and she looks down at the front of the panties where they pouf out a bit over the hair she has there, and blushes again. Everyone will know she doesn't shave it off. She can see Sam's panties lying flat against smooth skin, and there are no little hairs coiled around the edge of the elastic.

But Sam is delighted, claps her hands. "Ooooooh," she yells, "Raizl's wearing white! She's going to win the wet underwear contest!" Sam grabs Raizl's hand and starts running with her toward the water.

In seconds they are in the cold shock of the waves. Sam tugs her in deeper, and Raizl's down, rolling in waves and swallowing saltwater. A nauseous fear rises in her because she doesn't know how to swim, but then Sam grabs her up and her stomach settles. Sam is with her. Sam holds her tight. They are holding one another, their arms around each other's shoulders making a single body, a vessel for four cold nipples and laughter, the water dripping off the tips of Raizl's hair down her back and down her front, so icy and so good, and they stumble together, still embracing, back up the beach. And it goes like this, sitting and drinking vodka and then running stumbling to the water, and Raizl's body seems so much more naked than theirs because she has no tattoos. Only Raizl has bare skin, like a baby who has never made a choice, never decided what to do with her skin.

Late in the day, the sun drips down the sky, an orange so bloodshot that if it were an egg, Mami would throw it out, not kosher. They pass the bottle and over time her almost-nakedness is less and less. Her body just a body. Unclothed, her body is more free, but also less important now than it had ever been before, under all the clothing. It's so normal for them to sit here, to drink, to smoke cigarettes that they roll themselves, sprinkling the dried crushed leaves, cigarettes that smell sweet on the breeze. For the first time Raizl senses what it is to be just a person, not so much the names of what she is—Jew, Chasid, maidele—but something simpler, stripped, more essential.

The vodka goes around again, a bottle with a red label and onion-dome buildings, soon nothing but air inside that bottle, and Kurt and Solo make jokes, pointing out the tittes of other women on the beach. Sam ignores them. She puts on her sunglasses and lies down on her towel, patting the spot next to her where Raizl, too, can stretch out in the sun. Raizl has no glasses; she stares up at the sky. She is cold from their plunge in the sea but the side of her next to Sam is warm, and anyway, the sky is spinning overhead, she couldn't possibly stand or even move.

When she opens her eyes again the light has mostly seeped out of the sky, her teeth are chattering, and her head aches. Also, Solo is staring at her. Suddenly her nakedness feels, again, naked. The white panties cling damply to her. She doesn't see or hear Sam, and her head feels too heavy to lift and look.

Solo joins her on Sam's towel. "Oh shit, you're freezing," he says, and starts rubbing her arms, frictioning heat into her body. "I'm going to warm you up." Then he lies down on top of her, wrapping his arms over her head.

The slab of him is frightening at first, so heavy—too heavy! She can't breathe!—but his warmth is a gift. The heat sinks into her, and the fear loosens. She snuggles closer to seal out any tiny pockets of cold air between them.

"Sam?" Raizl asks.

"She went with Kurt."

"Yah," Raizl says. Even though she knows it's too Yiddishy and Solo absolutely does not speak Yiddish and she should use a different language. An idea floats through her mind of how Sam and Kurt must be on Kurt's towel, the way she and Solo are on Sam's towel.

"You're so beautiful, Raizl."

"Yah," she repeats.

He pulls his towel over them and then he really is naked, not just topless but shvantznaked, too. An idea floats through her mind that this doesn't matter at all because her panties are still on. His shvantz can't see her loch; it's like one person with eyes and one person without. Also the idea floats that his shvantz is real, not a video shvantz.

He pulls himself tightly against her, and she loves it. The shvantz holds extra heat, a smooth bar between them that rolls over and over her panties and her head is blooming with orange suns, melting and melting, warm against the inside of her skull, which is connected somehow to yene platz because she feels him on that place outside where his shvantz rubs and on the inside where the orange suns pour down. He kisses her, takes the moans off her lips with his. He wedges his fingers under the elastic and slides them over her klit, the contact unmediated by panties, while the shvantz is still outside, knocking against the white fabric. For a moment, he kisses her so hard she cannot breathe and then the orange suns burst and her back arches, the power of it bucking him off her, and he kneels so he can pull her panties down and without his body on top of hers the cold air rushes in and she is free, cold and free, but if she does this she cannot ever return from this freedom, she will be floating like this on a sand patch above a blue wave for always. Now he rubs his shvantz against her directly, and the top of it wants to go into her loch. He holds himself over her, bracing himself on his hands. In the dimming light the falcon spreads its wings and soars free of Solo's chest, its long feathers engulf her, its talons about to drop the key right onto Raizl.

"Nein!" she yells. "Nein!" She does not want this key from the falcon to fall on her. She ducks out under his arm and rolls to the side, off the towel and into the sand, which is chilly and damp and sticks to her, and Solo grabs her, pulls her back. Suddenly he is kneeling over her, saying, "Suck it, then," and he pokes his shvantz at her lips, a thick flesh that tastes of ocean and pish, a curl of ammonia mixed with salt. She tries to grow extra room in her mouth and make her lips open wider around the shvantz, like a woman in a video, but they never did show her how to do this, how to unhinge her jaw and block out smell and taste to be empty, a mouth-space. Solo is breathing fast and grunting; he holds her head and jabs his shvantz more fiercely into the back of her throat and gags her. A gush of the vodka comes up, a thick sour aftertaste of pickled alcohol; quickly she swallows it down. This closing of her throat brings Solo to his shpritz and she is swallowing, swallowing again.

He releases her. "I gotta take a piss," Solo says, and heads to the water.

Raizl panics. There is no one nearby; only a few shadows remain, farther down on the beach. She desperately pats around the edges of the towel, now mostly submerged in sand, searching for her backpack. Her clean underwear, her keys. Her challah. The last light is draining out of the sky, the air getting chillier. She is late for Shabbes.

This is what she will tell Mami when she goes home tomorrow night, when Mami cries and scolds and hugs her: that she went to visit a friend from school and fell asleep, that she didn't wake up until after sunset, too late to travel home because it was already Shabbes. She didn't leave home, no, she only waited until after Shabbes to return home.

Raizl finds her skirt in a damp pile and shakes it out, wraps it around her shoulders like a shawl, and keeps pawing the sand until her hand snags on a strap. Quickly Raizl unzips her bag, pulls out laundered panties and a clean shirt, softly singing the hymn to welcome the Shabbes bride as she gets dressed: *Come in peace, crown of her husband! In joy and jubilation . . . Enter, bride!* Then Raizl sits in the sand, tears off a piece of the challah, reflexively making the blessing. She takes great bites, fills her mouth with it. The eggy density of the bread wiping away the sour taste of Solo's shpritz.

Silver Treasure

Late Saturday night, so late that Tati and the rest are surely sleeping, Raizl creeps through the apartment to her room. The door opens and she panics—Zeidy's spirit! Welcoming her back!—but it's Mami. Holding the silver treasure in her hands.

"You came home," Mami says.

"Yah, Mami." Raizl takes the computer carefully from her mother. "Ah groysen shkoyech," she whispers, thankful to have the familiar heft of it in her hands. A longing courses through her, so powerful it makes her shudder, and she fears dropping the machine. She puts it on her desk, keeping it safe there, not wanting to open it in front of Mami, to appear too eager. Instead she turns away from it and gives her mother a tight hug, relief flooding through her and worry, too, of what will happen to her now that she has it back.

"Oof, Raizele, too tight," her mother giggles, suddenly girlish and nervous. "Turnishzugen far Tati."

"Don't worry, I won't tell him."

Her mother holds her by the shoulders. "Let me see a happy punim now."

What Do You Watch?

"You were so close to leaving home," Podhoretz says. "You did leave. But it seems you don't want to go. I'm wondering why?"

"You think I should go?" Raizl says.

"No, not at all." Podhoretz pauses. "Well," she says. She puts her two feet in their sensible one-and-a-half-inch pumps together on the floor and pushes so that her back straightens, her shoulders broaden against the chair. "What I think doesn't matter at all. Only what you think."

Another breath fills Pod's cheeks, then empties out. Pod, always asking a question in her sneaky way.

So: Why doesn't she go?

Raizl realizes with a shock that the question is familiar to her, that she has wondered something similar about Mami: How can she stay? Tati's rage, his moods on the scale from sullen to storming, a tiger prowling in the cage.

But many women have difficult husbands. Sick husbands. How many women wife even when the man doesn't husband? Stay, and take care, and don't ever leave?

That doesn't explain why Raizl stays.

"For Mami," Raizl says. "And Gitti and Moishe. For Shabbes. For Pesach." How will she hear Hashem if she leaves? This is where Hashem knows to look for her, to call for her, even if she has eaten what she is not supposed to. This garden of rules and prohibitions, this garden with its paths unscrolled.

"Sometimes I want to talk to Hashem," Raizl tells Podhoretz. "Not just praying, not just asking for help or praising Hashem, with Hashem far away. I want to call Hashem down here"—Raizl gestures at the room, at the air between her and the doctor.

Raizl can see Podhoretz doesn't think much of this.

"Hmm," the doctor says, recrossing one leg over the other. "And what does God say? When you call God down?"

Then Podhoretz blushes. "Does it offend you that I say God? Would you prefer that I say Hah-shem?"

Raizl lifts one eyebrow and says nothing. As if she, or Hashem, cared a hoot about what Pod calls the thing Pod doesn't think exists.

"Okay." Pod tries again. "If God were here—if you called and God joined us—what would you say?"

Raizl imagines the room full of a glowing opaque light, like the cloud above the tabernacle when the Israelites traveled the desert. Her questions wouldn't survive. The Presence would fill the space, undo her doubts.

Pod changes the subject. "Now that you have the computer back, how is it?"

"What do you mean?"

"Is the porn the same as before?" Dr. P asks.

Anger rises in Raizl. Because the answer is no. Porn now is nothing like what it used to be. The first night she had the computer back, she never slept, just watched video after video until morning. The videos looked awful, awful, not sexy. Not fun or beautiful.

"I hate porn," Raizl says. "I hate *you*."

Dr. P is nodding. A slow chin up, chin down.

"You ruined porn, but you didn't cure me. Not for five minutes did you cure me. I can't find any videos I like. I turn one on, I feel bored, I just want to see the next one."

"What are you looking for?"

"I'm not looking *for* anything. I just want to get on to the next one, and the next."

Raizl watches as much as she used to, before Tati stole her computer, before Mami gave it back. If anything, she watches more now, because she doesn't try to do schoolwork, and doesn't want to think about her job. She watches more, but it seems as though there's nothing to see. The men do all the usual things to the women, and the women have all the usual reactions. Same moves, same sounds, same expressions, which seem more fake with every repetition.

But she still can't bring herself to stop watching. Always, always the first moment holds a tingling hope. Every time she goes online, the promise of that first scene embodies the hope of seeing something different, something just as new as the first time she watched porn, and holds the possibility that she might, tonight, feel electrified again.

"I have to keep hunting for the one that will surprise me. I have to watch *more*, to find the one that's real." Raizl stops. Adds: "You bitch."

Podhoretz barely flinches, shrugging it off.

The word hangs in the air. Raizl's never said it before. A word from the mean porn, a word from a video where a man hits a woman and throws her down on a bed, on a floor. As soon as it's out of her mouth, though, she knows it's true. Dr. P is a hateful bitch. She has an urge to hit Dr. P. Shake her, mess up her hair, mess with her head. Taste of her own meds.

"There's a name for the phenomenon you're describing," Dr. P says. "Tolerance. When apathy and appetite merge. When you need more and more porn to feed the addiction."

Raizl says nothing.

"Do you still want to stop?"

"Yes, I want to stop coming here."

"That's not what I meant."

"Actually, it's none of your business, whether I want to stop watching. That has nothing to do with you anymore."

Raizl crosses her legs, doesn't realize she's doing it until after it's done: mirroring the Doc. Who still wants to help the girl who walked into her office six months ago. Raizl's foot kicks the air as she uncrosses her legs.

There's goodbye in the air. Like a special shrink perfume.

"You don't have to come back here."

"You want me to go?"

"I want you to stay, but you are free to choose. No one makes you come here."

"Mami wants me here."

Tch. Podhoretz clicks her tongue again. *Tch.*

"The minute you tell her you're done," Podhoretz says, "your mother wipes her hands and gives you a kiss. One less bill to pay for the woman who pays them all."

Raizl says nothing because at least on this, Poddy's got it right.

"So. Why are you here, Raizl?"

Another question like a cage, showing her the bars she can't escape. Of all the people Raizl speaks to each day—her sister, her mother, her father, a professor or two when she was still going to college and the other students, the butcher or cashier at the kosher grocery—of them all, not one knows her. Sam knows a little bit, but she cannot know everything. No one can.

So Raizl comes willingly into the parlor of gloom, Dr. Podhoretz's office that is more elegant than the front rooms of any apartment she has ever visited. This is the Slope. Leather armchairs, Persian rugs, the fancy furniture in which Jews who don't believe in G-d save those who do.

Podhoretz is worse than porn. Podhoretz is a betrayal of her faith, of the word of G-d. Raizl should have gone to a rabbi, as the Doc suggested at the beginning. A rabbi would tell her not to watch. A rabbi would save her from herself. Like her father, pounding the table, delivering the law and thunder. A confiscated computer, and it would all be over.

▼

"My parents sent me to therapy, too," Spark had told Raizl a few months back, when Raizl confessed to her and Sam what kind of appointment she had to get to after class. "It's what parents do when they can't come up with anything else. But don't worry, you can shit the shrink."

And Raizl has shit the shrink. That was fun, for a while. Now it's too much effort. Exhausting.

What's awful is that Mami sent her here for help. Mami, deceived into thinking this would cure her fear of getting married. And she herself, deceived into thinking this would cure her fear of never getting married.

There is no cure. All that lies behind the mirror of this question is another question, and another.

▼

"What about you, Dr. P?" Raizl turns the tables. Raizl asks the questions. "What do you watch?"

Podhoretz keeps her head even, her gaze level.

"Girls with girls? Or young boys with older women like you?"

Dr. P's stillness is lizard-like, but then she moves her lips. "What makes you think I watch?"

Raizl wishes she had a pen and a notepad. This could be fun. She sees then the job's appeal.

"You watch porn to see how other people do." Anger boiling up in a Yiddish-sounding rage. "Everything what I see, shvantzes mit shmundies, you see it, too." The fury so strong, she's dug her nails right through the cracked leather of the armchair and made holes in the foam.

"You watch porn because it's so much easier than dating and you don't need to buy better shoes." Raizl points, with her toe, at Podhoretz's bargain pumps. "You watch porn because, you tell yourself, it's important for you to understand me."

"Aren't you making a rather big assumption about me?"

This time, Raizl snorts. "*Everyone* watches porn. You said it."

Podhoretz raises an eyebrow. "Really? Aren't you here because watching porn has made you different? Aren't you here because most people in your community *don't* watch porn, and now that you do—all the time—you don't fit into your own neighborhood, your own family?"

"But you're not religious. Why shouldn't you watch?"

"I choose not to. I decide what to spend my time on, what I want to read and listen to, what images I want to stream into my mind. I choose what I do."

"I don't believe you."

"Does it bother you, Raizl? That I choose not to watch? That I have choices?"

"Choices?" Raizl sputters. "You're not *free*. You're too busy proving you're in control to be free. The only thing you choose, what all your control gives you, is being a bitch."

Podhoretz flinches this time.

Raizl gets out of her chair and heads for the door. But she doesn't walk out. She hits the lights. Stands in the shadowy dark. Only the desk lamp with its green glass shade casts a glow over Podhoretz. The light turns her blouse transparent; Raizl can see the outline of her right arm within the filmy fabric. Podhoretz's face is dark, and Raizl is dark to herself, she can feel her body but not see it. Until she flicks the light on again.

With a sweep of her arm, the light goes off again.

She flicks the switch up down up down up down up down up down up—

Snail in a Suit

The matchmaker must have smelled the fear on her mother because the next boy she sends to Raizl is a clammy snail in a suit.

"I'd like to see you again," he says, though he hasn't seen her even once—they only just started their seltzer waters. His lip quavers, but it's not sexual desire. What is it? A terrible shyness. Until this minute, he hadn't made any eye contact, and she had planned to tell Mami that it went badly, it was awful, he didn't like her at all.

But now Chaim Leib says, "Would you like that?"

He is asking her what no man has ever asked, no woman, no one. She stares at his thick, mobile, pale lips, visible through his scraggly beard, posing the question to her. Would you like that? A question to ask if there was a camera behind her, someone watching to see what she likes.

But there is no one. Only this skinny boy in a coat far too big for him, asking.

His question opens a door inside her: what she would like. So much is on offer, in the world, in the vast, internet-imitating world outside, with its fantasies and possibilities, its positions and devices, and beyond that the music and paintings, the books without G-d, books that are neither the word of Hashem nor the interpretation. The world outside offers infinite choice—but not to her.

What is on offer to her is this particular boy, his lip-tremble, his smeared collar, his poor hem. And to the question *Would you like that?* she looks down, but she says yes.

"Yes, I would like that very much."

"Burech Hashem." His lips turn up. The smile burns through her doubt, the answer she gave to save him.

▼

Raizl twists in the armchair. A little maroon-colored tape where she'd gouged the holes last time. The chair was never comfortable, but tonight it's much worse. Hard, lumpy, ridged and valleyed from a million tucheses before hers. Tucheses riding the upholstery into an oblivion of thinly cushioned soul-searching and despair. Tucheses pressed with unhappiness into this chair.

She never wanted to sit here again. She thought she would never come back! But she's made this enormous mistake—saying yes to Chaim Leib, leading him to expect something when she can give nothing. Someone has to help her out of this.

Quitting therapy is as hard as quitting porn.

"Is something wrong, Raizl?"

"No," she says. Nothing wrong. The wedge of upholstery, the space between other people's legs where the cushion has stayed firm, rises tauntingly between Raizl's legs. She squeezes it with her thighs.

"Chaim Leib," Raizl says, finally. "He's not going to like me."

"How do you know that?" Dr. P says this gently, as if she's pushing on a bruise and doesn't want it to hurt too badly, just enough to show: the bruise is here.

"Come on, Dr. P. He's not going to. He's so Chasidish, too Chasidish for me. I can't fake—".

She stops.

She eyeballs the diplomas of Dr. P. The framed poster of yellow flowers tilting and falling out of a vase. The office tchotchkes she's looked at for hundreds and hundreds of minutes. Thousands.

"He's going to see through me."

"Wait a minute, Raizl. What were you going to say? You can't what—fake it? Do you think he'd want you to fake it?"

The first time Raizl realized a woman in a porn video was faking—she looked right at Raizl, instead of at the man, while she was moaning *oh, oh, oh*—Raizl instinctively shut the computer. The woman had seen her; she'd been caught watching. It took Raizl a minute to recover, to reassure herself there was no way the woman could have seen her. She opened the laptop again, and there was the woman, her smile frozen, her stare unblinking. That was when Raizl understood that the sex was faked, or at least the pleasure. Manufactured, in the video, for the audience. After that, when the woman or women seemed to be having fun, Raizl felt uncertain.

Would you like that?

There was no way to know for sure—not what she likes, not what the women in the videos like.

Did married people fake it that way, too? How many women were there, married to their own Chaim Leibs, saying, *oh, oh, oh?* Or saying nothing, but wishing for something else. Wishing they hadn't said yes, when they'd meant *no*.

A deep sadness came over Raizl. She didn't know how to tell all this to Dr. P, and even if she could tell her, it wouldn't matter; Dr. P already knew, or would pretend that she'd already known. The door was open now, to all that was fake and the doubt that it could ever be real—the door to doubting everything. Dr. P was paid, and the beautiful women in the porn videos, and even the ugly ones, got paid, in money or fame or some other currency Raizl could only guess at.

Chaim Leib had tricked her, with his question: *Would you like that?* Foolishly she'd gone through that door, foolish and hopeful, but she'd realized soon enough that even if his question was sincere, her answer wasn't. This is the worst doubt of all, doubting herself. If she marries Chaim Leib, he will be paid, too, like the people in porn. He will be paid in gifts, her dowry—a suitcase full of towels and tablecloths, six months' rent on an apartment—her parents persuading his parents, and his persuading hers, that all is in order.

You Pick for Me

"You're refusing a second date with Chaim Leib? We already said yes!"

"So now we're saying no." No to the shattered-snail expression that Raizl imagines on Chaim Leib's face when he gets the news. "I'm not going."

"Oy, Raizele." Mami sighs a horrible sigh.

"Can't you pick one for me?" Raizl asks. "Just go to the shadchen and look at the photos, and whichever you pick will be the one. Anyone else, just not Chaim Leib."

"What? You don't want to pick a chussen for yourself? But you're so modernishe." Her mother tsk-tsks. "It will not be good if I choose."

"Yes, Mami, I want you to choose. Don't make me go. Don't make me do it."

"What are you talking? I never heard a girl who didn't like to go out on a shidduch-date! You went on what, three dates? And you're giving up? You're going to live a lifetime with a man, and you can't be bothered to meet him first to see what you like, what you don't? Finally Tati agreed for you to have a shidduch-date, and you're saying no?"

"Please, I'm begging you. Pick someone for me so it can be done."

"Narishkeit," her mother mutters. "Just go one more time. The next one will be the one."

Date-Moishe

This date is different. His beard is neatly trimmed, and his moustache, too, not swallowing his lips, all very distinguished looking. His payes fall in perfectly smooth curls, the way Raizl wishes her hair would curl, two elegant locks of a dark reddish-brown. If there is a redhead in his family, her own coloring is not an obstacle. Above his long, fine nose are two enormous brown eyes that sparkle when he greets Raizl, bowing slightly. Moishe—the same name as her brother. Strange, but maybe a good omen. Perhaps he is her soul mate, her ziveg.

Date-Moishe holds open the door to the hotel for her and asks her questions as they walk through the lobby, as if she is some kind of puzzle and when he gets enough pieces, he will put her together.

"What do you study?"

"Accounting. For my job."

"Where do you work?"

"Forty-Seventh Street."

"But not in diamonds?"

"No, accounting."

"You must be the diamond in accounting," he says, in a not-sappy way, grinning because he knows it could be sappy if he wasn't grinning. Raizl, smiling back.

The lobby stores hold no interest, they pass without stopping. Date-Moishe swaggers. He walks in a way she recognizes, but not from another yeshiva bucher. He walks like he has weight between his legs. Weight answered by a pulse between her legs.

Raizl remembers what Podhoretz said about yeshiva boys watching porn, too. Does he or doesn't he? It's not something she can ask. And it's not something that can be discerned from a look or manner— at least she prays it's not, G-d forbid he should be looking at her and knowing what she does at night. He thinks she studies accounting by day and Torah by night. And she doesn't want to destroy that image of herself; no, she wants to play that character of a religious girl, a bas Yisruel, so completely that the lie will rub off on her and become true.

He is tall and decent looking. Better than decent. Raizl catches a glimpse of his profile in the mirrored wall as they continue through the lobby and wants to stop, stare, look closely, as if she were alone with his image. But then she would start hallucinating pornography, and she can't let that happen. Not here, not now. Three o'clock on a Sunday. People all around them.

"I know you from somewhere," he says when they are seated in the lobby restaurant.

"I don't think so."

"Yes, I'm sure of it."

"Don't you think I would know it?"

"You will know it. It will come to you," he says with certainty.

▼

The waiter arrives, a young man with a long white apron, asking what they'd like and returning with two tall glasses on a tray. He places a glass in front of Raizl with a flourish, like it's a fancy meal rather than the plain, unquestionably kosher seltzer they've ordered, and she nods with a smile. When the matching glass is set in front of Moishe, he looks directly at the server and says, "Thankh-you," clearly, not mumbling or muffling his Yiddish accent, as if it doesn't the least bit embarrass him. Perhaps he never even tried to make it go away.

Just as the server turns to leave, Raizl speaks up. "Thankh-you!" The server looks startled, maybe she's a little too loud, but she had to try it. She had to see what that kind of voice would be like.

"You're both more than welcome," the waiter says, bowing slightly and tucking his tray under his arm.

And then the most astonishing thing: before Moishe takes his first sip, when the glass is in his hand an inch from his lips, he closes his eyes. The whispered blessing is no surprise, of course. But the closed eyes, the furrow of intention across his brow when it's not even Shabbes. It's not even a meal! Tati and her brothers bless everything before eating, and Mami and all the women do, too, but everyone with eyes open. Sometimes they don't even pause what they're doing—reading, cooking, talking on the flip phone, the blessing inserted as if it's just another line of conversation.

Shehakoil nihiyeh bidvuroi. Raizl makes her bruche, but in her ears the blessing rings hollow compared to Moishe's. He continues his meditation, slowly releasing Hashem from the glass of seltzer. Meanwhile she's already drinking, the little bubbles bursting in her throat as if it's the blessing she swallowed. At last his eyes open and, holding his hat to his head, Moishe leans back for a long drink.

After that he never takes his eyes off her.

He asks about her family, and she tells him about her brothers and her sister. Will he mind that her brother is also named Moishe? Not at all, and he laughs when she says that Moishe is her favorite brother. "And would you mind if I have a sister named Raizl?"

This catches her off guard. She hadn't considered such a possibility.

He laughs again, but it is a gentler laugh. "Oh, please, don't worry, I'm only joking. I have a cousin also Gitti, but you are my only Raizl."

Is she becoming who she is supposed to be? If he sees her as his kalleh, his beautiful and graceful bride, then surely that is who she is. His intention releasing the bride in her.

He says he wants a big family. He is one of ten and he prays for this for his children, that they, too, will have nine people who love them as much as he loves his brothers and sisters. Ten children to take care of their parents when they are old, the way he and his siblings take care of his father, a widower.

When he says it that way, she has a strange vision of the two of them, old and feeble, walking side by side with walkers, eight wheels and four plodding feet between them, and ten strong children dancing around them. A wedding of two elderly people surrounded by their own grown children. It's easier to imagine this than to picture what it will take to make this family—ten pregnancies, ten births, ten babies. Such numbers make her head spin.

"Do you want a large family, too?" There's hope in his voice. An invitation to join him in this family, this future, which gives her courage.

She smiles at him. If Hashem wills it, then yes. She finds herself telling him that Mami couldn't have more than five—was only supposed to have four, but then Yossi came, a gift from the Creator. "Mami and Tati didn't choose the number."

"How wise you are, to know that only Der Bashefer chooses the number. Wise and lovely," he says.

Does he really think that? She blushes, but she also doubts what she hears. Doubts him. Doesn't believe in her own loveliness, so doubts him for seeing it.

"Not always wise," she says. "Nisht eibig klieg."

"No?"

"No."

She takes a breath and plunges forward. "One time, I watched a video of some music. With Gitti."

"Goyishe music?"

"Nein!" Raizl exclaims. "For Chanuka was that song, but not Chasidish. Not haimish."

She watches him absorbing this.

"And now, when it's not Chanuka, you're still watching this music?"

"Not anymore," she says, and it's true, she hasn't watched a music video in months.

"Then this is from the past. Who was always wise? No one can claim this. A child is forgiven for being a child."

Right then, Raizl starts to love him. Not that she forgives herself, or thinks of herself as a child, or imagines that he would view her in this way when she turns on the porn videos, foolish and forgivable as a child. She is long past such easy forgiveness. But here is a man looking to forgive. Finding reasons for compassion. A man who recites not the law that applies to this situation, but the lenience.

"Yah," she agrees. A child is forgiven. And an adult, too, can change. Can do tshuvah and return. She sees this possibility through his eyes, sees the bride she might be. Covered in white, the past like a long train on a dress that flows behind her, that others will carry so she can walk forward, with their help.

Moishe orders two more seltzers, and they continue talking. Raizl has already heard from Mami, who heard from the matchmaker, that Moishe is progressing rapidly through his Talmud studies—"Faster than most," the matchmaker said, emphasizing his intelligence.

He tells her he's reviewing the laws about marriage. He'd studied them years earlier as part of his regular yeshiva learning, but now he's going through the codes on his own, more deeply this time, with more commentaries. "To get ready," he says, his eyes cast down at the table so he doesn't have to meet her gaze as he admits this.

Raizl contemplates a man who studies a topic in order to live it. What do all the men do who get married without such a review? And what does Moishe think he knows about marriage, about how to be a husband, from all his studying? She wants to dismiss such an idea, that the Talmud could have foretold some personal truth through the disputations of rabbis arriving at decisions that, thousands of years after the debate, she and Moishe will follow.

"Everything is in it." This is what the Talmud says about the Talmud, among the bits Raizl knows from listening in on discussions between Tati and her brothers. They believe this. They trust that their studies give them access to the wisdom required for life. An instructive window through the examples of their ancestors regardless of how they met their ends, hideously flayed and burned by the Romans like Rabbi Akiva, or passing from ill health, or from old age like Rav Nahman, his soul drawn from his body "like a hair from a cup of milk."

But everything is not in the Talmud. Raizl is not in the Talmud. Her fear and desire—her fear of her desire—are not in the Talmud. No matter how minutely Moishe studies the text, it will not warn him that she knows more than he does about their bodies, what their bodies might do to or with each other. The book does not leave room for surprises; that is the job of the body, her body.

Does Moishe think he already knows *her*? Or will he be willing to study her, too, to learn her, a fresh page? Around the same time that Moishe started to review the marriage laws, deepening his knowledge, her habits began. All the nights he has spent studying in preparation for his wedding—those same nights, she has spent in shmutz.

"What's so funny?" Moishe asks, his head tilted to the side, his gaze kind and curious.

She isn't laughing, but her expression has given her away. What can she tell him to explain this situation that isn't funny but makes her want to laugh in desperation?

"I'm afraid to tell you," she says. It's the only truth she can say, without saying the truth that scares her.

He considers this. "It's normal for a kalleh to be a little bit afraid. The chussen, too," he adds, and though his cheeks are covered with beard, Raizl knows the skin beneath is turning red—blushing at the implication that they are bride and groom ahead of any such agreement. He looks down and presses the pads of his fingers against the wooden table as if there were a tablecloth to smooth, as if it were a page of Gemureh, fabric, or paper, anything with a ridge or a wrinkle that he could flatten.

When the waiter returns, Moishe asks for the check. Then, once again, Moishe insists that they've met before.

Raizl tells him right away, she's not buying it.

"I don't believe in this stuff."

"You don't have to believe it," he says, standing. It seems that he is finished, leaving. She feels a sense of relief that it's over.

But then he says, "Whether you believe it, that's not essential. Weddings are made in heaven—"

"So we don't have free will?" she interrupts.

He looks hurt, but only for a moment. He draws his tall body straighter and doesn't break eye contact, doesn't move toward the door. He is not leaving yet.

"It can be true even if you don't understand it," he says. He sits back down, looking at her intently. " 'Believing,' in the way that you say it, is not necessary. Only your consent is necessary."

Consent? Already? Nerves twang in her gut.

"If there were a possibility that the matchmaker calls your parents tomorrow and asks if they want to continue with this match, what do you think they will say?"

Now it's Raizl's turn to look down at the table in embarrassment. It's unheard-of to make a marriage proposal directly to the girl.

"Of course you don't know what they would say. Whether they would give permission. But if you don't mind telling me, what would you guess?"

Raizl looks away, still uncomfortable but also thrilled that he has offered this loophole, a way for him to ask and her to reply, to skirt propriety without rupturing it. When she glances at him, she finds that his dark eyes are still on her. Patient, certain, demanding, confident.

She nods.

▼

"You said yes?"

Raizl focuses on Doc Pod, whose face is full of questions. Did she say yes? Under the doctor's scrutiny, Raizl almost doubts it.

"I didn't *say* yes. I mean, not the word. I couldn't talk, I didn't know what to say after that. He called his parents, and they called the shadchen, and the shadchen called my parents. So it's done."

"Wait, Raizl, hold on." The Pod brushes the air over her head impatiently, clearing away details to get to the important part. "You're marrying him?"

"Yes?" Raizl says with a questioning lilt. This seems to be the wrong answer, though it is true. "I am."

"That was fast," Doc Pod replies, looking a little taken aback. After all her encouragement to keep dating—what did she think would happen?

Shifting against the tush-valleys in the chair, Raizl switches to offense. "Don't you want to hear about the date?"

"Yes, I do."

"We were at the table for almost two hours, and it was like nothing. The waiter came a few times to see if we wanted something else. Moishe asked for the check, but then he got so intense, and said that we must have met before. 'I know,' " Raizl intones in a mock deep voice, her eyes wide open, " 'our souls were together before tonight.' "

"Can you believe that narishkeit?" she says. "Foolishness," she explains, answering Podhoretz's lifted eyebrows. "It's silly."

"Whether I believe it isn't important, Raizl. Do you?"

"Of course not." Raizl snorts. Though she has to admit, to herself only, that she does have the feeling of knowing him for longer than just one date. Moishe's mystic bent appeals to her. Maybe magic is the answer. Maybe Moishe's strange kabbalah of the soul will do for her what all the rest—Torah, porn, therapy—can't.

"He sounds like an intriguing young man," Podhoretz says, with her talent for the boring observation. "Why would he say he knows you if he doesn't?"

Raizl shrugs. "We drank the seltzer and then he ordered another one so we could talk more. He asked me about my classes—"

"You didn't tell him you stopped going to school?"

"Why would I do that?"

"Just asking."

"I'm going to go back." Raizl sniffs.

"Good to hear that. You haven't said that before."

"Well, I'm not going back *now*. I can't now. I'm getting married.

"Yes, of course." Doc Pod recovers quickly. "Mazel toff!" The Pod breaks into a smile, and Raizl can't help feeling embarrassed for the doctor and just a little bit proud of herself.

▼

The engagement takes place a week later at her home. As soon as Moishe and his father and siblings arrive, Gitti bubbles with hyperbole: "Oh, Raizy, he is the most handsome. He is the smartest." No longer does Gitti avoid Raizl; she doesn't leave her for a second. "His suit is the most beautifully tailored," Gitti says, "and he is the most kind!"

"Stop, Gitti, he can't be the 'most' of everything."

"Yes," she insists, "he has to be, he is for you!" And after the guests leave, Gitti spins around the dining table, still loaded with food. Every time the guests took a bite, Mami brought out more, so that the table never lessened, never emptied. Gitti fills a huge plate with stuffed cabbage and three different kugels, all the festive foods Mami made for this occasion. Then Gitti takes another plate of cookies and thick slices of cake, eating the quantities she's turned away for so many weeks now that her appetite is finally back.

Self-Therapy

It's like learning to make a French braid on the back of your own head. No—harder than that. Learning to make a fishtail braid, the kind with four strands, not three. All those fingers required, and you can't watch them, have to work by feeling and memory. But it can be done. After having it done to your hair for so long, it's not impossible to braid yourself.

So why not unbraid yourself? Unburden, untie the knots inside your head.

Now, before she gets married.

That is what Raizl decides to do, after so many stubborn months of porn + therapy. She's going to cure herself. A strand over, a few strands under. Watching porn has more strands than four. But she's ready. She asks herself Pod-like questions in the most Poddish tone:

So what happens when you watch? How do you feel?

Raizl opens the computer, determined to conduct her own analysis, report the findings to herself. She will be watching not just the video but the time stamp running at the bottom of her screen so she can note the critical moment—the flipped switch, the turned corner—the "on" of addiction. If she can observe that moment, she's sure she can change it all. She can turn it off, the second before the second she can't.

This is her plan. To outfox that critical minute. And to be sure of her plan, she scrolls through the torture videos, the ones she hates and does not watch, has sworn off. Won't that make it easier to use for her cure?

A strange thumbnail image catches her eye, of two women tied up with ropes—on tables, or some kind of machine—facing each other. They stare deeply at each other but cannot speak because they are gagged, red balls distorting their mouths into wide Os. The women's legs are suspended in the air behind them, each ankle bound in a metal clasp with chains that attach to black chokers around their necks. Both women are naked, but no one is getting shtupped. One is being whipped by a third woman in high-heeled boots. Raizl grips the laptop with both hands, holding on in a mesmerized terror. She searches each face: the woman being whipped; the woman bringing the whip down, over and over; and the tied-up woman spared from whipping, at least for the moment, watching the other captive in her agony. The long, black lash fascinates Raizl. It's like the gartel her father and brothers wear, a black sash with tassels at the end, though surely the whip in the video is made of twisted leather, not silk. The ritual belt worn by Chasidish men separates the heart from the lower part of the body, a requirement for saying the name of G-d and preparation for prayer, while the gartel-whip confirms the body's dominion, unites the flesh in one sincere gasp each time it lands on the tuches of the tied-up woman. Along with her cry, she jerks against the taut chains, and Raizl silently prays for the shackles to burst but of course they don't, and this, too, is satisfying—the longer the prisoner remains chained, the more Raizl is convinced that she desires those restraints. The whip is as necessary for the woman's pleasure as the lull between lashes, when her face relaxes. Meanwhile the woman wielding the gartel-whip struts around with a tantalizing freedom, alternating strokes between the two who are bound. Suddenly she changes the angle of lashing, brings the gartel-whip down not on the prisoner's tuches but between her spread legs, and Raizl instinctively flinches.

Only then, with her eyes briefly shut, does Raizl realize she missed it: that moment when she slipped from watching herself to just watching. In fact she's been watching for quite some time without making any observation of herself or untangling herself from the video. As a therapeutic endeavor her self-session is the utmost failure, but as pornography, as the desire to inhabit another world or insert herself into other people's desire and in this manner find her own, the self-help is entirely fulfilling.

When her eyes open she does not X out. She replays the video to see it all again from the beginning and not miss a single second. She could touch herself—the thought flickers—but her insides clench against it. Her thighs lock together with a new kind of stress. The tightening in her gut, a constriction that is desire mixed with fear, or fear injected with desire, a tense turmoil, a war inside her. She doesn't want to see it but she can't turn it off, repulsed, compelled, paralyzed and shivering as though the machine is not warm against her thighs but has encased her in ice.

Cured

Her parents put a deposit on the wedding hall. Is it possible to get married in less than three months? Yes, says Mami. Why not? says the matchmaker. They will be married before Rosh Hashanah, and start the Jewish New Year in their new home.

Seven weeks unfold in the manner prophesied by the matchmaker—a swirl of dress fittings and bridal preparations through the hot weeks of summer. Raizl is never alone, going to stores for clothes, for furniture. Her little bedroom and the room she'd shared with Gitti are filled with hatboxes and extra cardboard wardrobes for her trousseau. Raizl feels the ghostly presence of her betrothed, Moishe.

And she misses him! How is it possible to yearn so desperately for someone she's seen only twice? She alternates between longing and doubt, worried that he will change his mind or, fearing that he's not the right match for her, that *she* will change *her* mind. She knows she's not supposed to see him until the wedding, but she begs Mami to arrange a meeting. Please, Mami, don't you need him to bring something from the store? With enough tears and cajoling, Mami allows it.

He stands in the hall just outside her room for a minute, while she sits amid all the boxes she is packing.

"Vus iz dus?" Moishe points across the room, his finger aimed like an arrow at her desk.

"Maan komputer."

Raizl's stomach twists. Earlier she'd hidden it in the usual way, under some papers and a few old notebooks from high school, but somehow these had gotten packed or thrown away, and here is the laptop, exposed.

"Farvus?" Moishe asks.

"All my college work is on it."

"Mazel tov," he says, "you're not going to college now."

"I use it for work, too," Raizl says.

"Work, you'll do at work. Home is for our family."

"But—"

"We're not having a computer in our home."

And like that, her porn-watching is over. The laptop packed in a box with her girlish tchotchkes, not moving to the new apartment with Raizl and Moishe.

▼

Will she ever go back to college? Will she want to watch videos again? The questions seem far off in the future, and Raizl remembers Podhoretz had once said with assurance that if she wants a computer, she will find one. For now, though, Raizl brushes the questions aside; this abrupt cure is a relief. Raizl pledges herself to the home she and Moishe will build together; she borrows his certainty and throws herself into the preparations. If only she could tell Podhoretz. But the therapy, too, has ended. Raizl's expenses will become her husband's expenses, and Raizl can't be transferred to her husband with this extra cost. Of course her mother never mentioned to the groom's family that she'd been in therapy—tantamount to telling them she had two heads or a third breast, a genetic mutation. No, that was an omission in the name of modesty, in the name of the people of Israel, an omission sanctioned by the matchmaker, who silenced Mami the minute she brought it up.

"That's all over," said the matchmaker. "No need to mention. That would be like telling the chussen that Raizl had tonsils removed when she was three. The groom does not need to know this. He is going to see the real Raizl, the Raizl of today, not the Raizl of the past. Put your girlhood troubles behind you." The matchmaker had cupped Raizl's chin in the palm of her hand and looked at her intently, with the certainty of a cure that Podhoretz had never offered.

"Now you are a bride."

▼

At night she dreams of a new kind of porn, starring herself and her groom: Raizl wearing one of her new dresses, Moishe taking it off. Slowly peeling one long sleeve off her body, then the other, until the dress pools at her feet, and she is naked. In the dream, Moishe is silent and frightening, with a stern expression, a sign that she has displeased him. He wears an elegant tailored bekishe; the fine fabric creases across his broad shoulders, across his hips. He is clothed, but she knows what is under the long coat.

In the morning Raizl wakes from the dream of being married into the dream of getting married. The fears of the night dissolve in the anticipation and bustle of the day; from morning till night she *does*, and does not think. It almost seems to Raizl that she had never been in therapy. The way the sessions recede so quickly into distant memory confirms how little substance they'd had. She agrees with the matchmaker: she need never tell her betrothed. What good had therapy done her? Did those sessions ever help? Not the least bit. They'd made her questions stronger, her yearning worse. Therapy was no more useful than a dream, and the few moments of relief were revealed, upon waking, to be transient.

But she does wish she could tell Podhoretz what it's like to be getting married. Partly because she wants the therapist to be happy for her, happy with her. But also, she wants to rub it in Poddy's face—*Ha! You couldn't cure me, but I will be cured. I am cured! Not because of you, in spite of you.*

Though Raizl knows Dr. P wouldn't give her any satisfaction. She would sit in her chair, pen in hand, too professional to smile, her nodding punctuated by an uplifted eyebrow and a mildly inquisitive, mildly judgmental *Hmm?* Letting Raizl imagine the doctor's rejoinder. *Who told you, Raizl, to go on another date? Who told you, Raizl, not to give up?*

Sheitel-Shopping

Mami takes Raizl to the sheitel-macher to buy the wigs she will wear as a married woman. On the first visit Raizl will choose colors for her wigs, and try the different kinds of hair, synthetic and human. She will return for another appointment to have the wigs cut, and then again just before the wedding, to have them styled. At first Raizl is transfixed by the mannequin heads wearing wigs. They are all white, their Styrofoam eyes, cheekbones, and noses all perfectly shaped but expressionless, and it frightens Raizl that the heads can be so pretty and have no feeling. When she puts on the wig, will she put on that face, too?

The wigs all have shoulder-length hair in dark brown, light brown, and lighter brown.

The sheitel-macher squints at Raizl's red hair, her lips compressed. "Something a little darker, yes?" the sheitel-macher says.

Mami and Raizl both nod right away. At last, she won't be a redhead!

"Which do you like?" Mami asks.

Before Raizl can answer, the sheitel-macher points to one. "This is very pretty, very becoming." She pulls it off the mannequin and places it on top of her left hand, which she has balled into a fist. When the wig is balanced atop her knuckles, she strokes the hair with her other hand. "Feel how nice," she says, holding it closer to Raizl.

The wig is strange. The hair is smooth, which Raizl likes, but also stiff. It reminds Raizl of a doll's hair, and she has an unpleasant feeling of suffocation, of time folding over itself, of getting older and growing up to get married but also getting younger and growing down, as if she has become a large version of a doll she played with as a child. The wig is not supposed to feel like this, or is it? Raizl touches Mami's sheitel, touches the back where it comes out from under the little hat that she wears on top of her wig, and then the bangs in the front. Mami's sheitel is smooth, the bangs shaped to her temple, not so stiff.

"Yah," Raizl says mechanically. "Pretty. I want it." But she doesn't look at it.

"Feel," the sheitel-macher says again, turning now to Mami. "Feel how nice!" she insists.

Mami runs her fingers through the wig, appraising. "Vi fil?"

"A toaznt finef hindert," says the sheitel-macher.

Mami snorts. "A toaznt!"

Raizl knows this is a synthetic wig. For a thousand dollars, or even the fifteen hundred the sheitel-macher is asking, all they can get is a synthetic. A human-hair wig like Mami's would cost three thousand or more.

The sheitel-macher refuses to go lower than thirteen hundred.

Raizl stands beside the human hair wig. Without waiting for permission, Raizl strokes the long, light brown, almost golden hair.

"She can see it?" the sheitel-macher asks Mami.

"Of course!" Mami says, offended, as if human hair has been her plan all along.

Raizl will need at least three wigs to start out in married life. Mami unwraps a rubber band from a roll of bills, ready to peel off twenties and negotiate the deposit.

While Mami handels with the sheitel-macher to get a better price, Raizl quietly sets the luxurious wig over her hair, balancing long, straight, golden-brown hair atop her own impulsive red coils. A mixed-up, two-haired clown, silly, telling her nothing of what she'll look like married. Raizl digs into her scalp, tucking and then shoving her own hair under the wig, but it won't stay. This will be easier after Mami shaves her head, on the day after the wedding. When she has no more hair of her own. Suddenly the face looking back at her from the mirror turns pale, white as Styrofoam, imagining her temples and scalp, all of it white. The mosquito-whine of the razor as Mami buzzes away curl after curl. What will she look like, not red? Who will she be, not curly?

Raizl is relieved when Gitti joins them in the shop. Gitti is excited to help; she holds the sides of the wig while Raizl twists her hair into a single long coil as best she can and jams it under the base, a strange skin of filament against her scalp.

The smell of Raizl's own hair, flowery from the shampoo with a slight tang of oil, disappears under the dead scent of wig hair like a puff of dust. One red curl refuses to stay tucked in, and Raizl loves that rebellious curl. Could she keep just the one? But that would ruin everything. Determined to see what the straight hair looks like uninterrupted by red, undisturbed by curls, Raizl fishes a tiny scissor out of her bag and snips off that stubborn strand. She doesn't care if it will look odd, there's so little time left until the wedding.

There. The mirror shows her who she will be, a married lady.

"Burech Hashem," Gitti says, circling Raizl to see the sides and back. "Gorgeous!"

The mirror holds something they've never seen: how Raizl looks with straight, flowing brown hair. Hair the way her cousins have hair, the way the girls at her high school always had their own straight brown hair until they got married and styled their wigs with straight brown hair. *This is what it's like to have straight hair.* Raizl turns her head side to side, and the hair turns with her. It's hers now, but she is someone else. She shakes her head again to watch the hair dance. She's seen women do it in videos, shaking out their hair so it swirls around them. This sheitel falls just to Raizl's shoulders. Within the bounds of modesty, but still, the sheitel is a new Raizl, a perhaps beautiful Raizl. The sheitel shows, maybe even more than porn, that it's possible to change everything.

Moishe's Gift

Shabbes is over. Raizl still wears her Shabbes dress, though covered by an apron, careful not to get the polish on herself. All the silver wine cups and the candlesticks are out on the dining table for Raizl to clean. Next Shabbes, before the wedding, they will have guests, and everything must shine. Gitti studies at the far end of the table, wrinkling her nose at the polish smell. Mami is in the kitchen scrubbing the long metal trays from the Shabbes kugel. Tati sits at the dining table with his tea and the open Gemureh.

A tap at the front door is followed by a more definitive knock. "*Tch*, Eliyuhi Hanavi!" Tati says—who else but Elijah the prophet would be visiting?—and goes to answer the door.

"Ah gitte voch, Shver."

"Ah gitte voch, Moishe."

As soon as Raizl hears Moishe's voice, she jumps up, tearing off the apron. There's no time to run to the bathroom, no time to fix herself. She smooths her hair with her hands, useless against the curls that bounce right back where they were, and bites her lips to make them red, Sam's old trick.

"And you're here," Tati says, "for what reason?"

Raizl winces. Why are they talking in the doorway? Why doesn't Tati let him in? What if Tati *won't* let him in? They aren't supposed to see each other until the wedding!

Moishe clears his throat. "I brought Raizl a gift," he says with conviction.

"A gift you had to bring yourself? In the whole yeshiva you couldn't find a healthy pair of legs to bring this on your behalf?"

Raizl sinks into a dining chair, despairing. She knows Moishe should have sent the gift with someone else. But since he's here, at least let him come in!

"Forgive me," Moishe says. "I brought a tehillim." A plastic bag crackles and Raizl imagines it, a book of psalms drawn out of the bag for her. "I didn't want to give it to anyone else to bring. It was my mother's, may her memory be a blessing—" Moishe's voice cracks, and Raizl's heart overflows. "I've had it with me all the time since she passed. I couldn't give it to anyone else to deliver."

"A tehillim!" Tati repeats, mollified. "To deliver a tehillim, you are always welcome, Moishe."

Now their footsteps echo through the hall.

"Raizele, your chussen is here," Tati bellows.

Whatever it is that Moishe has in mind, he will have to accomplish with the family all around them. Tati returns to his Gemureh; Gitti continues studying; Mami picks up the rag and polish for the silver where Raizl left off.

Moishe and Raizl stand in the living room, in the bright glare of Saturday night, when every light is turned on. They stand with a few feet between them, close enough to talk softly, not close enough for an accidental touch. Mami won't even offer him a tea. They have two or three minutes at most, before Tati ends this visit.

Speaking urgently, barely above a whisper, Moishe says, "On the day of the wedding, I want you to have something from me."

Raizl watches his lips as he talks. His wiry moustache and beard move with every word and nearly obscure his lips but she finds them, red and smooth and mesmerizing. Who is this Moishe? At their meeting he was lighthearted, almost impish, more like her brother Moishe. Now he looks a bit wild-eyed and slightly unkempt, his white shirt wrinkled, the collar off-center. This is another side of Moishe, intense, filled with an end-of-Shabbes longing. Is this always in his heart, just set loose tonight by the scent of cloves, the fire of slivovitz?

Moishe holds a miniature book between his thumb and index

finger. It looks especially tiny in his large hand. "My mother had it at her wedding, and I want you to have it at ours."

Raizl feels Moishe's terrible loss, and wants to comfort him. It's a pity that his mother passed away, that their children will be missing a grandmother. Although, according to Mami, it might also be a blessing, since Raizl won't have to please a mother-in-law. But also a curse because it's harder to fight with a ghost.

They stand in silence, the molecules darting between them, the current of energy extending from each of them and clustering around the little sefer held in his hands. The cover is printed with pink roses in an oval frame, the word "tehillim" embossed in gold.

"Shkoyech," Raizl whispers, nodding solemnly.

"Take strength from the tehillim," he says. "Soon my strength will be in you."

His words send chills up her back, a particular vibration. The story opens between her legs, and the promise of his strength in her stirs a longing for exactly that. The O of her where he will fit.

And where he fits, there she belongs. His eyes are on her, he doesn't look away, not even to blink. All the places she has wanted to fit but couldn't, they don't matter anymore since she belongs with Moishe. Blushing, Raizl looks down and sees his fingertips are white from gripping the tiny book. Will he grip her this tightly? Tightly enough to hurt just a bit, but not too much? She wants to be held this way, after so many months of slipping, coming so close to slipping away entirely. She is bound now in his gaze, and in a week's time she will be tied to him by word and deed. She wants to be tied—not to the bed or the wall, only to his body. The week seems far too long to wait. She can't bear the thought that after this brief visit they will be apart until their wedding night, that such profound separation is required to launch them into perpetual union.

Tati closes his Gemureh rather loudly, pushes back his chair. Their time is up.

Moishe puts the tehillim back in the bag and places it on the sofa. "Ah gitte voch," he says quietly.

"Ah gitte voch," she echoes.

The psalms are hers. Moishe is hers.

The Dress

Though far from Moishe during this long week, Raizl is never alone. According to custom, the bride-to-be is treated like royalty, and must be accompanied at all times like a princess with her court in attendance until she is crowned queen. Also, if she is left on her own, the evil spirits might interfere in the plans for the wedding. And so a small troupe sets out for Raizl's final dress fitting: Mami and Gitti and Meema Freidy, her aunt an extra chaperone to assure that she is not alone even when Mami and Gitti need to leave.

When they arrive in the seamstress's shop, Raizl's gown is hanging from a hook on the ceiling. It takes Raizl's breath away, it's so beautiful, and it spins a little in the passing breeze, as if there is already someone wearing it. There are chairs around the shop, for everyone to sit, and a large three-way mirror in the center of the room with a small step stool for the bride.

Raizl hurriedly takes off her clothes, and her twinge of dismay at having to show this entourage rather than Moishe himself dissolves in excitement. Mami and the seamstress each hold a side of the dress as Raizl steps into it, feeding her arms through the long sleeves of satin and lace that extend over her wrists and nearly to her knuckles. Mami deftly fastens the row of pearl buttons that travels up her back to the nape of her neck while the seamstress hovers in front of her, smoothing the bodice and fluffing out the skirt.

What will she look like? Who will she be? In this dress, a Raizl who has never before been seen. A Raizl who has never walked or breathed.

A Raizl unknown—a Raizl revealed. At last the seamstress moves and Mami stands to the side and Gitti claps her hands in glee.

"Ah sheine kalleh kaneinehora!" Meema Freidy exclaims.

The dress is glorious and Raizl, looking at herself in the mirror, feels the power of it coursing through her, as though the white satin and lace are also inside her, liquid, a white blood giving her a fierce white energy, and the little step stool has lofted her into the air so that the glow of the dress—of her being—radiates to the four corners of the room.

Raizl steps off the stool and begins to promenade. But Mami wears an expression of displeasure and points to the extra fabric that bunches around Raizl's hips when she walks. "Like a secondhand dress!"

"Nein," says the seamstress, shaking her head. "She looks beautiful! Almost *too* beautiful!"

Mami glares until the seamstress sighs and gets her pincushion and helps Raizl step back on the stool. Down on her knees, the woman pushes straight pins through the dense fabric where she will make a few small darts. And when she reaches her hand beneath the skirts, lifting the gown from below and brushing Raizl's thigh, Raizl remembers a porn video, where the best man shtups the bride before her wedding. Even a porn-bride wears a beautiful gown, though of course the dress of a shmutz-kalleh has a plunging neckline and no sleeves at all. When the best man kisses her, it's shocking but also makes sense, because she is so lovely, and the shmutz-kalleh slaps him, which also makes sense—the chutzpah!—but then the shmutz-kalleh clasps the man's face in her hands and kisses him back! Next the shmutz-kalleh's tittes *pop!* out of the gown, and best man is licking them and squeezing them, and then the chussen knocks at the door, his white carnation on his lapel, and the kalleh hides the chutzpadik best man under the billowing gown. While the shmutz-chussen tells his kalleh to hurry and finish getting ready, the best man shtups her with his finger and licks her klit! This is what Raizl remembers as the seamstress sticks her hand under the gown, her arm across Raizl's thigh, and Raizl shudders.

"Oy!" shouts Mami. "What happened? You stuck her with the pin!" she accuses the seamstress.

The seamstress quickly moves away. "Nein!"

"S'iz git," Raizl says, recovering herself. Standing tall again. With the added darts, the dress will be perfect. She is desperate to leave the seamstress's shop yet she can't stop staring at the mirror. A fantasy: What if Moishe were under her skirt, Moishe hidden in the folds of satin, Moishe with his finger deep in her shmundie, his lips on the pink leaf of her klit? Could it possibly be? If she had never seen porn, such a thing would never have occurred to her, but she has seen it, and it cannot be undone. She doesn't want it undone.

Now, in this last week before the wedding, when the computer is gone and she can neither watch porn nor see Moishe, the porn memory is even more precious. Is all she has. And she relishes it, the remembered images becoming the seed of new desire as the video characters become roles for Moishe and for her. What if she held up her skirt, dared Moishe to crawl under there; what if she hid him inside her fantasy?

"Raizele," says Meema Freidy. "For the seamstress to work on the dress she needs you to take it off. Give the mirror a rest."

Raizl lets them strip the dress away, steps back into her ordinary, not-a-queen clothing. Meanwhile, her mind is full of shmutzige images, a barrage of bridal shtupping: A bride in her white gown alone with the groom's father and suddenly they're shtupping. Or the bride alone with a bridesmaid, and then there are two satiny gowns pushed up, two smooth-skinned shmundies.

"You look flushed," Meema Freidy says. Mami agrees: Raizl needs to go home and rest, but Mami has to settle the bill with the seamstress and then go with Gitti to the bakery.

"I'll take her home," offers Meema Freidy. Raizl doesn't feel like royalty, more like a prisoner, as her aunt grasps her arm and marches her home.

Last Day of Work

Raizl convinces Mami to let her go to work without a chaperone, since she will not be alone in the Rebbetzin's office. And she cannot miss this day of work. Today is payday.

Raizl doesn't want to tell the Rebbetzin it's her last payday until after she gets the cash, however, and this is why, even though she's getting married soon, even though she has quit a hundred times in her mind, has already walked out of the office and down Forty-Seventh Street for the last time in her imagination, she is in fact lying facedown across the Rebbetzin's desk.

The Rebbetzin has never been this demanding, this brazen. What can she possibly want now?

Raizl wants to leave. But she stays where she is. *Today will be the last time,* she tells herself.

The Rebbetzin seems somehow to intuit that Raizl's employment is almost over, and she draws out the ritual longer than usual. She refuses to let Raizl do any work at all. Any accounting work.

"Leave that on your desk," she says of the ledger. "I need you here." She beckons Raizl to stand next to her.

An entire subgenre of porn is devoted to office shtupping. Blinking computer monitors, multiline phones, and bulletin boards are the decor; swiveling armchairs and of course the desks, substitute beds, are the centerpieces. Varnished wood that somehow doesn't stick to the tuches. Women with their thighs spread, and someone licking there.

The Rebbetzin tells Raizl to reach across the glass-topped desk, to the folders placed just above a photograph taken at a fancy banquet. In Raizl's view, with her eyeball nearing the glass, the men's faces are distorted, their features dissolved in small, pale voids between dark hats and dark beards. Which one is the Rabbi, Raizl wonders, and what passed between him and the Rebbetzin if this, now, is what she wants?

The Rebbetzin is more and more odd. When Raizl begins to straighten so she can pass the folder, the Rebbetzin tells her to stay and lays her cane across Raizl's back. Not to hit her, just to hold her there, almost gently, so Raizl is lying flat, with the cane against her spine, her tuches.

What is the Rebbetzin doing behind her? If Raizl were watching this, if this were a porn video, Raizl would know; the camera would pan from Raizl's face against the desk back to the Rebbetzin.

This is life, though, not video, so the scenario is flipped: Raizl sees nothing and tries to feel nothing, to shut down the imagination and even the senses. Raizl keeps her mind filled with noisy thoughts.

What Raizl focuses on, while she lies across the desk, is having her own money. Before work Raizl had checked the places she banks: between the sole of a certain shoe and the inner lining; in the zippered garment bag that holds a white dress Raizl wears only on Yom Kippur; tucked into the spine of an old prayerbook whose binding had torn loose at the top; plus the money banked in various corners of Zeidy's room, now her room—Raizl has stored three thousand one hundred and seventy-two dollars, her savings from years of babysitting and then her work for the Rebbetzin. A kind of work that does not fit in any other category. It's not porn—there is no camera here, this isn't a public act. No one will ever know about it but the two of them. And it's not sex, of course, not the way she will be with Moishe, Hashem willing, in a few days. This is not porn, not sex, not accounting. Just work. And she is compensated. She has earned enough for the necessary purchase.

Raizl wants this work to be over. She starts counting in her mind. Counting not dollars but seconds. Without her meaning it to, Raizl's breath comes out in an audible whimper. The cane goes away, but Raizl doesn't move, waiting to see what will happen next.

When Raizl finally decides to stand up, the Rebbetzin hands her the envelope. "Shkoyech, Raizl," she says.

▼

Later that night, after work, Raizl cries on the toilet. She's locked the door, and Mami tries to cajole her out.

"No, Mami, no. I can't get married."

"Oy, Mamaleh, don't cry. Keep your skin clear for the photos."

"Tell Moishe, no chasseneh. I can't."

"What you're worrying, this is what every kalleh worries. Soon, you'll see. The glass will break for you, too."

But Raizl's fear is not the same as every bride's fear. She did not quit; the last day of work is not this day. She couldn't tell the Rebbetzin she's not coming back. How would she explain quitting her job to her family, to her chussen? He is counting on her income for their new apartment. For his future studies. For their future family.

In these last days before the wedding, with no contact from Moishe, the images of him do not leave her. The darkest picture: she lies beneath her husband, unable to breathe; she can't support his weight, his mechanism, his jabs. In her nightmare Moishe brandishes a cane. He pins her to the bed and won't let her up.

The Kalleh-Teacher

"What's important," the kalleh-teacher says, "is that you know how to make your chussen happy. Can you cook?"

Raizl thinks about this. "I know a few recipes," she says. She knows how to prepare the noodles and lay them in the pan for a kugel. She knows how to roll the spiced meat and rice in the big cabbage leaf and tuck the edges so the stuffing doesn't fall out, which Mami says is the hardest part. But there's still much more!

"Chulent?"

"Not as good as Mami's."

"Kokosh cake?"

"Can't I get that at the bakery?"

Tch, tch. The kalleh-teacher shakes her head. "If you don't know that at the start, it's not *so* so terrible. You'll learn, while you're a newlywed."

The kalleh-teacher takes a deep breath, her large chest rising and falling. She takes a tissue from inside her sleeve and pats her moist cheeks and brow, then tucks the tissue back in by her wrist. "Now," she says, looking sternly at Raizl. "You understand what the kalleh needs to do?"

"Yah," Raizl nods. Then, catching herself, remembering that she's not supposed to know anything yet—she shakes her head no. "Ich veiss nisht. Can you tell me what to do?"

There is a glass on the table. The kalleh-teacher had asked for water when she first arrived; the heat of the day swept into the room with her. Raizl brought her water with ice, and she drained the glass at once, leaving only the melting cubes at the bottom. Now even those are gone.

The kalleh-teacher swallows the cool puddle from the bottom of the glass, then holds it sideways. She weaves the index finger of her other hand through the air into the glass and then away, into and away, into and away. A tiny, final drop of water slips from the glass to the floor.

"I'm a glass?" Raizl asks. The kalleh-teacher sets the glass down abruptly, ending the demonstration.

"Not just a glass," she protests, wagging her index-shvantz-finger at Raizl. "You're a *vessel*. Burech Hashem, you will be first a bride, then a mother. You will take care of your husband and family."

The kalleh-teacher pauses, staring at Raizl. Appraising her.

"I think you know enough already. I can see, you're a smart girl. You don't need anything more from me."

"Shkoyech," Raizl says. Relieved that she doesn't have to pretend, anymore, not to know.

Raizl can think of several ways to make her chussen happy. For this information, how to please a man, the internet is excellent. Moishe might not know they'd make him happy, but she's certain they would. She will show him what she saw on a video. Special ways of using her hands, pretending she's wringing out a towel, with her mouth on the top of his . . .

Suddenly she's worried, thinking of ways to make him happy that, she's pretty sure, would be painful for her. "Remember to give him your ass," a video advised. "Fuck him oh so sweetly." These videos, she might not mention.

"I have a question," Raizl says. "If it will make me unhappy, but it will make him happy, do I have to do it?"

"I don't understand. Why would something that pleases your chussen make you unhappy?"

How to say this? "If it hurts me," Raizl begins, "but he likes it, am I mechiyev—am I obligated to do it?"

The kalleh-teacher loses her patience. "No chussen wants to hurt his bride," she huffs. "He's not going to hurt you."

The kalleh-teacher resumes her sweet voice. "The first time—mayyyybe—a little pinch, just like this"—she snaps her fingers—"and it goes away, like nothing. Your chussen will not hurt you. Don't worry."

The kalleh-teacher checks a little notebook she has, then picks up her bag. She seems ready to go.

"Shkoyech," Raizl says.

Tch, tch. The kalleh-teacher shuts her eyes as she shakes her head against this. "Don't thank me. This is for shulem bayis, for peace in your home. Raizl, you say you don't know but you do know. Trust me. You know all that you need. Don't ask for more. Your chussen will lead you, and you will follow him. And that is the peace of your future, the happiness you seek."

The kalleh-teacher asks her, "Are you ready for this joy l'shem shumayim? The true happiness for the sake of heaven?"

Somehow the teacher is asking her the questions now. And there is only one answer, yes, her happiness for the sake of heaven, yes.

"And now, Raizl, it's time for me to go. Mazel tov!"

Forces of Evil

"Go out by yourself? Chas v'shulem!" Meema Freidy exclaims and spits over her shoulder. For a woman who is not so old, she is very superstitious. "Going alone is an invitation for the forces of evil to join you. I will not permit it."

But Raizl is determined to run her errands, two days before her wedding, without a chaperone.

"A wedding we can plan, a birth happens when it happens," Raizl says. Her cousin Chaya, on Tati's side, is due any minute, and Raizl has promised to buy a baby monitor for her. Raizl has her pocketbook and a raincoat on, ready to go.

"Yah, yah, I know the family," says Meema Freidy. "A good family. Isn't there a monitor she can borrow?"

It is unusual, Raizl agrees, that among all the friends and cousins, and all the babies, there is not a secondhand baby monitor to be found. No one buys new! But it seems that all the baby monitors in circulation are still in use, or else too old and got thrown out in the last Pesach cleaning. Thus it is upon Raizl to do this good deed, and do it today.

"What if the baby comes tonight?" Raizl says.

"You're right, a mitzvah like this cannot wait. I'll go with you," says her aunt.

"Meema Freidy, I want you to come. A mitzvah for both of us! But I'm thinking here of you, and the terrible storm predicted for this afternoon. I heard it will be a thunderstorm. It's so hot already! And your arthritis!"

"So humid," her aunt nods, wiping her cheek with the back of her hand. "Well, if you're going to do a mitzvah, the evil forces won't be able to stop you. I will have a little rest while you're gone."

Her aunt sits on the sofa. Raizl brings her a pillow from the bedroom to put behind her head. "Hurry," Meema Freidy says, "and come right home."

"Yah," says Raizl, and sets off, running, on her errands.

Goodbye

Raizl doesn't know how to say goodbye to Sam, only that it will involve eating ice cream. Maybe ice cream with marshmallows in it, a last bit of traif and sweet before she gets married. In addition to the distraction of ice cream, Raizl hopes there will be music Sam likes—she's grumpy and brittle when the music is not to her liking ("fucking-capitalist-pig-Billboard-Grammy-crap" is what Sam says, and Raizl had to search online for the meanings of these curses except "fucking," which she had searched before she met Sam).

"Getting married, hunh? Cool," Sam says, sitting across the booth from Raizl in the Dunkin' Donuts–Baskin-Robbins. Spooning some rocky road out of the pint Raizl bought. Sam seems almost light-hearted today, her normal all-black uniform disrupted by a T-shirt turned tank top, sleeves scissored off unevenly, black background covered in a print of hot-pink lips, as if Sam's been kissed a hundred times.

"Yah," Raizl agrees. "Koo-ul."

"Who's the dude?" Sam asks, intently digging a trench around the perimeter of the pint. When she passes the carton to Raizl, there is an island of ice cream in the middle, with the plastic spoon sticking out of it like a spear. Raizl digs a crater in the rocky road.

"His name is Moishe, just like my brother. He's the one." She blushes.

This would be the juncture when anyone else, certainly any girl

Raizl grew up with, would squeal, and ask when is the wedding, and demand a close inspection of the ring.

"Can I have the ice cream?" Sam says.

In a way it makes things easier. Raizl passes back the sticky, chocolate-fingerprinted carton, their friendship sealed in sugar and stabilizers, cocoa and almond slivers. The marshmallow goo. Raizl doesn't have to say a word about can't invite Sam to the wedding, can't ever introduce her to Moishe, no apology for this too brightly lit Dunkin' as the locale for their last meeting, for a while or forever. There's no way to know, so Raizl decides it's best just not to bring it up, not to say, this is goodbye.

"Are you still with Kurt?" Raizl asks.

"Who?"

"You were with him at the beach," Raizl says.

"Yeah," says Sam. "Naw. I haven't seen him. He's not around."

The next time Sam reaches across the table to take the ice cream back, Raizl sees a patch of bright red skin on the inside of her upper arm.

"What is it?" Raizl asks, not giving up the pint just yet, letting Sam's outstretched arms reach just an inch or two farther, to reveal what appears to be "Billy" in a strange blue script.

"What? Nothing," Sam says. "I met him a couple weeks ago, and I thought it was going to be a serious thing." Sam pulls her hands back and hugs herself so the writing isn't visible. "You have the ice cream," she says.

Now Sam starts pouting. She rolls her eyes. "As soon as I can get the money together, I have to get it removed. That was stupid-me the other night. No drunk driving, just drunk tattooing."

Raizl pushes the ice cream over to Sam's side of the table. So she can finish the pint without reaching.

"Can you believe this idiotic crap?" Sam jabs her spoon in the air over their heads, pointing at the music as if it's a physical thing she can puncture. " 'We can do what we want to,' " Sam mimics the song. "Fucking Smiley Cyrus. Rich girl can do what she want to."

"How much?" Raizl asks. "To take it away?"

"The tat?" Sam contemplates this, and the time it takes her to answer makes it clear that any number, from one dollar to one thousand dollars, is more than she can afford. "Dunno. Laser costs a lot, but at least the tat's not very big. Maybe two hundred dollars?"

Under the table, with as little motion as possible so Sam won't notice, Raizl opens her purse and pulls ten twenty-dollar bills from her wallet. She still has enough in there for her other errand today. This much she can do for Sam.

"Here," Raizl says, tapping Sam's hand with the edge of the rolled-up bills. A goodbye present, the gift of taking something away.

Sam puts the spoon down and takes the cash. She looks genuinely surprised, and then a huge grin spreads across her face as she tucks the roll into her bra. "Wow, Razor! Thank you! Moneybags bride!"

Raizl smiles—she loves making Sam happy like this, there's nothing better than seeing Sam's scowl disappear, the purple-black-lipsticked lips turn up, eyes brightening under the fierce black eyeliner—but inside Raizl cringes. Thinking of the work she's done, what she'll continue to do, for the rolls of money that buy a little relief, a little room to maneuver.

Sam gives her an impish look. "So are you going to devirginize?" A dab of chocolate smears Sam's lips as she takes another bite. "Solo said you wouldn't do it with him." The plastic spoon makes a scraping noise, and Sam tilts the carton to get a better angle. "Saving yourself for—what did you say his name is? Moy-sheh?"

"Yah," Raizl says. "Moishe, like the moving company." She guesses that Sam has seen it painted on the trucks.

"Why didn't you do it with Solo?"

"With him, I didn't want," Raizl says.

"Well, so are you going to do it with this Moishe dude? You have to, right, if you're getting married?"

Have to. Want to. Have to. "Yah," Raizl says.

"Do you have to do it through a hole in the sheet?"

"A hole?" Raizl says.

"On *Oprah*, I heard that Hasids fuck through a hole in the sheet, and then the Hasid women on the show said it wasn't true. That would be a total pain in the ass, so I hope it's not true. Anyways, congratulations."

"Thank you," Raizl says, feeling flustered, and then she doesn't know what to say. When they don't talk, she can hear the scrape of Sam's plastic spoon against the carton.

"What are you taking this semester?" Sam asks.

"I'm not taking anything. I have to work full-time," Raizl says.

"What? I thought you were going to quit that job. But I guess that's why you've got the bucks."

"I wanted to quit. But I didn't. We need the money for rent."

"Don't we all," Sam says quietly.

"You're not staying at your cousin's?"

"No." Sam looks away. "You want more ice cream?"

"I can't." Raizl shakes her head. "You know, the dress."

"Right, the dress. Is it tight? Sexy?"

Raizl blushes again. The wedding dress is, if not exactly tight, at least a little more shapely than her other clothes. She hopes Moishe will think she's sexy. And that Sam, if she could ever see the dress, might also think she's sexy.

There's a rolling feeling inside Raizl, the bottom of her stomach dropping, and it's not because of the ice cream. What will it be like, with no more Sam? With no one to ask her, is it sexy?

"You'll be okay, Razor," Sam says. "I don't know about this dude, but you're strong. Very strong."

Raizl's cheeks are burning so hot she feels the skin might peel off. This seems like the longest conversation they've ever had; it seems like they might stay in this little booth with the fluorescent lights humming above them forever. It seems like the conversation might never end.

And then suddenly, it's over.

"Let's go." Sam pops out of the booth. "Damn, I don't have an umbrella."

The humidity has finally turned into a downpour.

"We use mine," Raizl offers. "We go together." She pushes open the door, putting her full body weight into it to fight the wind.

They stop for a minute, realizing just how hard the rain is, how certain it is they will get drenched. Then, under the double sky of the umbrella and the store awning, Sam kisses Raizl. A not-accidental, not-brush-by goodbye. It's a full-on-the-lips, wet-with-wanting kiss. It's salty and sweet, almonds and marshmallows, chocolaty and sticky and Raizl wants more of that kiss, wants the carton not to be empty, wants the goodbye not to be over. But then Sam links arms with Raizl and pulls her across the sidewalk, running toward the train.

The End of Dating

Professor O'Donovan, though he had failed her, had taught Raizl an important rule: if the play ends with a wedding, it's a comedy, not a tragedy. But under the wedding canopy, Raizl is afraid. She's been fasting all day, and now that it's past sundown, her face is covered and her mother leads her toward her groom, and then around him seven times. Dizzy from the fasting and circling, Raizl grips the tiny psalm book Moishe gave her, though she doesn't look at it. She whispers tehillim by heart under the opaque veil, the psalms of David rising inside the heavy fabric like a second, shimmering scrim. Finally the circling stops, and she feels even less steady standing still. After the blessing over wine, she hears Moishe swallow, and then a scuffle of shoes as her mother approaches to lift the veil, and the cup is at her lips. This is the comedy, the dance of who can touch the bride and who can't, to ensure that she fulfills the legal requirements, the cup tilting too quickly, the wine spilling off her chin as if she's a drunkard, and she feels like a shiker, tipsy and full of crazy ideas. She could run away! Run out of the hall and never come back! Change her name not to Moishe's but to something no one (Chasidish) has ever heard of, Rosie O'Malley, Rosa Sanchez, any Rose at all, but not Raizl, daughter of Feiga and Zalmen, that girl named in the wedding contract—not her!

The rush of wine sets off fear inside her like none she has ever experienced. She prays fiercely, but the psalms don't calm her.

For so long she was scared of what she knew, but tonight a far more awful fear takes hold of her; she shakes with terror because she knows nothing. All that she has watched has not prepared her for this blindness, for the vast unknown of a man beside her. Of the thickness about to be upon her, she is scared. She feels small and frail and worried that her body will not be up to the task of wifing a man. This will not be like Solo at the beach: she cannot roll away, she cannot shout *nein!* at the top of her lungs. And what if somehow Moishe can sense all that has preceded him—all the porn, or the Rebbetzin's terrifying cane, or Solo in her mouth? What if Moishe can see her memories, the way Zeidy could see her dreams? The shame mixed with dizziness nearly makes her faint. She wishes she could talk to Podhoretz here, under the chuppah, under the heavy veil, and a few words would come back to her—not words of prayer, not the binding phrases of the wedding contract, not blessings, not a sermon, no—words of inquiry. Talk that offers no answer but opens possibility, clues pointing in the direction of herself. If Podhoretz were here, Raizl would hold nothing back, she wouldn't monkey around, trying to make Podhoretz guess. She would tell her everything, finally. How she cannot see Moishe but she feels him with all of her being, the outline of his body as a source of heat, the smell of him warm and musky cutting against the scent of hot candle wax and more faintly the roses that once, on a day that might have been years ago, she had selected from photos of floral arrangements. She would tell Podhoretz how his voice sounds on the other side of the veil, melodic but not soft, determined and clear as he announces that she is made holy to him in the faith of Moses and Israel. That she likes the feeling of his fingers pushing the ring down her finger: his first small finding of her body.

But right away he drops her hand. He has other matters to attend to, a glass to smash. There is a moment of silence, and Raizl pictures it: Moishe's knee raised in preparation as he is about to bring his foot down.

Do you feel like that glass, Raizl?

Her teeth chatter though she is not cold, the sweat pools in her armpits under the satin chiffon, and tears fall in stripes down her cheeks. Wrapped in a white dress like a white napkin, about to be stamped under heel of manhood and tradition, she wills it on herself:

let the weight of him smash her. Let her shatter, let the shards of her cut worse than glass, let the vessel that carried her through the past be vanquished, let there be no way ever to put her back together in the old form, may her undoing be utterly complete, psalm of the porn-bride, let her be broken and new.

The crash comes, and the thunderous "Mazel tov!" She is married. It's too late to back out; all these people are too happy and the veil is being lifted but not quickly enough, she is being pushed in a direction that she cannot see, then at last the veil is up and the faces of her parents wash over her, her brothers, the blurred past, her sister kisses her and pushes her on, on, toward the dressing room where two plates of food are set out, and schnapps, and two chairs, inviting them to be alone, inviting them to taste what they have never.

You sound happy, Raizl. And a bit frightened.

Podhoretz was never one for reassurance. Podhoretz didn't believe in false promises. She never said, *It's going to be all right* or *You'll figure it out.* It was probably better for the Doc's business that nothing turned out all right.

But what about this time?

Look, she would tell Podhoretz, *the treatment worked. I'm married!*

But Podhoretz ends, as always, in silence. The session is over. As always, the truth under the truth is what's left at the end of therapy. The place in her mind that she keeps from Dr. P, the place Raizl barely knows herself. The thought that doesn't exist. Only the fact: a smartphone sewn into the stuffing of a sanitary pad and put back in the box with the rest, the internet safe in her toiletry case, a space that her new husband won't touch, a space Podhoretz would never think to look. The seichelphone is hers. The bill prepaid in cash.

Raizl takes a deep breath and settles the train of her dress on either side of her chair as Moishe pours the schnapps.

▼

Raizl smiles at him and takes the glass. "Shehakoil!" they say in unison, and the burn of schnapps makes Raizl feel strong and alive. Giddy, too, after a day of fasting. Moishe says Hamoitzi and passes her some bread, and they eat a few bites in hungry silence. They don't have much time; soon there is knocking on the door, a reminder that hundreds of guests are waiting to dance before the bride. "Ein minit," Moishe calls. He takes a small, fine kerchief from his coat pocket and wipes his brow, then puts on his shtreimel. So handsome he looks with the glossy ring of sable on his head, tall and regal.

The beautiful new hat doesn't sit straight, though, and Raizl wants to fix it. "May I?" she asks, pointing.

And without quite waiting for his answer, she steps very close to adjust the shtreimel the way she's seen Tati do it. Her body presses against Moishe, and she senses the surprise passing through him, an inhale that lifts his shoulders, a tremor through his beard. But she stays steady against him, and he doesn't pull away. When she tilts her head up, he finds her lips for a kiss, and Raizl feels the strain under his long silk coat and trousers, the strength he has promised her. His tongue hot in her mouth like a flame in a fire.

Glossary

Adoin Oilam: Master of the World (literal); a Jewish prayer

ah freilechen Purim: happy Purim

ah gitte voch: a good week; traditionally said on Saturday night after Shabbes, to mark the start of the new week in the Jewish calendar

ah groysen shkoyech: thank you very much

ah sheine kalleh: a beautiful bride

ah sheine maidele: a pretty girl

ah yiddishe kop: a "Jewish head," from the German "kopf" (literal); smart (slang)

ah ziesse kind: a sweet child

alte moyd: old maid

asisa: from Aramaic, an expression to wish someone good health ("bless you")

azoy: is that so

b'li neder: without making a vow

b'show: traditional Chasidic date; takes place in the home, with parents in a nearby room

bruche(s): blessing(s)

burech Hashem: thank G-d

chasseneh: wedding

chas v'shulem: heaven forbid

chazzer: pig

chevrah kadisha: Jewish burial society

chilul Hashem: a desecration of G-d's name

Chimesh: the five books of Moses; the Old Testament

chumetz: bread and wheat products that are not kosher for Passover and must be removed from the premises

chuppah: wedding canopy

chussen: bridegroom

chutzpadik maidele: insolent girl

chutzpah: impudence, rudeness

daan shvester: your sister

davening: praying

Dayeini: enough for us (literal); from the Passover Haggadah

di maaseh: the deed (literal), the story; sex (slang)

dortn: there (literal); pussy (slang)

ein minit: one minute

erev Pesach: the day before Passover

farshteist: do you understand

fleishig: of or relating to meat; in a kosher home, where meat and dairy foods and utensils must be kept separate, "fleishig" refers to dishes and utensils used for meals with meat

gartel: black sash or belt worn by Chasidic men

G-d: a way to avoid writing the divine name and thus avoid the sin of taking the divine name in vain

gelt: money

gematria: in Jewish mysticism, a numerological system in which Hebrew letters correspond to numbers

Gemureh: classical Jewish text with rabbinic commentary on Jewish religious law, traditionally printed in leather-bound, oversize volumes. Together, the Mishnah and Gemureh comprise the Talmud (200–500 CE).

gonif: thief

goyim: people who are not Jewish

goyishe kollej: non-Jewish college

goyta: woman who is not Jewish (also, goya)

gurnisht: nothing

gurnisht mit gurnisht: nothing with nothing (literal); you get nothing for nothing, worthless

haimish: cozy, homey; following Chasidish tradition

handels: bargains to get a better deal or lower price

Hashem: the name (literal); religious Jews refer to G-d this way to respect the prohibition against taking the name of G-d in vain

hub nisht chasseneh: don't get married

humentash(en): triangle-shaped cookie(s), typically filled with jam, for the Purim holiday

ich hub fargessen: I forgot

ich ken nisht: I cannot

ich veiss nisht: I don't know

intershmutz: the internet of porn

kalleh: bride

kaneinehora: no evil eye, an expression to ward off bad luck

kishkes: intestines, guts

klopping: beating the breast with a closed fist, a traditional gesture of atonement

klotz: clumsy

kokosh cake: flat, dense Hungarian variation on babka

limidei koydesh: study of Jewish texts and laws (literally, holy studies)

loch: hole (literal); pussy (slang)

lushen hora: evil tongue (literal); gossip

lushen koydesh: holy tongue (literal); Hebrew

maan tochter: my daughter

mazel: luck

Megillah: the Book of Esther, which is read on Purim

meshiggeneh, meshigge: crazy

mezuzah: scroll containing the Shema prayer, traditionally affixed to doorposts of Jewish homes

mikveh: ritual bath

mirtzeshem: Yiddish contraction for the Hebrew "im yirtza Hashem," meaning if G-d wills it (literal)

mirtzeshem bei dir: if it pleases G-d, you, too, will get married (in this context)

mitzvah: good deed; a Jewish ritual commandment

moal: mouth

Moishe Rabbeini: Moses our teacher; traditional reference denoting respect

Moshiach: the Messiah

narishkeit: foolishness, silliness

nebbish: a timid, meek person who is scorned or pitied

nein: no

nisht: not

nisht geferlech: not urgent, not terrible

oyse-mukem: that place (literal); refers to vulva

parnussa: a living, income

pecklech: packages, bags

pish: urine, piss (*n*); pishen: to urinate, to piss (*v*)

pulkes: thighs; chicken drumsticks

punim: face

prost: coarse, vulgar

rebbetzin: rabbi's wife

rekel: long coat worn by Chasidic men

seichel: brains, smarts, intelligence

sfurim: classical Jewish texts and commentaries

shaayleh: question about Jewish law

shadchen: matchmaker

shalach munes: gift packages of food exchanged on the Purim holiday

shehakoil nihiyeh bidvuroi: by whose word all things came into being; part of the Jewish blessing that is said before eating some foods

sheitel: wig worn by religious women after they are married

Shema: listen (literal); the first word of the essential Jewish prayer said daily during morning, evening, and bedtime prayers. The Shema affirms monotheistic faith (Shma Yisruel: Hear, O Israel, the Lord is our G-d, the Lord is one).

sheyfele: little lamb (term of endearment)

shidduch: an arranged marriage, or a match for the purpose of marriage

shiker: drunk

shkoyech: thank you

shmundie: pussy

shmutz: dirt , stain, or filth (literal); smut, pornography; something lewd or profane (slang)

shmutzig: dirty

shmutz-kalleh: porn-bride

shmutzlecht: pornlight

shmutzvelt: pornworld

shpritz: spray

shteindele: pebble

shtick: piece (literal); comic bit, prank, gimmick

shtup: to push (literal); to have sex (slang)

shul: synagogue

shulem aleichem: peace to you (literal); welcome

shvantz: tail (literal); penis (slang)

shvantz-fresser: penis-eater (literal); fresser: glutton, person eating hungrily

shver: father-in-law

shvigger: mother-in-law

simchas: happy occasions such as weddings and bar mitzvahs

smicha: rabbinic ordination

Talmud: classical text of Jewish religious law, dating from the fifth century

tchotchkes: knickknacks

tehillim: psalms

Torah: the Jewish Bible (the five books of Moses)

traif: not kosher

tshuvah: repentance

tsunoyfshtoys: crash

tuches: buttocks, ass (*pl.* tucheses)

tuches-potching: spanking

tumeh: impure, spiritually unclean, profane

turnishzugen far Tati: don't tell Tati

tush: rear end, behind (Americanized version of "tuches")

tzadeikes: righteous woman

tzedakah: charity

tzitzis: ritual tassels or fringes tied at the four corners of a garment, traditionally worn by Jewish males

tzuris: troubles

ushamni, bugadni, guzalni: we have trespassed, we have betrayed, we have stolen; the first three words of the confession prayer recited on Yom Kippur

vi fil: how much does it cost

vilde chaye: wild beast (literal); rambunctious or wild person (slang)

vilde loch: wild hole (literal); pussy (slang)

vus iz dus: what is this

vus machsti: how are you

yarmulke: skullcap; a round head covering traditionally worn by religious Jewish men and boys (and worn by Chasidic men underneath their hats)

yeitzer hora: evil inclination

yene platz: that place (literal); refers to vulva

yeshiva: religious school for boys and young men to study classical Jewish texts

yeshiva bucher: teenager or unmarried young man who studies at a yeshiva

Yidden: Jewish people

yontif: holiday

Yoshke: Yiddish diminutive form of the Hebrew name for Jesus, used by those who want to avoid saying it (also, Yoyzl)

zaa mir moichel: I'm sorry

zaftig: plump

zchis: merit, honor, credit

zeks in draasig: thirty-six

zetz: a blow, a smack

ziveg: soul mate, spouse

Acknowledgments

How beautiful that books have their own gratitude practice, a list of begats chronicling the lineage of a birth in print.

Thank you to the extraordinary Ellen Levine at Trident Media, for your vision and advocacy, and to Martha Wydysh, Audrey Crooks, Nora Rawn, and Marianna Sharp. Many thanks to all at Simon & Schuster who have cared for this book: editors Lindsay Sagnette, Natalie Hallak, and Jade Hui; Laywan Kwan for cover design and Kyoko Watanabe for interior design; production editor Sherry Wasserman; and the publicity and marketing wizards Gena Lanzi and Katelyn Phillips. Special thanks to Daniella Wexler for welcoming *Shmutz* into such a wonderful home, and to Fiora Elbers-Tibbitts.

Deep gratitude to the many writers in my life, especially my adored writing group: Therese Eiben, Pamela Erens, Philip Moustakis, Lynn Schmeidler, and Joanne Serling. To Leslie Margolis, for your final read and your friendship. To Liz Ayre, for the final-final read and thirty-five years of cross-pond alliance. To Susan Greenfield, for the gift of your wisdom on writing and life. To Shelly Oria, for knowing what street corner I'm at, and crossing with me.

I'm blessed to be part of the Columbia School of the Arts community. Thank you to the MFA faculty, especially Deborah Eisenberg, Rebecca Godfrey, Lis Harris, Margo Jefferson, Heidi Julavits, Sam Lipsyte, Ben Metcalf, Darcey Steinke, Lara Vapnyar. Rebecca, thank you for invoking the power of the antiheroine. Deepest thanks to Binnie Kirshenbaum, Bill Wadsworth, and the Joseph F. McCrindle Foundation for their support.

I'm also grateful to the Vermont Studio Center for giving me an artist's space where I could tape the entire first draft on the walls. To Jonathan Rosen, for the magnificent book *The Talmud and the Internet*. To the Jewish Women's Archive. To writers and muses Alex Chee, Sonya Chung, Dylan Landis, Joanna Rakoff, Lore Segal, Rachel Sur, and Stephen Wright. To inspirations Marlon James, Maggie Nelson, and Abby Chava Stein. To the memory of writers Ellis Avery, Vicki Hearne, Tom O'Brien, Carol Prisant, and Norma Rosen.

My thanks to Rabbi Amichai, for observing that I live in Jewish time, both a descriptor and a blessing. To Ed Lederman, for the photos, and Lauren Bergman, for the long walks and deep talks. And to the others who have walked with me and contributed to this book in ways small and large: Ann, Carlo, Camille, Brian, Debbie, Elizabeth, Eva, Gili, Isaac, Joel, Keith, Laura, Megan, Nathalia, Pamela, Rifky, and Yvonne.

Thank you, Mariza, for your friendship and intuition; David, for the possibility of transformation; Leo, for erev Shabbes calls; and Tova, for lifelong friendship and faith. Thank you, Michael, for excellence in all things. My love and gratitude to Abby and Mychal, sisters of my soul. To Felice, Jonathan and Kristen, Mom and Joe. To my sons, love beyond words. And to Esther, may her memory be a blessing. In loving memory of my father, grandparents, and namesakes Feigel (Fanny) and Beila Dina, may their memories be a blessing.

About the Author

FELICIA BERLINER has an MFA in creative writing from Columbia University. She lives in New York City. *Shmutz* is her first novel.

Shmutz

FELICIA BERLINER

This reading group guide for Shmutz *includes discussion questions and a
conversation with the author. The suggested questions are intended to help
your reading group find new and interesting angles and topics for your
discussion. We hope that these ideas will enrich your conversation and
increase your enjoyment of the book.*

Topics and Questions for Discussion

1. When you first saw the cover of *Shmutz*, what did you think? What ideas did you have about the book, based on the cover? After you read the book, how did your understanding of the cover shift? How did it stay the same?

2. Who is Raizl's community, or "tribe"? Is it her family? Other Hasidim? Straight-A students at her college? The students wearing black or dark clothing? In a time when social media and the political climate can contribute to a sense of unbridgeable divisions between people, what is the value of having a tribe, of belonging? What are the core values that motivate you and others in defining/choosing your tribe? Do you have more than one tribe?

3. "A child is forgiven. And an adult, too, can change." In what ways does Raizl change over the course of the novel? In what ways does she stay the same?

4. After the ending of the book, what do you think is next for Raizl? Will she follow the path of her parents? If not, how will she shift her own marriage and relationships?

5. The characters in *Shmutz* confront several important and controversial topics, including addiction and abortion. How does the secrecy around these subjects affect them?

6. Is there any aspect of discovering shocking things on the internet (sexual or otherwise) that you can relate to, or that you've seen other people experience?

7. Abortion is permitted in Jewish law, and is required to protect a mother's life and health. Yet in Raizl's family and community, discussion of abortion is taboo. Raizl and her mother both perceive her mother's abortion as something unusual and potentially shameful. What is the impact of secrecy and shame surrounding a medical procedure that is legal and necessary for the mother?

8. If you were raised in a religious family or community, what influence did religion have on your views of sex and sexuality? What influence does religion have on views of sex and sexuality in society generally?

9. When you were growing up, did your parents talk to you about pornography? If you're a parent, how do you talk to your kids about porn?

10. What's your view of the Rebbetzin and her influence on Raizl? Is the Rebbetzin purely malevolent, or are there aspects of her role that might have been positive for Raizl?

11. How did you relate—or not relate—to Raizl and her family's way of life? Can you picture your life without a computer or smartphone? What would that be like?

12. Toward the end of the book, Raizl gives up her relationship with her friend Sam. Why does Raizl do this? Were there other alternatives for her? Have you ever given up friendships, and, if so, what factors influenced those decisions?

13. As the novel opens, Raizl is worried that she knows too much about sex and that this knowledge may be an impediment to getting married. Have you ever felt that you knew too much about something? How could your knowledge be harmful? Later in the book, after Raizl reads an essay by Sherman Alexie, she feels she "understands what it means to be a child who wants to learn when adults around you expect you not to learn certain things. Don't want you to learn too much." Have you ever faced a situation where other people didn't want you to learn too much?

14. *Shmutz* has been called a "love note to Yiddish" by the activist and author Abby Chava Stein, a native Yiddish speaker. Is a language other than English spoken in your family? Who speaks the other language(s) and why? Is another language spoken all the time or only occasionally for a particular purpose? How do other languages shape or influence the English that is spoken in your family? And vice versa: How does English influence the other language(s)?

A Conversation with Felicia Berliner

Shmutz follows one young woman's coming-of-age story in her Brooklyn Hasidic community as she grapples with her porn addiction, the clash between the traditional and modern forces in her life, and ultimately figures out what she truly wants for herself. What drew you to this story and these characters?

Raizl, the protagonist, loves her family and feels deeply connected to God. When she stumbles onto pornography online—she discovers shmutz—and starts learning about sex, she's thrown into a terrible conflict.

In many communities across the United States—not just in the Hasidic community—young people are being told not to read certain books and not to discuss sexuality. Young people (and adults, too) constantly get the message that you need to be a certain way to belong in this society, to fit in. My book is about the struggle of a young woman who has to choose between her sexual exploration, her sense of self, and her family and community.

I chose to write from the perspective of a young ultra-Orthodox woman who had been sheltered from the internet so that the full force and shock of online porn could be represented. And I was drawn to her story because the stakes are so high—in her community, the internet is forbidden and sexual information is generally not discussed, so she has to keep her exploration a secret.

Raizl's story gave me a way to celebrate a woman's curiosity, desire, and pleasure.

What was your toughest challenge writing *Shmutz*? And your greatest joy?

The biggest challenge was finding a way to resolve Raizl's dilemma. I understood how to dramatize her conflict—her love for her family and her faith, and her longing for sexual knowledge and experience. But what would she do, in the end? How would she choose? Readers of early drafts had a lot of opinions about this, and I continue hearing from readers who get into debates about the ending. This, to me, is a sign of success: when readers have different interpretations of a character's path after the end of the book.

Do I have to pick just one joy? I'll talk about two great joys. One was finding a way out of the big challenge (see above) to write the ending. After sitting with Raizl's dilemma for so long, when the ending came to me, I wrote it in a great whoosh, several hours straight of writing, of knowing at last how Raizl would be true to herself at the conclusion of the book. That was a relief and a pleasure.

Another great pleasure was writing the various dreams that are woven throughout *Shmutz*. There is a kind of Jewish magical realism in the book. Even though Raizl lives in Brooklyn, and most aspects of her life are recognizably realistic, the dreams are one way that I was able to put much more of the spiritual and mystical dimensions of her experience on the page. Raizl prays a lot, and that might be engaging for some readers and not for others. But dreams can come to mystics and realists. And having Raizl's grandfather, her zeidy, be a dream-teller who sees and interprets other people's dreams was a way to give him a superpower and have him be connected to Raizl on a spiritual plane. The dreams show that a mystical force animates this seemingly ordinary family in Brooklyn.

How did you know you wanted to be a writer? What does the publication of your first novel mean to you?

I've wanted to be—have been—a writer since I was a kid. It's thrilling to publish my debut novel and keep the promise I made to my eight-year-old self! My message to all the would-be writers: go for it! It doesn't matter how many years you didn't write your first book; you can start today. Sit down and write one paragraph. Or take a walk, and talk that paragraph into a voice memo on your phone. That's how it works: one sentence at a time, one word at a time.

What other books and writers inspire you most? Are there any books currently on your nightstand right now?

On my nightstand now is a gorgeous debut novel, *A Tiny Upward Shove*, by Melissa Chadburn, which is told from the point of view of an aswang, a shapeshifter in Philippine folklore, that enters the body of a murdered woman. I'm also reading *Human Blues* by Elisa Albert, which is hilariously funny and devastatingly on point about women's reproductive dilemmas, along with an anthology of writing about reproductive freedom, *I Know What's Best for You*, edited by Shelly Oria. For inspiration I also dip into a very thick book in the pile, *Tales of the Hasidim*, compiled by Martin Buber, and some books of poetry, including *The Great Fires*, by Jack Gilbert, and *Bright Dead Things*, by Ada Limón (our current U.S. poet laureate), with its wonderful opening poem, "How to Triumph Like a Girl."

If there's one thing you most hope readers take away from reading *Shmutz*, what would that be?

One way to read *Shmutz* is to see it as a protest against the requirement to give up parts of yourself in order to fit in. An epigraph in the book comes from the author Maggie Nelson, who wrote that "it's the binary of normative/transgressive that's unsustainable, along with the demand that anyone live a life that's all one thing." So many of us have multiple identities, and this demand to be "all one thing" is often a source of great pain for people who don't want to live in one category, in one box.

Raizl is a devout young woman, and she's also a sexual human being. What Raizl discovers is that she can't be just one thing. She can't live her life that way. So even though Raizl is a unique character, the themes of her story are universal. Many readers relate to Raizl through experiences of conflict between their sense of self, their sexuality or curiosity, and the expectations of their family and community, or what other people say their faith requires of them. The message of this book is: Be whole! Be all the parts of yourself.